T0194056

FIND A SCOUT

FIND A SCOUT

And Make Him Your Friend

L.M. CHAMPION

FIND A SCOUT
AND MAKE HIM YOUR FRIEND

iUniverse books may be ordered through booksellers or by contacting:

iUniverse
1663 Liberty Drive
Bloomington, IN 47403
www.iuniverse.com
1-800-Authors (1-800-288-4677)

Because of the dynamic nature of the Internet, any web addresses or links contained in this book may have changed since publication and may no longer be valid. The views expressed in this work are solely those of the author and do not necessarily reflect the views of the publisher, and the publisher hereby disclaims any responsibility for them.

Any people depicted in stock imagery provided by Getty Images are models, and such images are being used for illustrative purposes only. Certain stock imagery © Getty Images.

ISBN: 978-1-5320-7092-1 (sc)
ISBN: 978-1-5320-7781-4 (e)

Library of Congress Control Number: 2019908745

Print information available on the last page.

iUniverse rev. date: 07/12/2019

PROLOGUE

Last Fall

Kendra and Walt Williams hosted a going away dinner party at their home for their neighbor, Jake Alder, with a few close friends and neighbors. Walt steadily drank himself into a stupor that evening.

Kendra quietly closed the door behind the last of the guests, then she and Jake got Walt into bed—a task that had become the norm, rather than the exception. It had been a long week and a trying evening for Kendra. She smiled uncertainly as she instinctively touched Jake's hand—a smile and a gesture of both embarrassed frustration and honest gratitude.

"Thank you for being here, Jake. Thank you for always being here when I need a friend."

The stress and dejection she felt were apparent in her voice and on her face. "I don't know what I would do if I didn't have you and Kelli to lean on."

Jake Alder was their close friend and neighbor. Kelli Sinton was her best friend and her neighbor.

Jake hugged her shoulders comfortingly. "That's what friends are for."

"His drinking has become intolerable. I don't know what to do. And I'm so unhappy."

As tears welled in the corners of her eyes, Jake instinctively drew her into his reassuring embrace where she leaned against his chest and wept quietly. When her tears passed, she sniffled, swiped at her eyes, kissed his cheek and softly said, "Thank you."

He kissed her forehead reassuringly. "I'm here for you anytime. I hope you know that."

He felt her nod of acknowledgment as she laid her head back on his chest. She looked up, into his eyes, and said softly, "Jake, I …" *Oh, Jake, you've always been here for me. You've always listened. I wish you could take me away from here.*

Jake could read the pain and frustration—and the need for comfort—in her eyes. She looked utterly forlorn. He wanted so much to be able to help her, but he didn't know what to do. He nodded and paused, then gently kissed her lips. "I understand."

Wrapped in his warm embrace, she slipped her arms around his neck, hesitantly returning his kiss. He gently parted her lips with the tip of his tongue and she tentatively accepted his overture as they pressed against each other, holding and imagining. She perceptibly trembled, as willow leaves tremble in a gentle summer breeze, surprised by the warm tremors that surged throughout her. She involuntarily arched, pressing against his strong chest, and she tingled wonderfully.

"Do you," she implored softly. "Do you really?"

"I think so." Again, he kissed her tenderly and she returned his kiss.

Suddenly, she gasped.

"Oh, no," she moaned softly, backing away. "I can't do this, Jake. I'm still married to him. I can't do this to him. It isn't right." She looked into his eyes. "I'm so sorry. Please understand."

Jake was embarrassed and chagrined—for both of them—that he had put her in such an awkward situation. "I do. It was my fault. I'll leave."

"No. Please …" she said as she took his hand tentatively. "I don't want you to go. Please stay a little longer."

"Yes. Of course." He said, confused, but he smiled understandingly.

"Oh, Jake. I'm so confused." Tears again appeared in her eyes and Jake didn't know how to react. She went for a tissue and dabbed at her tears and her makeup. "I'm sorry," she said softly

Touching her cheek, Jake smiled sympathetically. "There is nothing for you to be sorry for."

She smiled uncertainly and blushed. "It isn't that I don't want to."

She paused, a pensive expression on her face. *Oh, Jake, if only you could take me away from all this. If you only knew how much I want to be with you.* "If things were different …" she looked down and whispered very softly, "If only things were different."

PART ONE

ONE

Five minutes into the second half of the second game of the second season, the tension on the field was obvious. The game had been intensely physical since the initial kick off. Tempers had flared and fists had flown since the first play of the game. Walt Williams had been double-teamed on every play that came his way, but had still managed three solo tackles and an assist.

Houston took the kickoff to start the second half and drove to their opponent's thirty yard line in eight plays. It was third and six. The defense blitzed and the Houston quarterback took a devastating late hit that got the defensive player who committed the foul ejected. But it stopped Houston's momentum. Houston moved the ball to the twenty-five yard line, but stalled and turned the ball over.

On the first down, the opponent's offense ran an option play at Walt, and once again Ohulu and Morgan were bearing down on him. He feinted Ohulu and moved toward the ball carrier who had just taken the option pitch from their quarterback. Walt feinted away from the ball carrier and toward Morgan. But instead of completing the feint, Walt drove into Morgan with a massive forearm to Morgan's chest that knocked him off his feet. Walt dove over Morgan and made the tackle at the line of scrimmage.

Morgan scrambled to his fee and trotted past Walt, never looking at him. "That's the last fucking tackle you'll make in this game, Williams," he said low enough that only Walt could hear the threat.

"Hell of a play, Williams," was repeated several times as Walt joined the defense's huddle while the television announcers enthusiastically praised Walt's effort on that play and throughout the game

The next play was a mirror of the previous play, except that Morgan moved inside the play and out of Walt's peripheral vision. Ohulu's massive bulk loomed in front of Walt, between him and the ball carrier. Again, he feinted Ohulu, intent on moving to the ball carrier, but as he did he felt the full impact of Morgan's two hundred and forty pounds coming from nowhere and crashing at full speed into one knee, then the impact of Ohulu hitting the other knee. The pain was excruciating.

Walt had been an All-American, a highly touted college linebacker who signed with the NFL. He had a storybook first season—leading the team in tackles and second in the league in tackles and sacks—and the sportswriters sang his praise. He received a substantial performance bonus, which Kendra invested wisely, and they eagerly looked forward to his second year in the NFL.

Unfortunately, he never made it back after the devastating blow to his knee, despite surgery followed by physical rehabilitation for nine months. He wasn't prepared for the demands of physical therapy and rehabilitation, and he didn't take rehab as seriously as needed. When his career dream ended abruptly, he felt sorry for himself and sought solace in the bottle.

All Walt knew how to do was play football. He had not earned a degree. He was now on his third job and that would probably end soon if he didn't get his drinking under control. By nature, he was irritable and short-tempered, and those traits increased with his inability to rehabilitate his knee. The team doctor enrolled Walt in a counseling program and Kendra encouraged him. She dutifully attended meetings with spouses of alcoholics in an effort to be supportive of Walt. When he abandoned the counseling sessions, she tried to get him into Alcoholics Anonymous, but he refused, and railed at her whenever she suggested AA or more counseling.

TWO

Jake Alder had been a promising college baseball pitcher—tall and lean with a blazing fastball and a dynamic slider—but an unfortunate ligament injury in his pitching arm his senior year ended his hopes of playing professionally. He underwent Tommy John surgery, but the rehabilitation had been slow and tedious. While recuperating, he interviewed for jobs.

His athletic prowess combined with a business degree and a high grade point average, as well as his good looks, confidence, and an affable, sanguine personality had been instrumental in his being offered a lucrative job with a major athletic equipment company. He stayed the course, worked hard and saved his money. After three years, he bought his first home. It was in a desirable new neighborhood of young professionals. The streets were lined with live oak trees and attractive houses on large lots. The fall of that same year, Kendra and Walt bought the house directly across the street from Jake. The three of them quickly became good friends.

Two years later, he and two co-workers bought a small subsidiary of their employer and quickly turned it into a very profitable and popular entity.

Jake's career was going very well, so a year ago he bought his current home. It was a custom home under early construction at the time he discovered it. It was near his first home and was in an enviable gated community with large, wooded lots. He made some practical changes to floor plan and added a pool in the spacious back yard. With the aid of a decorator and Jake's own good taste, the home was comfortably furnished in warm colors, with polished hardwood furniture and floors, well-chosen thick rugs, appealing artwork, and pleasing fabrics. It was a handsome home that exuded an inviting atmosphere of comfort, masculinity, and welcoming warmth.

Construction was complete in August. On the Labor Day Weekend, Kendra and Walt organized a going away dinner party at their home for Jake with a few close friends and neighbors.

In the first two years of their friendship, Jake and Walt had played golf together frequently, but as Walt's drinking increased, the golf decreased, then ceased. They had little in common these days, but Jake and Kendra remained good friends. He thought of her often, and the night of the kiss played significantly on his mind. Jake was concerned, confused, and curious. He was sure that his kiss a month ago had made her uncomfortable in his presence. That had to be why she now seemed so distant.

You really stepped in it that night, Jake, old buddy. She had enough problems in her life. She didn't need you making a pass at her. She has a husband—a poor excuse for a husband, but still her husband. Don't cause problems for her. She needs a friend, not a lover.

THREE

Kendra Carter Williams was five feet eight inches tall, slender and shapely. Her smooth, light almond skin was unblemished. Her long, raven black hair was thick, lustrous and hung gracefully to her shoulder blades. She had perfect white teeth and large, sparkling hazel eyes set in the whitest sclera imaginable. Surprisingly, she really had no idea how attractive she was. She always appeared quietly friendly, cheerful and happy.

Kendra and her brother, Callen, inherited the best features of both of her parents, Sam and Mei Carter. Mei was Asian, slim, pretty and intelligent. Sam was a lean, rugged looking man who had been an Army officer serving in Viet Nam. While there, he met Mei, who served as an interpreter for American forces at USARVN Headquarters. Kendra and Callen were Army brats. As a result, their childhood had been peripatetic, creating a strong bond between Mei and her children, and between her and Callen.

Kendra was highly intelligent; and Sam and Mei had gone to great lengths to ensure that both of their children were well educated. She was an associate professor of math and computer science at the University of Houston where she had recently earned a Master's degree in Artificial Intelligence. She consulted with several computer hardware and software companies, tutored gifted students, sang in the church choir, jogged, did yoga and exercised regularly. She enjoyed reading and was a Scrabble addict. Kendra had a superb voice—low, dulcet and mellifluous—a perfect contralto that seemed to draw others to her.

The Carters were strong believers. That and the repeated relocations in her life brought her to the church as a focal point in her life. It gave them all a pleasant means of meeting the families they encountered in each new environment.

Since the night of Jake's kiss, Kendra chastely tried to ignore what surfaced deep within her when Jake was near—but there was always that persistent little fillip that seemed to wriggle teasingly through her core. It had always been there, just below the surface. Until Jake first touched her the night they kissed, she just hadn't recognized it for what it was. It wasn't a feeling that she had ever experienced with Walt, but she felt it rise from deep within each time she saw Jake or spoke with him.

That night was an emotional epiphany. Kendra began to admit to herself that Walt was not, and never would be, her fairy tale prince charming. And she knew that it was different with Jake. As time passed, that realization overwhelmed her.

Kendra, you've already made your choice. You've chosen your path; you can't change direction now. You have a husband—and Jake has all the beautiful women any man could want. He was just being a comforting friend that night. Don't do something foolish that you will regret.

She avoided Jake for a month after that kiss, confining her need for support to Kelli. She didn't call Jake and because he feared he had embarrassed her, he didn't call her. Then, they met accidentally outside the entrance to the grocery one evening. She was polite and congenial, but they didn't touch. Jake asked how she was, and it was obvious from the tone of his voice and the look on his face that he was asking about the night of the kiss. She told him she was fine, but emotion churned within her.

They chatted for a few minutes, then Jake said, "You've been distant since the night we put Walt to bed. I'm sorry if I made you uncomfortable. I didn't mean to damage our friendship."

She looked pensively at Jake for a moment. "It isn't like that."

Oh, yes, it is. It just isn't uncomfortable in the way you think it is, Jake.

"I'm going through a lot right now, Jake. I'm not trying to make excuses. I know I've been distant and I'm sorry. From the beginning, you have been a wonderful friend and confidante. You didn't damage our friendship. I'm just very confused right now."

Well, it's about time you admitted it, Kendra. You can't tell him why, but you can talk to him. He has always been supportive of you and listened.

"I think I need to step back and take an objective look at my life." She paused pensively.

Oh, Jake. This isn't the right time or place, but I wish you could just take me in your arms and hold me for a few minutes. I wish I could tell you that. I wish I could tell you how I feel.

Jake quietly gazed at her for a moment, then said, "When you need to talk, I'll listen."

"Thank you, Jake Thank you for being my friend. Please don't stop being my friend," she asked softly as they parted.

You always listen, Jake. And you're always supportive. I'm sure you can't imagine what I want to say to you—and I can't say it.

FOUR

A week passed. She didn't call Jake, although she wanted to. She and Kelli had talked often. Finally, she called. Jake answered and the sound of his voice made her insides squirm happily.

"Hi," she said, "have I called at a bad time?"

Jake chuckled "Never. This is a pleasant surprise. It's nice to hear your voice."

Suddenly, she got cold feet. *You're going to embarrass yourself, Kendra. This was not a good idea.* "No, really; I can call another time if you're busy."

"Actually, you called at a good time," Jake assured her. "I'm up to my ears in contracts and I need a break. We bought a company that makes basketball uniforms and have inherited a couple of very attractive contracts with two school districts. I'm reading final drafts. We're scheduled to close the deals on Tuesday, so I'll be in Indiana all next week."

"I'm happy for you. That's wonderful news. I'm really impressed with what the three of you are doing."

"Thanks. We're a little overwhelmed at the moment."

"Tell me about it."

"It is a family owned business. Dad and mom ran the business. They have two sons who hold enviable and lucrative jobs in other fields. Dad died suddenly. Mom can't and doesn't want to run it by herself, and both sons don't want to leave their jobs. So they decided to sell."

"How did you find out about them?"

"That's the surprise in all this. One of the sons had read about us and did some research on our company before his father died. He called us and asked if we were interested. They wanted a quick sale and were asking a realistic price. We looked at their financials and their contracts, visited their facility, and made them an offer within a week. It just came to us out of the blue."

Kendra felt an unexpected surge of happiness for Jake swell from within her. "Oh, Jake. That's wonderful," she repeated. "I'm so happy for you."

"Thank you. So, how are you doing," he asked.

"I'm good. Your news makes me happy for you. School has started and I'm busy. We have a new department head and I really like him. Our old head was nice, but hadn't been in the classroom for so long that I think she lost touch with the life of an instructor. Our new head seems very in tune with what we need and the challenges we face."

"Ah, that's good news. I'm happy to hear that." He paused and she was silent. "Are you stepping back and looking at life, as you said you wanted to do?"

"A little at a time. Getting ready for the new school year has kept me busy. But, yes, I'm trying to do some thinking."

"Any time you want to talk, feel free to call."

She paused quietly, then spoke, her voice sincere. "Thank you, Jake. I know you mean that. Give me some time."

"Sure," he replied. "Whenever you want. I'll be back in a week."

"I won't keep you. Get back to your contracts." She paused again. "It's nice to hear your voice. Please call me when you get home and let me know how it all went."

Jake called a week later and Kendra was excited to hear his voice. He told her about the closing on the new business. She told him about her classes and the new department head. They were friendly and polite, but neither gave away what was going on inside each of them.

A week later, she called him after a particularly bad week with Walt. He listened and was concerned, knowing she just needed to talk. As she ended the call, she said quietly, "Thank you, Jake. Just hearing your voice is reassuring."

FIVE

Halloween fell at the end of the week that year and Kelli and Scott hosted a small Halloween Party Saturday night. Kelli called to invite Kendra and Walt. She said it would just be a small group of friends and Jake was invited as well.

Kendra hesitated to speak. *Don't say yes. Don't let Walt embarrass you in front of Kelli and Scott and a room full of friends. You do not want to do this.* Then, reality struck. *It isn't that. You just don't want to see Jake with another woman, do you?*

Kelli said, "We've only seen him briefly a few times since the night of the going away party. And he says he has only seen you once since then. I know he would like to see you. He told me he worries about you."

When Kendra was slow to respond, Kelli had said. "It will be fun. Dress casually. Scott will grill steaks."

"Thanks; it sounds like fun. It will be nice to see Jake," she said perfunctorily, but wistfully. *What do I do? I know I have feelings for Jake that I don't want to admit. Get a grip, Kendra. Get these thoughts out of your mind. One awkward kiss doesn't give you a claim on Jake.*

Saturday came. Walt woke with a hangover and was testy all morning. As she expected, he told Kendra to go that evening without him as he left for the golf course. He played golf and drank beer all day.

She debated begging off, but she wanted to see Jake and Kelli. She did not, however, look forward to seeing Jake with another woman.

Her phone rang as Kendra was preparing to leave for the party. She answered and a voice she knew well said, "Hi, Mrs. Williams. This is Tommy."

"Hi, Tommy. Is he passed out again?"

"Yes, ma'am. He's in a chair in the locker room. I just wanted you to know. If he's still here when we close, we'll let him sleep. He knows how to get out after hours."

"Thanks, Tommy. I'm so sorry for all the inconvenience."

"It's all right, ma'am. I just wanted you to know where he was when he didn't come home. He drank a lot, but at least he wasn't rowdy this time. He'll probably sleep all night. We're used to it."

"Thank you, Tommy," Kendra said as she made a mental note to remember the clubhouse staff at Christmas for all they did to help her with Walt.

"You're welcome, ma'am. Have a good evening."

Kendra retrieved her purse and left. The evening was pleasant, so she walked the short distance to Kelli and Scott's home, passing some Trick-or-Treaters on the way. She saw Jake's car on the driveway as she approached, and she felt a knot begin to grow in her stomach. Kelli saw her coming and met her at the door. Kelli's eyes questioned and Kendra replied, "He's passed out in the locker room. He'll sleep it off there. Just me tonight."

They hugged and, relieved, Kelli replied, "Fine with us. It's so good to see you."

Kendra was dressed in a fetching milkmaid costume, complete with dirndl and white stockings. Jake was there, dressed as the devil, all in black with a handsome black cape. His date, Anya, was vivacious and confident—tall and long-legged with flowing, lustrous auburn hair, dressed as a she-devil in high black boots, fishnet stockings, and a skintight devilish red leotard that superbly displayed her perfect figure. She wore a tiara sporting two red horns. She had an enticing smile, a mellifluous voice, smooth skin, perfect teeth, and sparkling hazel eyes.

Kendra was angry with Jake before she realized what was happening to her.

Jake is going to get laid tonight!

The thought shot through her mind with the impact of a bullet through a plate glass window. She was overcome with hot jealousy—and surprised at herself for using a phrase she had heard, but never before in her life used—but she allowed nothing to show on her face.

Kendra, you're angry ... and your mother taught you better than to think like that. Get a grip. Jake has a right to have a life.

The night was difficult for her, despite how welcome it was to be with old friends. She was cordial to Jake and the she-devil, but avoided them as much as she could. Once, she found herself next to Jake in a group. He leaned to her and said quietly, "You look great! Love your costume." She smiled her thanks and her heart sang at his notice of her.

One time during the evening, Kelli caught her arm and whispered, "What do you think of Jake's date?"

Before she could stop herself, Kendra replied, "She's a little obvious, don't you think?"

Kelli laughed. "Jake knows how to pick them, doesn't he?" she replied good-naturedly.

Kelli's comment tore through Kendra. She felt as though she were going to be sick to her stomach. Kelli looked at her and asked, "Are you all right? You look tense."

She nodded, excused herself and escaped to the bathroom where she fought the urge to vomit as tears came uncontrollably.

A week later, she was still upset, but she realized that Jake wouldn't understand if she didn't call him soon. She called. They talked politely about his business, her work, small talk until she said, "Anya certainly was eye-catching. She's a striking woman. Have you known her long?"

"Two or three years," Jake replied.

"Really? Do you have feelings for her?"

"She is a friend of my sister," he replied enigmatically.

Kendra asked no more questions, but the thought of Jake with Anya upset her.

SIX

Thanksgiving came and Kendra went alone to her parents' home for the long weekend. She called Jake before she left to wish him a happy holiday. He was spending the holiday his family. She was glad she wouldn't be home alone with Walt. And she was secretly glad Jake wasn't spending the holiday with another woman.

Kendra returned from Thanksgiving and found Walt sitting forlornly in a darkened living room, just staring blankly ahead. Surprisingly, he was sober—but for how long, she had no idea. He apologized to her for his past behavior and told her he was going to start counseling again the next week. He told her he had missed her and had done a lot of thinking. She was very surprised, but assumed his parents had reached the old Walt over the holidays.

Oh, God. Now what do I do? I can't continue thinking of Jake. I have to be supportive of Walt.

True to his word, Walt had arranged to return to counseling the next day. He told her he didn't want to ruin the Christmas holiday for them. He avoided alcohol for a week and his spirits were better. He told her he was going to call the coach and ask to join the team on the sidelines during the next home game. Kendra didn't think it was a good idea, but she was supportive, all the while torn between desire and duty.

The next day, Walt made the call. Kendra heard the excitement in his voice as he made his pitch to the coach. Unfortunately, he was told no. The coach believed the risk of having a drunken Walt appear on the field was too great. The rejection broke his fragile resolve. Two hours later, he was sloppy drunk and soon passed out.

Kendra called Jake in tears. She explained what had happened, and he was incredibly understanding and sympathetic. She vented, cried, vented some more, but never felt sorry for herself or whined. When the call ended, Jake called Kelli and told her Kendra needed a friend. Kelli immediately walked to Kendra's home, gathered her in her arms, and walked her to Kelli's home, where they talked late into the night.

The next weeks were unhappy and uncomfortable for Kendra. Life with Walt was erratic, with constant mood swings and far too much alcohol. Kendra went to her parents' home at the beginning of her Christmas break and stayed through New Year's Day and the rest of that week. She called Jake to wish him a Merry Christmas.

Kendra talked to Jake twice in January and three times in February. She talked to Kelli regularly, but said little about Jake. Once she asked Kelli if Jake was seeing anyone and Kelli told her he was now dating a banker.

Between her disillusionment with Walt and her thoughts of Jake—knowing that he was again with a new woman—she was despondent and angry with herself. She vacillated between being angry at Jake and wanting to hear his voice. She pondered her life constantly, with growing resolve

SEVEN

It was the first Thursday of March. By noon, Walt was well on his way to being over-served. He had kept one unsuccessful appointment that morning, was home before noon, and had just finished his fourth beer. He had closed the drapes and sat morosely in the darkened living room, holding his empty beer can. When the doorbell rang, he cursed and decided he wasn't going to answer.

The bell rang again, accompanied by a rough knock on the door itself. When he still ignored the intrusion, he heard a voice call out, "Mr. Williams. This is Constable Evans. I know you're home. Please open the door, sir. I need to speak with you."

What the hell is this about? He strode to the door and opened it. There, on the front porch, stood Constable Evans in full uniform. "Mr. Williams, I'm Constable Evans. May I come in for a moment, sir?"

"Whaddya want?" Walt responded. "I was just on my way out."

"I have some documents, sir; and I need to explain them to you. Would you like to sit down?"

"I'm fine. Whaddya got?"

"Sir, the first document is a Petition for Divorce. I'm serving this on you at the request of Mrs. Kendra Williams and by order of the Court."

"What the fuck!"

"Sir, the second document is a Temporary Restraining Order of the Court and a Request for Protective Order." Evans handed the documents to Walt, who took them reflexively without looking at them.

"What the hell is this, anyway?" Walt groused.

"Sir, you are being sued for divorce. That is the first document and it is self-explanatory. I suggest you retain an attorney to explain that document to you." Walt spewed a stream of invectives and Evans waited until he finished.

"The second document is an order of the court. In summary, you are to gather some clothes and your necessary items, turn all firearms in your possession over to me, and leave the home immediately. You are also prohibited from coming within one hundred fifty feet of Mrs. Williams and from communicating with her in any way except through her attorney. Please show me your firearms now."

"You're kidding me!"

"No, sir. Please tell me now what weapons you have in the home or in your possession." Evans opened a sheet of paper with typing on it and looked at it without showing it to Walt. "Before you speak, I advise you that it is against the law for you to knowingly make a false or misleading statement to me, particularly about the weapons you possess."

"You little shit! I'll kick you off my property!"

Walt was a big, muscular guy, now going to fat—but still big. Evans looked capable, but was far from being a physical match for Walt.

Evans put his hand on the flap of his holster and replied quietly and evenly, "Mr. Williams, this can happen one of two ways. You can withdraw that threat, and peacefully do as I ask. I will wait while you arrange for transportation since it appears that you have had too much to drink to drive yourself. Or I can arrest you now, cuff you and lock you in my car, search your house for weapons, take you to jail, and your attorney can arrange for your belongings. Your call, but decide quickly."

Walt stared at Evans with hard eyes, but didn't speak. Evans waited quietly, a hand on his holster.

Finally, Walt capitulated. "What the hell. I have a deer rifle, a shotgun, a forty-five and a nine millimeter in the closet in the bedroom. Follow me."

Walt relinquished the firearms, packed two suitcases, a traveling bag and his golf clubs, and called his brother, Mitchell. When the firearms were stowed in Evans' cruiser and his bags were waiting at the front door, Walt went to the fridge and got the two remaining beers from the six-pack.

"Want one?"

"No, thank you, sir. Can't drink on duty."

Evans collected Walt's house keys and garage door opener after Walt parked his car on the street in front of the home.

Mitchell arrived and drove Walt to Mitchell's home. Walt brooded quietly the entire drive. Mitchell knew his brother. When Walt yelled and cursed, he was angry. When he became taciturn, he was stoking the fires of his anger and a storm was on the horizon. Mitchell settled Walt into his spare bedroom.

Walt and Mitchell were PKs—preacher's kids—who had a stable, but restrictive, childhood. Their parents were earnest, pragmatic persons who found fulfillment in the church, and who assumed their sons did, as well. Walt struggled to be a low average student, was rebellious and socially inept with girls, but an excellent athlete who attended college on a football scholarship. Walt did not graduate from college, in contrast to Kendra's academic scholarship and summa cum laude graduation.

Mitchell, a year older than Walt, was tall and stocky, like Walt. They looked alike and they sounded alike when they spoke. He was a nice looking man, but going soft quickly. Mitchell was highly intelligent and eclectically curious, awkward with women, not athletic, and had a saturnine disposition. Mitchell had earned a degree in Business Administration and had a good job as an independent programmer, which provided him a nice income and the flexibility to work at home and set his own hours. Both brothers hunted and liked guns—their only common ground.

It was Mitchell who looked after his brother, cleaned up his messes, and mended fences when Walt offended others. Mitchell ensured that Walt graduated from high school and maintained scholastic eligibility in college, although the influences of his coaches had a lot to do with his barely passing grades as well. But, it was Walt who shone in his parents' eyes, to Mitchell's chagrin.

EIGHT

Constable Evans returned to the precinct and checked Walt's guns into the evidence room for safekeeping. He completed his perfunctory return of service report, filed it and called Kendra. Fortunately, he called on her break period and she answered.

"Mrs. Williams, this is Constable Evans. I called to advise you that Mr. Williams has been served and has left the residence. I have made him aware of the terms of the restraining order and I have taken possession of all the firearms that he identified."

Kendra breathed a sigh of relief. "Was it difficult?"

"He had been drinking and threatened me, but I threatened him right back and he settled down. I have his house keys and a garage door opener. If you can stop by the precinct later today and sign for them, they will be turned over to you."

Kendra said she would do so and thanked Evans for calling her.

"Yes, ma'am. Mrs. Williams … just remember, that restraining order is just a piece of paper. If he comes around or violates the order, don't hesitate. Call us. Restraining orders don't always keep the peace or work as intended. Please don't take any chances."

Kendra thanked him for his advice and reiterated that she would come by the precinct later. She hung up, sat at her desk and cried. Some of her tears were for her failed marriage and the failed dreams and hopes that she had taken into the marriage. Some of the tears were for Walt's inability to control his drinking and the two times he struck her when he was drunk.

And, some of her tears were simply relief that what should have been—but never was—a storybook marriage was now over and she would have her life back.

She dried her tears and quickly realized that she wasn't going to be able to do her students justice that day, so she dismissed class early with a wish to them for a good weekend. She returned to her office and called Kelli.

"Hi. It's Kendra. Did I call at a bad time?"

"No. Actually, I'm just packing up. It's slow and I'm going home early." Kelli paused. "Are you okay? You sound like you have something on your mind."

"I do. Do you have some time to talk this evening?"

"Sure. All the time you would like. Scott is out of town tonight. Our house, your house, or meet somewhere?"

"It's been weeks since I've been out of the house except for work. It would be nice to go somewhere. Is it okay if we meet for dinner? But someplace quiet where we can talk."

"Sure. Let's go to Timpano. The food is good and it's usually quiet there. We'll be early enough to get a booth, and maybe we can get that really quiet booth back in the corner. Five thirty?"

"That would be nice. See you there."

NINE

Kendra checked her face in the mirror. The bruise on her cheek was still dark, but she had hidden it well with make-up and it wouldn't show much in the subdued light at Timpano. The bruises on her arm and shoulder were covered by her blouse.

She retrieved Walt's keys and garage door opener from the Constable's office, and arrived at Timpano promptly at five-thirty. The back booth was open. At her request, she was seated there just as her phone sounded the alert for a text. She looked and read, *Small brush fire. On my way now. Order an apple mojito for me.* She ordered two apple mojitos and an appetizer of mushrooms and shrimp, telling her server that her friend was about ten minutes away, so there was no rush.

Kelli arrived just as the drinks and appetizers were delivered. "Perfect timing," she quipped with a laugh.

They toasted and Kendra asked, "How are you doing? And Scott? Is everything good for the two of you?

"It couldn't be better," Kelli effused. "Life is so good. Scott just got a promotion and a nice raise. My job is good." She paused. "We've decided we aren't ready yet for children—and we laughed when we found out that it was a mutual feeling because each of us had been afraid tell the other. So, we're going to France and Italy in June to celebrate the promotion and our decision to keep it just the two of us for a while longer."

She took Kendra's hand. "I'm sorry. I'm just rattling on. And you have something on your mind. You talk; I'll listen."

"Don't be sorry. I asked because I wanted to know. You're my best friend and I want you to be happy."

"Thank you. I know you mean that. I know things have been difficult for you. Tell me what's going on."

"I filed for divorce."

A look of surprise, then concern filled Kelli's face. She was silent for a moment, then took Kendra's hand. "Are you okay?

It was Kendra's turn to be silent. She looked thoughtful before she spoke. "Yes. I'm okay. I'm sad, but I'm okay. I've been contemplating divorce for a while, but I've kept it to myself. When Walt struck me the second time, I knew it was the right thing to do."

"Oh, Kendra! We knew things weren't good, but we didn't suspect that."

"I'm okay, but I'm very sad that something I believed—hoped fervently—would be wonderful actually wasn't. Part of me feels responsible because I didn't know how to be a good wife. Except for one boy in high school, I never even had a steady boyfriend. I had never been with a man. I was caught up in the mantra of saving myself for my husband.

"I think Walt had been with other women, but I don't think he had much experience either. I didn't know what to do for him or with him and he never took the time to help me. He wasn't a romantic man. And he was always so wrapped up in football and golf. Even when he was home, he had little time for me or for us."

As Kendra sighed and tears slipped from the corners of her eyes, Kelli took her hand. "He never just took me in his arms and held me, or listened when I needed to talk. I think the problem was really a lack of good common sense at the beginning. I think I married Walt because he was a football star, popular and well-known, who asked me to be his wife. I think he was more interested in how I looked on his arm than how he felt about me. At first, I was happy being on his arm. And, I really liked his parents and they seemed to like me.

"So, I'm sad that our marriage never became what I hoped it would be. But, I realize now that was never going to happen, even if he hadn't gotten injured. We had very little—nothing actually—in common. We met at church in the middle of our junior year in college. We dated until graduation, and then married. I thought our religious upbringing was good common ground for a marriage, but Walt really didn't accept the church as his parents did.

The circumstances are sad, but I'm happy that I will have a chance to start over and I'm happy that I won't be a single mother. Does that sound cold?"

"No. I'm glad you made the decision before you were hurt worse or became pregnant. I think you're doing the right thing. Do your parents know?

"Yes. They are fine with my decision and they're happy for me. They were always very amiable and accepting with Walt, but I know they always had reservations."

"Do they know he struck you?"

"Yes."

"How did your father take that?"

"I told them by phone. It's probably better that I couldn't see Daddy's face. But I could tell by his voice that he was very angry."

"Are you afraid Walt will hurt you again?"

Kendra paused a long moment. "Really, I'm not sure. He has changed with the drinking. He's quick to get angry now and he gets verbally abusive when he is drunk. I think he is just frustrated and I'm the convenient outlet. I've done everything I can to help him cope with his life, but he just pushes me away.

"He has always gotten everything he wanted … including me. Now he is in a situation where only he can fix the problem and he seems afraid to try. For a man who attacks so relentlessly on the football field, he seems afraid to confront his problem off the field. I think he is waiting for someone to fix it for him, just as someone has always done for him."

Their waiter returned. They quickly scanned the menu, ordered dinner and a bottle of good pinot noir.

TEN

Kelli reached for Kendra's hands and squeezed them gently. "I'm glad you called. You need to talk and I'm happy to listen." Kelli nodded her head and smiled invitingly at her friend.

"How can I help?"

"You're right. I need to talk. You're my best friend. You're the only person I can talk to about this and I know you will understand."

"Talk, girlfriend. Please. Whatever I can do to help."

Kendra paused and took a deep breath. "The night of the going away party for Jake, Walt drank so much he passed out."

Kelli nodded. "I remember."

"That night I was really frustrated, hurt, angry at Walt. We had just put him into bed. Jake literally had to carry Walt over his shoulder down the hall to the bedroom. I felt so alone. I knew I was going to miss having Jake just across the street.

"Jake hugged me. We talked. Somewhere in all the talk, Jake kissed me and I returned his kiss. From the time we first met, I knew there was something special about Jake, but I always kept that thought to myself. He took me in his arms and we kissed again."

Kendra paused and Kelli looked at her. "Is this about Jake?"

Kendra nodded. And Kelli nodded sagaciously.

"Kelli, my experience with men has truly been minimal, but I had <u>never</u> been kissed as tenderly or touched as gently as Jake did that night. I literally trembled all over. I backed away. Jake apologized and said he would leave, but I asked him to stay. He did, and we just talked for another hour. But, the thing about that night is that I know I would have given in to him if he had only pressed me just a little. I know I would have regretted it, but thankfully, Jake was a gentleman and didn't persist.

"Despite all my upbringing, all the good moral background I thought I had, and my respect for marriage and the church, I knew when Jake touched me that night that I wanted to be with him. I knew it the moment he kissed me and I've known it ever since. It was like being doused under the Gatorade cooler after the big win. I was suddenly immersed in a feeling I had never experienced ... and never expected.

"I get butterflies whenever he is around me. I want to be close to him. I want to be wrapped in his arms. I'm Walt's wife, but that isn't where my heart is anymore—not since that night. I know that's terrible, but I can't help it. My marriage was never what I thought it would be or what I hoped it would be."

Their dinner was served, and the wine was tasted, approved and glasses were filled. When they were again alone, Kelli spoke.

"That's ironic. You've never given yourself away, but Jake told me once when we were all together at his home that Walt was a fool to treat you so thoughtlessly and that he was—quote, unquote—literally clueless to what he had in you. I thought Jake was just being a good friend, but I can tell you, his tone was grimly serious. Later, when I recalled the tone of his voice and the look in his eyes, it made me speculate about what he was really thinking."

"Thank you for telling me. Since that one night, he has never ... expressed interest in me except as a friend."

"Well, he never lacks for company—and they are always beautiful and well-educated. But, no matter how strong his feelings might be for you, I think that night was out of character for him. I don't think Jake would ever intentionally approach another man's wife, especially the wife of a friend—albeit a drunk who seems bent on alienating everyone around him.

"But, for that very reason, I think the fact that he actually kissed you is a strong indication that he has feelings for you."

Kendra nodded. "We've known each other for nearly four years now—for more than three years before that night. I think I know who Jake is pretty well. It has been five months since that kiss, and I think about it all the time. When my lawyer called me and told me the divorce petition was filed, my first thought was of that night. It's all I can think of. And I know it's a futile thought because, as you say, Jake wouldn't intentionally put me in that position."

Kelli laughed softly. "Pardon my saying so, but I think, if you were single, Jake would happily put you in any position you wanted."

Kendra looked puzzled for a moment until the innuendo of Kelli's comment sunk in. She blushed and was at a loss for words.

"I'm sorry, Kendra. I didn't mean to embarrass you."

"It's okay. I shouldn't be embarrassed. I'm a grown woman. But … I'm still naïve in many ways. You and Scott seem so happy. I want to find that kind of happiness, but I don't know how. Jake's sister once told me that Jake knows how to please a woman, which must be true because he certainly doesn't seem to lack for female companionship."

Kelli looked at her thoughtfully. "Anya upset you, didn't she?"

Kendra was pensive, then nodded and softly replied, "Yes," with a look of chagrin. "I'd like to know what would have happened that night if I hadn't backed away from Jake. But, I don't want to ruin the friendship that we have."

She looked morosely at Kelli, who replied, "I think we both know Jake wouldn't have let it go much farther than you did that night because you were married and he was in your home. And now, you want it to actually happen, but you don't know how to go about making it happen. Is that right?"

Kendra paused, looking into space for a long moment. She looked back at Kelli and nodded. "Yes. But, even if it happens, I'm afraid I will disappoint Jake … and it will be awkward between us."

"Because you have little experience?"

"Yes."

"What's the worst thing that will happen if he's disappointed?"

"I'll lose Jake's friendship."

"I don't think Jake would be that shallow. If anything, I think he would let you down gently and help you convince yourself that he wasn't the right man for you."

"Oh, Kelli. I'm so confused right now. I don't know what to do."

"Let me relate a little personal advice that I was once given.

"Scott and I dated for nine months, then lived together for six months before we bought our home. We lived in our home for a year before we married. My parents have always liked Scott and they quietly accepted us living together.

But I have an aunt who is a bit of a character. When my aunt learned we were living together, she took me aside. She asked if I thought Scott might be the one for me, and I said yes, but only time would tell.

"She grasped my hands and gave me this huge grin and said, 'That's exactly right, my dear. You're doing the right thing. You know, there's a good reason why a girl tries on a pair of shoes and checks them in a mirror before she actually buys them.' I laughed, but her comment made sense to me."

Kendra laughed, and Kelli took her hand. "You might consider my aunt's comment. You aren't a virgin anymore, and relationships are different today. Test the water. Whether or not Jake is the one for you, my guess is he is the perfect one with whom to learn. I certainly encourage you to … ah … influence him in the right direction.

"You want resolution. I imagine Jake does as well. Give it some time. Stay busy and keep your mind occupied. Get the divorce behind you. Then, make a decision. This is the twenty-first century. It's okay for you to take the initiative. Let Jake know you want to be with him. Call him. Invite him to have a drink or dinner with you. Get tickets to a play and invite him." Kelli paused. "Or just tell him how you feel—that you want to finish what the two of you started that night.

"My father always told me, 'The worst that can happen is that the answer will be no.' I don't think Jake will say no, and I don't think he will hurt you … or allow you to hurt yourself. I have a lot of respect for Jake.

"And remember, sex is a two-way street. Don't expect your partner to read your mind. Tell him what you like and what you want."

Kelli paused, then laid her hand on Kendra's arm. "I may be out of line—and you can tell me if I am— but think about this. It is much easier for a woman to satisfy a man than it is for a man to do so for a woman. Unless we show our pleasure, it's often difficult for a man to know that his attentions were successful or appreciated.

"On the other hand, many men just take what they want without giving back. I don't think Jake is like that.

"Making love is not just having sex. Truly making love is the greatest expression of devotion and acceptance two persons can give each other. It's okay to be vocal and physical and emotional. If he pleases you, show him and tell him—celebrate like it's your birthday. Don't try to keep it bottled inside. If he makes you giddy with anticipation, if he makes you tremble all over, it's okay to quiver and bounce like a puppy, buck like a pony, scream like you're five years old and your daddy is tickling you. Be effusive and vocal and enjoy the pleasure he gives you. Don't light a firecracker when you really want to use a skyrocket.

"Personally, I think the two of you could be good for each other. John Greenleaf Whittier once wrote, 'For all sad words of tongue and pen, the saddest are these: It might have been.' You might give that some thought."

Kendra nodded, sighing morosely. "I'm so confused. Thank you for listening. I appreciate your concern and your advice. I guess I have a lot to think about. I don't want to appear needy to Jake, … or desperate … but I want to know what might have been that night."

Kelli offered some insightful thoughts and some practical suggestions. Kendra paid close attention and was thoughtful as they finished their dinner. As the plates were being cleared, their waiter asked if they would like to finish the wine and they agreed. There was enough for exactly two glasses left in the bottle.

Kendra looked up, raised her glass and said cheerfully, "Thank you. I appreciate what you've told me. Thanks for being my friend … and my mentor.

"Here's to you and Scott and your upcoming vacation. I hope you have a wonderful time." As Kelli touched Kendra's glass with hers and thanked her, Kendra invited her to tell what they planned for the vacation.

When she returned home, there was a message from Jake, asking how she was. Uncomfortably, she returned his call, told him she was fine and very busy preparing a mid-term exam to give before spring break. He said he would be out of town the next week on business and told her to call him if she needed anything. She said she would. She hung up, knowing she had maintained her façade, and happy at hearing his voice—but distressed with herself.

Except for that one night, Jake has never shown any interest other than as a friend—and, despite that, you're as giddy as if he had asked you to the prom. His kiss was nice, but it was probably just platonic. You can't make Jake be interested in you by wishing it were so. You've made much more of it than it really was. To Jake, you're just the girl who cries on his shoulder about her unhappy marriage and drunken husband. You want Jake to be your knight in shining armor, ride in on his white horse, and bring your unhappy life to its knees. But Jake isn't thinking about what Mr. Whittier wrote; he isn't thinking about what might have been. That moment has passed for him.

She was angry with Jake by the time she went to bed, but didn't know why. She cried herself to sleep that night.

ELEVEN

On Friday, Walt called in sick. Mitchell took him to retrieve his car. Walt went to the golf course where he played golf and drank beer until the pro on duty firmly suggested it was time for him to go home. When Mitchell arrived home, Walt was comatose on the couch.

Mitchell read the petition for divorce and the restraining order, knowing that Walt had not read them and had no idea what was in the documents that he needed to know. He made some calls to friends and got the name of a good attorney to represent his brother.

Mitchell called Kendra, telling her that Walt was with him. She explained what had happened and why she was ready to move on. He listened and was sympathetic. He solicitously told her he was there for her if she needed him.

Over the weekend, Mitchell worked to get and keep his brother sober while Walt railed against Kendra, the system, his boss and his injury. Walt vacillated between hating Kendra, threatening to harm her, and blubbering that she just didn't understand what he was going through.

On Monday, Mitchell got is brother off to work and hired a lawyer for Walt. On Tuesday, he took the morning off and drove Walt to the lawyer's office. He kept Walt sober until the upcoming hearing on Wednesday.

Kendra stayed busy. Sam and Mei arrived Tuesday night and the three of them went out for dinner. They voiced concerns for Kendra, but were very supportive and helped keep Kendra on an even keel that evening. Mei said that someday they hoped for grandchildren, but was thankful that

Kendra was not going to be left as a single mother. Kelli called that night and confirmed that she would be in court with Kendra.

Kendra had not spoken to Jake for two weeks. She was now even more uncomfortable—still excited by thoughts of him, but even more certain that their kiss had not meant as much to him. She decided that she was behaving like a schoolgirl.

Jake can have his pick of a dozen beautiful, intelligent women. Get over this, Kendra. Jake is a friend who has been there to listen, and now you want him to take the next step. He doesn't have an amorous interest in you. If he does, wait for him to take the first step. But, he isn't going to do that because he isn't interested. It's that simple.

That night, she again cried herself to sleep, upset by Walt, the divorce, her inability to keep thoughts of Jake at an emotional arm's length, and Jake's apparent indifference to her.

Wednesday morning, she and her parents ate breakfast together, dressed and Kelli joined them for trip to the courthouse.

TWELVE

Mitchell got a sober Walt to the hearing. They had difficulty finding a parking space and arrived late to court. The Williams case was in the middle of the docket, so it wasn't heard until after eleven o'clock. The courtroom was a packed house and he was forced to stand along the back wall until some of the early cases were heard and seats became available. It was hot in the back of the room and the longer Walt stood there, the more uncomfortable he became.

The case was eventually called and the parties came forward to stand with their lawyers before the judge. Kendra looked lovely and professional. She had done nothing to hide the bruises that remained on her face and arm. The judge commented on the bruises and the significant difference in the respective sizes of Kendra and Walt, which embarrassed Walt. Her parents and Kelli were there with her—and their presence embarrassed Walt even more.

Kendra testified truthfully and there was nothing Walt could say in his defense. The judge gave him no credit for his mumbled and half-hearted apology to Kendra. The restraining order became a temporary protective order under the same terms and conditions. The Judge ordered Walt into drug and alcohol counseling and ordered him to report to the court weekly. He was also ordered to pay Kendra's medical bills arising from the incident.

Walt was angry that his lawyer did not play on his football injury as the reason for his behavior, despite being advised that such an argument would only do him harm. He was angry that he could not return to his home. He was angry that Kendra could do this to him when, as he shouted in a tone of righteous indignation before his lawyer could stop him, that it was she who threatened to leave him.

When his lawyer advised the judge that Walt was to be out of state on business with his boss the next week, Walt was ordered to appear on Friday to discuss the matter.

Throughout the hearing, Kendra had closely watched Walt's face and listened to the tenor of his voice. Like a child who was caught with his hand in the cookie jar, Walt could only offer insipid comments intended to take the attention away from his own actions. By the end of the hearing, Kendra was even more convinced that she had made the right decision.

By the end of the day, Walt was an angry and frustrated man, but knew he had to toe the line. He ignored the positive that had come from the day. He had probably lost his wife, but he had gained a foothold in keeping his job and dealing with his alcoholism.

On Thursday and Friday, a coworker who was a Friend of Bill took Walt to AA meetings. He attended, but only with a half-hearted effort.

Walt appeared in court on Friday. He was given another tongue-lashing by the judge and a reprieve from reporting to the court the next week. He was embarrassed and felt that he had been treated like a child. He was angry, and blamed his anger and his perceived ill-treatment on Kendra.

By Friday evening, Walt was beside himself, but he knew enough not to start drinking. He and Mitchell went to dinner together. After dinner, Walt told Mitchell that he was going home to talk with Kendra. When Mitchell reminded him of the injunction, he blurted, "What the hell can that judge do to me. If Kendra tells me to leave, I'll come back here, but it's my home. I should be able to go to my own home."

THIRTEEN

Sam and Mei stayed with Kendra Wednesday and Thursday nights, but she sent them home on Friday morning, telling them she was fine and needed some time alone. On Thursday night, both Walt and Jake called while they were out.

Walt left her a curt, angry message that she couldn't just throw him out of his home and that he was getting another lawyer when he returned. His parting words were, "I'll get you for what you've done."

Jake left a message that he was home and asked if she were all right. The sound of his voice made her tingle, but she waited until Sam and Mei left on Friday to return his call.

On Friday morning, she called her lawyer and told her of Walt's telephone message. Her lawyer advised that she would call Walt's lawyer and inform him of the breach of the Court's order, and told her not to worry, but to be cautious. She assured Kendra that Walt's violence would come back to haunt him and that she would keep Kendra in her home.

Her dinner conversation with Kelli had been a catalyst that slipped the lock on all that she had sublimated about Jake. Kendra had been consumed with thoughts of him since she had actually talked about him,. Much of her imagination was dominated with youthful fantasies and imaginations, but her body was filled with the atavistic and unfamiliar yearnings and needs of a woman—and this was all new to her. Despite her fears and concerns, hearing his voice last night had set her mind aglow with thoughts of Jake, and her woman's body ached with unfamiliar newfound need.

After Sam and Mei were on their way and she was alone, she replayed in her mind her conversation with Kelli. She pictured herself in an unending loop, in Jake's embrace, his gentle touch, his tender kiss—just as she was five months ago—but the vision didn't progress. She didn't know how to move forward.

Finally, at four o'clock, compulsion prevailed over hesitation. After a week of indecision and debate with herself, Kendra's desire to see Jake outweighed her hesitation. *You found the courage to file for divorce. You can find the courage to call Jake.* She didn't want to wait until the divorce was final. She wanted to see Jake, to be close to him and to feel his touch. She had dutifully and naively spent nearly four years in a loveless, unhappy marriage. And she had spent five months thinking about Jake's touch and his kiss. Her mind was made up.

The worst that can happen is that he will say no. Isn't that what Kelli said? Can you live with his rejection? Is the chance that he will say yes worth the chance of rejection? Nothing ventured, nothing gained—isn't that a quote from Chaucer?

She bathed, shaved her legs smooth, applied oil and lotion, and took special care with her hair and makeup. She dabbed perfume in all the right places and examined herself in the mirror. She debated how to approach him, and what to wear to get his attention. All Walt ever wanted was short, tight and sexy. But she knew Jake's taste in women was much more mature and sophisticated that Walt's.

Occasionally, her mind's eye would picture Jake with one of the beautiful women with whom she had often seen him. Each time, she felt hopelessness sidle close to her, smugly nudging her shoulder, its cold breath on her neck, but each time she prevailed. She had to know if he remembered that night—had to know if it had meant anything to him.

She would do just as Kelli suggested. She would tell Jake she wanted resolution to what they had left unsaid and undone. She didn't know where to go from there. She would leave the next step to Jake. If he were interested, he would know what to do.

Then, the thought struck her like a bolt of lightning out of stormy, dark sky—*I should have called first. It's Friday. I've gone to all this trouble to get ready and he probably has a date tonight. I should have called first.*

FOURTEEN

Kendra's name appeared on the caller ID, and Jake answered his humming phone. Her voice was soft.

"Hi. What are you doing?"

There was a familiar undertone in her voice that he knew. *Walt must be drinking again. She needs to talk.* It had been two weeks since they had spoken for any length of time. He was concerned for her—and glad to hear from her.

"A little TGIF by the pool, reading a book and thinking about grilling a steak," he replied casually. "You?"

"Just wondering if you have a few minutes to visit?"

"Sure. Are you on your own tonight?" He was pretty sure Walt was either absent or passed out. That seemed to be his usual behavior lately.

There was a long pause before she said, "Yes, as a matter of fact. Just me. But don't let me intrude if you have plans."

"No plans."

Kendra heaved an inward sigh of relief.

"You can visit as long as you'd like. If you have time, I'll fix dinner."

"That would be nice. Thank you. I'll be there in twenty minutes. What can I bring?"

"Bring your bikini, if you feel like getting in the pool. And your appetite. Got the rest covered."

He quickly showered off the tanning oil and pulled on clean shorts and a soft polo. He inspected his home, but it was neat and orderly as always.

He opened a bottle of good pinot noir that he knew she liked, decanted it, and set it aside to breathe. He set his playlist to soft jazz.

He knew that she was frustrated in her marriage, and that she had outgrown Walt's lower intelligence level and constant self-pity. He believed that it was time for her to get out of the marriage. He hoped, for her sake, that was coming soon.

She arrived, looking terrific in a soft, salmon-colored silk romper and petite flat sandals. Her thick, dark hair was brushed to a glossy sheen and pulled high on the back of her head into a pert ponytail that cascaded down her back and swayed enticingly when she moved. She smelled of fragrant soap and alluring perfume.

"Hi," she said with an enigmatic smile as she kissed his cheek. "Thank you for inviting me. Actually, I guess I invited myself, so thanks for having me." She set her purse and a leather bag by his entry table, looking around. "I just love your home. You must be very happy here."

"Thank you. I am," he replied with a smile. "Would you like a glass of wine?

"That would be nice."

He poured, and led her into the den. They sat at opposite ends of his comfortable, leather love seat. She dropped her sandals and gracefully curled her legs beneath her, sitting quietly for a few minutes.

"How are you?" she asked.

"I'm great. Life is good. Business is good."

She sipped her wine, smiled approvingly, and asked about his trip. He said that it went well. He and his partners had met with the owners of two small businesses that they were interested in acquiring. She asked some related questions.

She paused, and took a deep breath.

"Are you seeing anyone?" she asked with seeming nonchalance. It was a question she occasionally asked him.

"No. Not seeing anyone." He smiled, and she inwardly brightened.

"What happened to the banker you were dating?"

"No sparks," he replied. "She was nice, but ..."

She nodded, relieved. They talked pleasantly, but indirectly for several minutes. She sighed, looking at him without speaking. Jake had put her at ease, as he always did, but she was becoming anxious. He waited, knowing she would speak when she was ready.

She was thoughtful. *You're going to make a fool of yourself. He isn't interested. Leave now.*

"Jake, this was a mistake. I'm sorry. I should go home." She set her glass on the table and started to rise.

"Kendra, relax. I don't know what has upset you, but you can talk to me about it. I told you. Whatever is upsetting you, I'm here for you."

She signed, uncomfortably. "I know you are. I feel a little guilty. I'm taking advantage of your kindness and good counsel. I seem to do that a lot."

"Not at all. You're very special to me. I think you know that. At least, I hope you know that."

She smiled and nodded.

"Whatever I can do, all you have to do is ask."

She chuckled softly and smiled, saying nothing. *Talk to him, Kendra. Isn't that why you're here? You need closure. Talk to him.*

Finally, she sighed deeply, and spoke matter-of-factly. "I filed for divorce."

He nodded, surprised, but happy for her. "Good. I think you know I support that decision. Do you want to talk about it?"

She nodded soberly, grateful for Jake's support. "Two weeks ago, Walt was being his usual drunk and obnoxious self. I finally had enough. I told him we were through if he didn't get himself into rehab and stop drinking. He got belligerent. He grabbed my arm and asked who I thought I was, telling him what to do. I told him I was his wife, but that was going to end if he didn't change his ways. He slapped me and pushed me down. I struck the coffee table and it hurt like the dickens. Then, he just got a beer and went to the golf course without a word."

Jake didn't say anything, but she saw his black scowl at Walt's behavior.

"Since then, I've slept in the guest room." She paused. "To be honest, I've slept there for the last year. That happened on Sunday. On Monday, I had bruises on my face, my arm and my shoulder. I called in sick. I went to the sheriff's office and filed a report. They took pictures. I saw my doctor about the pain and the bruises so that there would be a medical report.

She took pictures also, and X-rays. Then I retained that great attorney that Susan Ellis used last year.

"My attorney filed my petition for divorce on Tuesday and obtained a temporary protective order. Walt was ordered out of the house and not to come within one hundred fifty feet of me and not to contact me except through my attorney. He was served and evicted Thursday while I was at work, and the sheriff took his guns away from him.

"The deputy called me afterward and told me Walt was drunk enough to be obnoxious, and even tried to intimidate the deputy. When the deputy threatened to jail him, Walt got his things and left. There was a hearing Wednesday of this week and the judge ordered him into AA, and drug and alcohol counseling twice a week, and he has to report to the court each week. The judge chastised him pretty well in plain language.

"His boss had already put him on probation. He is supposed to be out of town all next week on business with his boss. When he told the judge, she said she would excuse the counseling for this coming week. So, he will be gone all next week.

"I know I should feel bad, but I don't. I have no feelings for him anymore. He isn't the person I thought I knew in college and he isn't the man I thought I was marrying. I've tried to be supportive, but he's so wrapped up in himself that he has shut us all out.

"Confronting him opened a door for me, and any feelings I had for him just walked out. I'm sad about it, but I feel as though a huge load has been lifted from me. I'm going to have my life back. And I'm very thankful we didn't have a child.

"Does that sound cold?"

"No. It sounds practical and realistic. I'm glad you've taken control of the situation. I was worried you would stay for all the wrong reasons. I'm sure I must sound callow, but I think you've done the right thing. I'm very happy for you. I know that must have been a difficult decision."

"It was … until he hit me the second time."

Jake did a double take, an incredulous and deeply troubled look on his face. "Kendra, why didn't you tell me before now?"

Kendra hesitated, dropped her head and spoke softly. "I didn't want to talk about it. I was embarrassed and ashamed. I didn't want anyone to know, especially you. When it happened the first time, I let it time go. When it happened again, I knew it was time to move forward with my life."

"Good for you," Jake nodded calmly, but inwardly he was seething at Walt. "Do you think you'll stay in the house, or is that a premature question?"

She looked up at Jake. "Right now, I really don't want the house. It doesn't hold good memories for me, but I like the neighborhood and it's close to Kelli and Scott. My attorney says I should stay there until school is out."

"It's good the school year will end in two and a half months. I guess you have a lot of planning to do?'

"Yes; but I don't want to make any hasty decisions."

"That's smart." He saluted her with his glass. "Get your feet back on the ground. You'll find someone. Things will work out. You're beautiful and intelligent. You have too much going for you not to have a wonderful life."

"Thank you."

FIFTEEN

She held her wine glass before her, eyes pensively on the glass. After a minute, she spoke, not looking at him. "What you just said … I'm not interested in 'finding someone' right now."

She paused and breathed out softly. "Spring break is next week. I'm free for a week and I'm going to do some things I've wanted to do. At least, I hope so."

"Good for you. What do you want to do?"

"There are things around the house I should do. There are some new things I want to try." She sounded hesitant, as if she wanted to tell him, but was unsure of voicing her thoughts.

"Is there something special you want to do?"

She stared into her glass for a few seconds, took a sip and was quiet. *Trust Kelli's advice. Tell him.* He waited.

She smiled and quietly repeated, "Something special?" She looked up, into his comforting gaze. "Yes—something very special—but … I'm not sure how to talk about it."

"It's just me. You can tell me anything. I hope you know that."

"I do. I know that, but it's still a little awkward." *Courage, Kendra. Don't stop now.*

She looked directly at him, and straightened her shoulders. "You're well aware that the last few years have been less than ideal."

He nodded somberly.

She paused, again looking down at her glass. "Oh, Jake … this is not easy." *The worst that can happen is that he will say no. But … what if he says yes?*

She slowly looked up, directly into his eyes and blushed. "I … I want the company and attention of … someone very special to me. I want some intelligent conversation … and … ." She blushed, paused for a long moment, and looked down. She inhaled deeply, looking up, again directly into Jake's eyes. "I want warmth … and intimacy. I'd like to know what I've been missing for the past four years."

She exhaled softly. "There, I've said it," she murmured very quietly, almost as if to herself. *Please, God; don't let me make a fool of myself.*

Her bluntness took him by surprise. As did the disconcerting intimation that there was another man in her life. He knew from things that had been said over the course of their friendship that she and Walt had little experience before they married, and that Walt wasn't a particularly romantic or affectionate man.

He chuckled. "Well, it's good to know you have a plan. You're too intelligent and beautiful not to have what you want from life." He cocked his head, raising his eyebrows questioningly.

"You smiled when you told me what you wanted and your face brightened when you mentioned 'someone special.' I assume you have someone special in mind?"

She smiled, and was quiet for another long moment, looking intently into her glass before she spoke. Without looking up, she replied, "Yes. As a matter of fact, I do have someone in mind—a man who is very special to me."

"Good. You're a wonderful woman—and he's a lucky guy. Have you known him long?"

She looked up and smiled. "Yes. For a few years."

He nodded, smiling encouragingly at her, but inwardly he was selfishly disappointed—and more than a little jealous. "I didn't know you were seeing someone."

She smiled at him, saying nothing.

"Have you told him your plans?"

She hesitated and was silent for a moment. "Yes … in a way," she replied enigmatically, with a pert smile and a twinkle in her eyes.

He again raised his eyebrows questioningly.

She tilted her head and smiled a gentle, wistful smile, holding his gaze. Jake didn't speak.

"I just did," she said softly, looking directly at him with that same wistful smile.

Once again, he looked at her quizzically.

"Do you think he's interested?" she asked softly.

"I'm sure he is. Any man in his right mind would be."

"Thank you." She continued, her gaze never wavering.

He stared at her, confused—confused by her words and by her steady gaze that didn't shift as she quietly sat opposite him. Then, the dime dropped.

He blinked, cocked his head and simply looked at her. She smiled gently and nodded ever so slightly.

Jake was overwhelmed. He opened his mouth to speak, but nothing came out. He opened his mouth a second time and said, "You … don't mean me?"

She nodded, smiling broadly. *Yes, Jake—I mean you.*

"Yes," she said, softly. "I trust you, Jake. We know we're attracted to each other—it seems to make sense." She paused, gathered her courage, and continued quietly. "I'd like to finish what we started last fall. I'd like to know if that night meant anything to you." *Please, Jake.*

She touched his hand as her courage began to wane. Her touch was warm and gentle.

"You can think about it. You can say no, and I'll understand."

She sighed, shaking her head fearfully. "Oh, God. I feel so awkward." *Don't quit, Kendra. Don't quit.*

"I'm … speechless." He ran his hand awkwardly over his hair and smiled. "I guess that makes me one incredibly lucky guy. Are you sure?"

She nodded silently. "You remind me a lot of my brother. You seem to be all the good things my brother is. My brother is an Eagle Scout. He recited the Boy Scout Oath and Law to me so many times, I know them by heart."

She raised three fingers in the Scout sign and recited, "On my honor, I will do my best to do my duty to God and my country and to obey the Scout Law …"

Jake smiled at the memories her words evoked. "And?"

"I recall you told me you were a Boy Scout—an Eagle Scout also, I think. My brother always told me, 'Find a Scout and make him your friend. Trust him and he will always be there when you need him. You won't be sorry.' So, I'm taking his advice," she said cheerily.

"We came close last fall. I think about that night constantly. But, if you aren't interested, just tell me." She looked into his eyes.

"Yes; we did come close. I've never forgotten that night either. And yes; that night means a great deal to me."

Oh, thank goodness, she thought, relieved.

She had caught him completely off guard. He had never met a woman who caught—and held—his interest the way she had. She was beautiful, intelligent, witty and personable. And he, too, often thought of that night last fall. But, she had certainly surprised him—in the most pleasant way.

He gently took her hand, touching her for the first time in five months, as he chuckled. "I don't remember anything in the Scout Handbook about girls and intimacy."

She smiled gently and said softly, "It's right there, in the Scout Law— trustworthy, loyal, helpful, friendly, courteous, kind, obedient, cheerful, thrifty, brave, clean, reverent—everything a girl could ask for in a man."

Jake thought about that. "Everything?"

"Well, good looking and exciting would be nice," she replied with a chuckle.

He laughed and nodded.

She squeezed his hand. "I'm an optimist. I guess we'll just have to see, won't we?"

"You may be disappointed."

"I doubt that seriously." A disconsolate look crossed her face. "Actually, you're the one who may be disappointed."

"Why do you say that?"

"I really like your sister. Once when she was here visiting and you guys were outside, we talked frankly. We opened up to each other. I told her about my frustrating marriage. She told me about herself and her life.

"She also told me that she had set you 'on the right path,' as it were." She made little quotation marks with her fingers. "Her words were," she blushed, 'I told him, if he was going to take women to bed, he should know how to please them properly.' She told me that you frequently escort her friends to events when they need a male companion, and that her friends are very fond of you."

"Anything else?" he asked with mock curiosity.

She hesitated. "She said it was too bad I wasn't single." Kendra blushed and continued quietly, "She said you told her that you found me attractive."

"I did tell her that." He smiled at her. "My sister can be very direct when she wants to be. She must like you a lot to have told you those things."

SIXTEEN

Jake's sister was a very competent executive in the world of finance. She was also a lesbian who traveled in influential circles. She and her friends kept a very low profile and wielded a measure of influence in the business and political worlds. Very often, when one of them needed a male companion for a special event, Jake was her date.

Kendra touched his arm. "Your sister gave me this sense that you know your way around a woman's bedroom, so to speak. I had no experience when I married Walt. He was the first and only—and I don't think he had much experience either. Romance and foreplay weren't in his playbook. I think it seemed good at first because … well, it was sex and I was married—and I didn't know any better.

"The night you kissed me, you literally made all of my nerve endings quiver. I had never been kissed as tenderly as you kissed me that night—or touched as gently. Despite my limited experience, I would have done anything with you that night if you had pressed me." She blushed. *As always, Jake is easy to talk to.* "I know I would have regretted it afterward. Thank you for understanding. But, I've never forgotten your kiss or your touch."

He nodded and smiled. "I'm truly flattered. My sister told you the truth. I've always been attracted to you, but—except for our one night—I don't get involved with married women."

"I won't be for much longer. My mind is settled on that issue."

Courage, Kendra. Tell him.

"That night is indelible. I'd like to know where it could have gone if we had let it. I feel as though we left something undone … and I'd like to finish it—but I don't want to ruin our friendship or be a problem for you."

"You could never be a problem for me." He smiled at her. "Are you sure this is what you want? No regrets down the road?"

Kendra paused and took a deep breath. She sat quietly for a moment, then looked up at him, nodding purposefully. "I'm sure. As soon as my decision about divorce was made and the papers were actually filed, I just knew I had to see you. In my mind, the marriage is over, even if it isn't official yet."

She touched his arm gently. "I'm not asking you to make a commitment, but I'd like closure to what we started. No regrets later. Hopefully, just wonderful memories."

He took her hand. "Maybe, now that you've actually spoken of it, it would be good to reflect for a little while. Are you hungry? I can fix dinner and you can think as long as you would like."

"Thank you. I'm too nervous to be hungry. But some more wine would be nice."

He stood, taking her glass. She followed him to the kitchen. She stood close as he poured, her fragrance and her smile embracing him. It was both exciting and disconcerting for him. He extended her glass, asking again, "Inside or outside?"

She took her glass, touching his arm. "Outside would be nice. Is that okay?"

He nodded. "You smell good," he offered as he gazed at her. "And you look wonderful."

"Thank you," she said, looking down. She looked up, into his eyes and held his gaze. "I'm glad I'm here. Thank you for not rejecting me out of hand."

He nodded and smiled warmly. "I'm glad you're here, too." He touched her cheek. "Very glad. Relax. Everything will work out as it should."

She smiled ingenuously and took his hand. They went outside and sat, watching the incipient pastel sunset begin. Jake's yard was beautifully landscaped, and accepted the softening evening light delightfully. They talked about dinner and the weather and this and that. They talked around the elephant in the room. There was an undercurrent of awkwardness between them for the first time since they had met—until he made her laugh. He saw some of her tension dissipate. Then he made her laugh again and she relaxed.

"How soon would you like to eat?"

She stood, stepping close to him, putting her hand on his arm as she stretched to kiss his cheek. "I'm too nervous to eat, but don't let me stop you."

He took her glass, setting both glasses aside, stood and gently pulled her into his embrace. "Just relax. There's no need to be nervous."

She put her arms around his neck and pressed against him, laying her head on his chest. *Relax, Kendra.* She felt his warmth as she pressed against him, and he felt her warmth against his hip. They held each other like that without saying a word for several moments as the burgeoning orange and pink patterns of sunset suffused the cerulean sky.

"Jake?"

He stepped back a half step and looked into her intent eyes.

"Jake, I've thought about this a lot. Please don't lead me on out of kindness. If you're looking for a polite way to say no, to let me down gently, you can tell me you aren't interested. I understand I've been pretty forward."

"Kendra … uuh … no," he stammered, shaking his head. "I'm trying to get my mind around this without jumping up and down and shouting for joy. I'm flattered. I'm ecstatic. I'm sorry if my hesitation seemed like rejection. I won't lead you on; but I don't want to lead you into a mistake." He put a finger under her chin and gently tipped her face up. "You're really sure this is what you want?"

She blushed, once again, and smiled almost shyly. "I'm sure, Jake. I couldn't be more sure," she replied with false confidence.

"You're still tense."

She nodded cautiously. "I'm still a little nervous."

"Would you like to slow down?"

Oh, my—he thinks I want all this tonight. Oh, my God. You need to go home, Kendra, and give this some time to develop.

"Jake, I … I didn't mean…I …" *What do I do now?* She was suddenly a bundle of nerves, and she began to tremble. *Oh, my God. Why wouldn't he*

*think that after what I've said to him. But, that's what I really want. That's
exactly I want. I'll lose my courage if we wait.*

"No. Just hold me for a minute."

He wrapped her in his arms, kissing her temple and stroking the back
of her head. She sighed and relaxed just a little.

Pressing her head against his chest, she was still for a moment, then
whispered, "I'm okay. It's okay now."

He kissed her very gently on the lips and she timidly returned his kiss,
just as gently. She was still for a moment, then again kissed him timidly.
She looked up and, when he smiled at her, pulled his mouth to hers. She
kissed him, slowly, two times. With the second kiss, he ran the tip of his
tongue across her lips, parting them. She responded readily, holding him to
her, and he felt the warmth of her breasts against him and the heat in her
against his thighs. They explored with their lips and their tongues, kissing
and making love with their mouths, enjoying the growing anticipation.
Each felt the incipient release of emotional fetters.

"I'm a little nervous, too," he said softly. "I never thought I would be
able to hold you and touch you or kiss you like this—but I've imagined
it often."

His words were a soothing comfort for her, reassurance that what was
happening wasn't one-sided, after all. She raised her lips to his and they
again made love with their tongues and lips.

*I won't let this get out of hand. But for right now, I just need to be close
to him.*

Inwardly, she thought of the first time she dove into the deep end of
the pool as a young girl. She was a little scared then, and a little excited.
She was a little scared now—and very excited.

He touched her gently, and his touch was warm and confident. A
tremor coursed throughout her body followed by a pervasive, but welcome,
feeling of warmth. *Leave now, Kendra.* But she knew she wouldn't—knew
deep in her core that this was what she wanted.

Jake kissed her as gently as he had that night months ago. His kiss sent
ripples of eager excitement throughout her entire body.

Oh, God. This is really happening. Trust him.

Jake felt her tremble as a small shiver of anxious anticipation ran
through her. He stroked her hair softly, reassuring her with gentle words.

She was nervous, breathing hard. Her breath quivered and slowed, but her mind was alive. She felt wetness between her legs and was surprised that her body was reacting involuntarily to Jake's presence. *Even on his best day, Walt was never this gentle and attentive.*

He held her close for a long moment. "You're sure?"

She pressed against him, pensive and uncertain. Finally, she made her decision. She nodded silently. *This is what you've wanted,* she thought. *You're not a virgin. Trust him. Let him lead.*

"We can go slower."

She shook her head and took his hand. "I don't need to be courted, Jake. Just be patient with me." *Make love to me before I lose my courage.*

SEVENTEEN

Jake led her to his bedroom where he closed the shutters and they turned down the bedcovers. In the subdued light, they undressed each other slowly—but eagerly. Kendra had never undressed a man before, but Jake helped and it seemed to happen naturally.

Gazing at her, he thought she was breathtakingly beautiful. He gently walked her backward to the spacious, empty bed. She sat slowly, then hesitantly lay back against the pillows, one knee up and a conflict of anxious eagerness on her face. Neither spoke a word, but their eyes communicated as he stretched out beside her.

Kendra's eyes were those of a sleek, graceful doe—wide, intent, curious, wanting to approach, yet ready to bolt at the first wrong move.

Looking into his eyes, she said quietly, "Walt was the only one. I … I'm not … I don't want to disappoint you."

"Shh." Jake took her into his arms and kissed her tenderly. "You're a beautiful woman, Kendra, and I want you more than you can know. Listen to your body and follow your instincts. We'll be fine together."

Oh, God. I'm in the deep end of the pool now. I hope I've done the right thing.

She was tense. She tried to relax, but couldn't. He kissed her gently and murmured softly to her. He stroked her very slowly, deliberately—adroitly calming her nervous fears and arousing her growing desire with his touch, his lips, his tongue, his warm breath and soft words.

At first, Kendra felt wooden and uncertain, but her timidity was gradually replaced with growing awareness and excitement. When Jake was certain she was ready, he gently moved to her. She inhaled sharply, her entire abdomen clenching as a bolt of white-hot awareness surged through her loins.

As Jake slowly pressed against her, she gasped and clenched. He stopped.

"Are you alright?" he asked softly.

She held him tightly, her breath quivering in her throat. It wasn't her first time, but it had never begun like this. Excitement filled her as she squirmed against him.

"Yes," she gasped very softly. "Don't stop."

Jake continued slowly. Kendra tightened again and trembled as he slipped inside her.

"Oooh," she murmured softly, closing her eyes and drawing the word out deliciously.

"Still alright?" he asked, gazing at her face.

She looked at him with glazed eyes. Kendra was astounded and thankful. Jake was gentle—not in a rush to pound away at her. There was no discomfort—only wonderful sensations that filled her core and coursed throughout her body. She quivered. *Oh, yes. I'm very alright.* She nodded, looking languidly up into his eyes.

"Yes," she repeated huskily with unforeseen pleasure and satisfaction in her voice as she involuntarily quivered and clenched again. "Don't stop."

As Jake began to move against her, she gasped, her breath catching in her throat. Her eyes hooded, closed and her head lolled back. She grasped his wrists tightly, moaning softly as her body involuntarily arched to him. They made love just as they had undressed each other—slowly, gently, but eagerly. Jake led Kendra as her uncertainty cautiously dissipated.

Kendra had never experienced making love as slowly and sensually as she now was with Jake. She may have been nervous and uncertain, but her body knew exactly what was happening—and it responded just as it was intended to do.

She felt the tremors and sensations surging within her and was unsure of what to do. She didn't want to embarrass herself, but she was mindful of Kelli's advice. She had never experienced a climax with Walt—by any means—but Jake was gentle and attentive to her.

Jake felt her tense—not from excitement, but from uncertainty.

"Relax. Let yourself go, Kendra. Listen to your body." He kissed her neck. "Let it all come out. It's okay. I need to know if this is good for you."

His words were what she needed to hear. And Kelli's advice rang clear in her mind. She gave herself to all that was happening in her mind and in her body. Kendra clutched Jake's forearms as her body and her breath quivered like a candle flame in the breeze. She groaned with unexpected pleasure as all her nerve endings tensed and released in sensual rhythm, sending an ageless message throughout her body, over and over. She involuntarily moaned and mewled, cried out and convulsed naturally as she peaked, breathing heavily. She felt Jake tense and heard his groan as she began her descent, murmuring happily with unbridled pleasure until her heart and quivering nerves slowed and she lay comfortably in his arms.

Tears filled her eyes and joy filled her heart. Walt may have been her first, but this was everything she had ever hoped intimacy with a man would be—and much more.

So this is what it's like to make love, and not just have sex. I've waited five years to experience this—and it was incredible. Thank you, Jake.

She looked into his eyes. *He isn't asleep!*

He smiled at her. "Are you okay?" he asked with quiet concern.

"I'm wonderful," she said softly. *If you only knew.* She kissed him hungrily. She raised her eyes, looking directly into his eyes as she whispered with happy conviction, "I've <u>never</u> felt like that before."

He smiled, nodded and lay quietly next to her, stroking her hair. After a while, despite the fact that he wanted her again, he politely asked, "Are you hungry?"

"Not just yet," she whispered, kissing him gently as she nestled herself firmly against his chest. *How could I possibly think of food right now?* She wanted him again, but her emotions were mixed. She still tingled everywhere—inside and out. For some inexplicable reason, a small, uncertain part of her wanted to simply grab her clothes and bolt. Another part of her wanted to revel in what had just happened inside her. But another, more demanding part of her wanted to experience him again.

Sex with Walt had always been just a single, hurried act; but with Jake, it had been so much more—and she wanted more. She kissed his lips and buried her head in the curve of his neck. They lay together quietly.

Want me again, Jake. Take me there again, please.

He kissed her and she pressed herself against him, parting his lips with her tongue, sending him an eager, undeniable message. As if he read her thoughts, Jake slowly, gently repeated everything they had just done, making her ready, leading her back into love. Kendra was still tremulous, but excited and eager. She was ready.

She slid her arms under his and grasped his shoulders as she involuntarily began to move rhythmically with him—slowly, tenuously, awkwardly at first, but with growing ardor until emotion again overwhelmed her. She shuddered, trembled and moaned, long and low and joyfully, pulling Jake tightly against her as complete fulfillment again coursed through her. She sighed and murmured happily to Jake.

Oh, my God! This must be what Kelli experiences with Scott. This is what making love should be. She was filled with reverie. *Oh, Jake, you know just how to make love to me.* Her body quivered with tiny aftershocks, and her mind raced with wonder and amazement at the physical pleasure that Jake gave her. She looked at him and smiled. *And … you're still not asleep.*

She thought about what Kelli had said to her at dinner. She kissed his ear and softly spoke what was in her heart. "Oh, Jake. That was wonderful. I love how you touch me and I love how you make me feel. Thank you for taking your time with me."

Jake grinned happily, kissed her gently and spoke softly. "The pleasure was all mine."

EIGHTEEN

They lay together until their breathing slowed and their hearts stopped pounding. They sighed and murmured to each other. As Jake started to move apart, Kendra gently pulled him back to her, and said softly, "Stay with me for a minute." Jake did happily.

She held him and kissed his neck. "Yes," she murmured, barely audible. After a moment, she sighed contentedly, then relaxed.

"Are you hungry now?" Jake asked

"Yes—" she giggled, "famished. I've been too nervous to eat today."

"He chuckled. "Steaks, salmon or chicken?"

"Salmon would be nice, if that's okay. What can I do."

"You can make the salad … and talk with me."

They dressed. "Give me your keys," he said. "I think it would be prudent to put your car in my garage."

They set about preparing dinner in his spacious kitchen. He didn't press her, letting her lead the conversation. She talked about her day, his house and mutual friends. It was easy small talk between friends that avoided the obvious, but at one point, she stepped to him, took his hand, laid her head against his chest, and sighed happily.

"Thank you," she whispered very softly. Her small act spoke volumes.

After dinner, they went to the patio and settled into comfortable chairs by the placid pool, enjoying the evening as the final waning pastel rays of sunset became twilight.

"You said you were going to do some things you had always wanted to do. What do you have in mind?"

She chuckled softly, touching his cheek with her fingertips. "We just did the most important one." *I just made love with my best friend, and I'm just as comfortable with him as I have always been. I saved myself for my husband. I spent four married years not knowing how good physical intimacy could be. And all that time, I've missed so much. I've done the right thing now.* She looked at him pensively. "I certainly hope there will be more—if that isn't being too presumptuous."

He chuckled and quipped, "I think you can rely on that, probably as much as you want."

"Then, I'm a happy girl." *Oh, yes! I'm a happy girl. I never imagined a man could make me feel this good.*

She heard her phone ring from within the house. She went for her purse, came to the door and said she had to return a phone call to her lawyer. She talked, ended the call and returned to the patio.

She told Jake about Walt's phone message and that she had informed her lawyer. "The judge called my lawyer at the end of the day. The judge is concerned that Walt will defy her order. She told my lawyer to let her know if there were any problems this weekend and gave my lawyer her home number.

"My lawyer suggested that I spend the weekend with friends until Walt leaves town, and that I verify that he actually leaves on Sunday as scheduled. I guess I'll call Kelli or Susan Ellis and ask if I can stay for a couple of nights."

"You can stay here, if you would like."

She was taken aback at first, the good girl in her recoiling—until she thought about making love with him. She considered his offer.

Well, she thought, smiling inwardly, *isn't this an unexpected and pleasant surprise. And timely. Do I have a fairy godmother, or is Eve tempting me with her apple?* She smiled and nodded as she took his hand and started to speak, then paused thoughtfully.

"Thank you. I don't want to impose …"

She saw the eager invitation in his eyes and in his smile. She made her choice. "But I think I would feel much safer here … and enjoy myself much more." Her warm smile said it all. "But, I really don't want to impose on you, and I didn't bring any clothes."

"You aren't imposing. I invited you." He smiled reassuringly. "You can get clothes and whatever you need tomorrow. Since your home will be unattended, get your jewelry, valuables and important items and bring them with you. If you need something to sleep in tonight, I have plenty of soft T-shirts."

Kendra smiled and was happy. "Thank you, Jake." She kissed his cheek.

They sat, enjoying the warm evening. She talked, and he listened. She obviously needed to discard some burdensome baggage, and he was attentive and encouraging. They refilled their glasses and returned to the patio. She was quiet.

"What else?" he asked, returning full circle.

She grasped his question immediately.

"Apart from feeling the earth move again," she replied with a satisfied smile, "I'd like to ride a horse. I haven't been on a horse for ten or twelve years. I'd like to go zip lining. I'd like to go to the Museum of Fine Arts. I want to sit in the sun, tan and read a good book. I'd like to create some flowerbeds and plant pretty flowers in the yard; although I'm not sure I can keep the house, or even want to. We've done nothing to the house since we bought it and it needs some attention."

"Those are good projects. I'm sure you can do them all in the coming week. Anything else on your list?"

She was pensive for a moment. "Maybe—but let's talk about that another time."

Enigmatic, he thought, *but she'll tell me when she's ready.*

Darkness had fallen, the moon was rising, and familiar night sounds and shadows filled the calm evening. Except for the soft music that was playing, the house behind them was quiet, immersed in darkness. Jake pulled her to him and they sat quietly for a moment. They heard a car coming slowly along the street. It stopped. It sounded as if it were stopping at Jake's house. A dog barked from somewhere outside, and soon the car drove away.

She looked at Jake and smiled. They kissed and touched, aware of where they had been and could now go again. As their shared need grew,

Jake stood, and smiled questioningly. Silently, she nodded. He took her hand in his and led her to his bedroom.

When they were spent and she was calm, she pulled his head to her, kissed him and nestled into the crook of his neck. She languidly said, "I think all the emotion and the excitement of making love have worn me out. May we sleep?"

He nodded, took her hand, kissed her, and she was asleep in seconds.

NINETEEN

Walt drove to their home and parked on the street just before eight o'clock. He rang the bell, but she didn't answer. That made him angry. *Where the hell is she? Probably with Kelli or Susan complaining about me. Or with Jake. She talks with him a lot. Or, maybe she's with some guy. That would make sense. Why else would she want a divorce?*

He took the spare garage door opener from his pocket, the one he had picked up from the kitchen drawer when the cop made him leave, and opened the big door. Her car was gone. He went into the house through the garage and began looking around. *This is my home, isn't it? Judge or no judge, I have a right to be here, don't I?*

He looked through the papers on the desk, but found only mail and court papers and school papers from her students—nothing that could explain her behavior. He looked through the kitchen, then their bedroom where he went into their closet and looked through her clothes, touching them and smelling her fragrance on them. He looked through her jewelry box and found the ring he had given her for her birthday. He picked it up and put it in his pocket. *She sure as hell doesn't deserve this.* He opened her drawers and searched for anything hidden among her underwear or clothes. He found nothing but noticed a new pair of small, black lace panties. *I wonder who she bought these for.* He stuffed the panties into his pocket.

He went to this trophy room where he sat on the couch, admiring his trophies, awards and accolades. His thoughts shift to the past week. *What a shit storm. My lawyer is a loser and that damned judge obviously has it in for me. What a bitch! And Kendra—she might be beautiful, but she isn't the woman for me. And marriage isn't for me. But look on the bright side. I can date again, all the pretty and sexy girls I want to date. Get my knee back in shape and get back in uniform—the chicks will be all over me again.*

But he was still angry with Kendra. She had embarrassed him in front Kelli and Scott, her parents, that damned judge, and a whole courtroom of people who knew who Walt Williams was.

I need to talk to her, get her to drop this lawsuit and then we can go our separate ways peacefully. She blind-sided me, just like Ohula and Morgan. I'll get even with them and I'll get even with her. She needs to know she can't treat me like this.

He thought about going to a bar, but had enough sense to know that would lead to losing his job. He couldn't get on that plane with a hangover. His boss would fire him on the spot. He drove around for a while, stopped at a restaurant known for its attractive waitresses, ordered pie and coffee, enjoyed the view and flirted with his waitress while he ate.

He drove by Kelli's house, then Susan's, then decided to talk to Jake about everything. *Hell, she's probably there talking to him about me.* He followed a pizza delivery driver through the gated entry into Jake's subdivision, but didn't see Kendra's car on his driveway.

He parked in front of Jake's the house and the neighbor's dog began barking. The lights were out and the house was dark. He sat for a moment. He remembered that Jake normally went to bed early and rose early, and thought that it probably wasn't a good idea to wake Jake. Jake was on her side, anyway. Jake had talked to him often enough about his drinking and about his lackadaisical attitude toward physical therapy after the surgery. He knew he wouldn't get any sympathy from Jake.

What the hell. I don't need Jake preaching to me now. Besides, Jake probably knows by now that I hit Kendra, and Jake would never excuse me for something like that.

He drove to Mitchell's, took an over the counter sedative and went to bed. He left the ring and panties on his dresser.

TWENTY

On Saturday, Jake woke first, made coffee, showered quietly and shaved. Contrary to Friday, the day was overcast. He took his coffee to the patio and watched the sky for the rain that was predicted to come. Kendra came to the door, dressed in her romper, a full coffee cup in her hands.

"Want some company?"

"Certainly." He smiled as she came toward him. He softly asked her, "Are you okay?"

She gazed directly into his eyes. She nodded, smiled a very happy, warm smile and softly replied. "Yes." She stood motionless, looking into Jake's eyes.

"Yes," she repeated. "I know I should feel guilty—but I don't. I feel wonderful. Last night was wonderful."

"Good." He took her hand and kissed it. "Good morning."

She came to him and kissed his lips. "Good morning," she replied warmly. "I hope you don't mind, but I helped myself to your shower."

He returned her kiss and she sat next to him. "I don't mind at all. *Mi casa es su casa*, as they say."

She laughed and touched his hand. "Thank you. I don't want to be in your way. I can go home."

"Nope. The judge said stay gone until we know he has left town. You're welcome here." He drank some coffee. "Do you know his flight number? Can you check to see if he's gone?"

"I know the flight number and time, but I don't know how to verify he got on the plane. I can just check the departure. But he'll be flying with his boss, so I think it's safe to assume he will be gone."

"I guess that's the best we can do. And you aren't going to be in my way. You're invited for the weekend. After that, we'll have to see if we have any ragged nerves."

She laughed again. "You're sweet. And a very accommodating host. I'm still on cloud nine."

"Good." He looked at her thoughtfully and nodded his head. "Very good," he said softly. "Did you sleep well?"

She smiled. "Very well. You don't snore."

"Does that surprise you?"

Everything about you surprises me, Jake. "I thought all men snored. My Daddy does. Walt did." Jake noticed that she used the past tense, and it pleased him. "Kelli says Scott does. It was a pleasant surprise. Or, maybe I just slept so soundly, I didn't hear you."

"Well, I've never awakened myself snoring."

She laughed.

"Would you like some breakfast?"

"Maybe in a little while. Right now, coffee is fine.

"I think it will be okay for me to go home for a few minutes. I'm sure you have things you need to do." Kendra retrieved her purse and keys. "I can get what I need and be back shortly. I'll be okay."

He agreed hesitantly. "Call me if there are any problems."

Fifteen minutes later, the phone rang and her name appeared on the ID.

"Hi. Is everything all right?"

"I'm not sure, but I think someone was in the house while I was gone. Some papers and things aren't in the same place that I left them. The door to the bedroom closet was partly open and I know I left it closed. I can't find the ring Walt gave me for my birthday and I'm certain it was in my jewelry case. And—this probably sounds funny—but I'm pretty sure that a new pair of panties is missing from the dresser. I checked the safe and nothing there has been disturbed."

"How do you think the person got in?

"I'm dumb. I locked the house, but not the door from the mud room into the garage. When the constable made Walt leave, he collected his keys and his garage door opener, but the spare opener that we kept in a kitchen drawer is missing.

"What should I do?" she asked.

"Gather your valuables and enough clothes for a few days, unplug the garage door opener, lock every door and come back here. When you get here, call your attorney and ask her advice. I suggest you also call a security company and have a system installed next week."

She returned with a suitcase and an overnight bag. She was dressed fetchingly in short shorts and a tank top. "I did what you suggested. What I have and don't want to lose is all in here."

"How are you doing," he asked.

"I'm not sure. I'm unsettled, I guess. I'm angry, partly at myself for not being more careful with the doors. I don't know whether to be scared or not. I'm glad I wasn't home last night when Walt—or whoever—came in. I wish now we had installed a security system." She touched his arm. "Thank you for giving me a safe haven last night."

"You're welcome." He could tell that her mind was awhirl at the moment. "Give me your keys. I'll move your car into the garage."

When he returned, she said, "Okay, all the little ones and zeros are back in place. Sorry for my silence. I guess I should call my lawyer … and arrange for a security system."

He smiled and nodded. "No problem. Relax. Talk with your lawyer." He showed her an empty drawer and closet space for her things. "I'll be in my study."

She called her lawyer who told her to file a police report, today if possible, if not, on Monday. They talked for several minutes about the incident and about the divorce. She called to report the incident and was told a deputy would come to her home within the hour. She looked at the name on the control panel on Jake's home security system and called the same company, arranging installation early Monday morning.

She told Jake about the call to the sheriff and he accompanied her to her home. They met the deputy who took her report, advised her that little could be done without more evidence, but promised to file the report in case there were any more events.

TWENTY-ONE

Walt woke at nine o'clock, Saturday morning. Mitchell was in the kitchen with coffee and a magazine on the table before him. He looked up and pointed to the coffee pot. Walt poured a cup and sat.

"I'm going to talk to Kendra today. She can't just evict me. It's my home, too."

"Walt, don't rock the boat. That judge sounds pretty serious. If you go over there and Kendra calls the police, you could be arrested and you would miss your flight tomorrow. You're not thinking clearly. You need this job, bro."

"Yeah, you're probably right. I guess I'll get some breakfast and go to the golf course."

"Better idea," Mitchell replied.

Walt drove by Kelli's home, Susan's, and followed a car through the gate into Jake's subdivision, but didn't see Kendra's car. He went for breakfast, frustrated and overthinking the matter. Despite Mitchell's caution, he decided to go to the house and talk to Kendra. He paid his check and drove to their house.

As he approached, he saw Kendra's car on the driveway and a Sheriff's cruiser parked in front of the house. *Well, shit. She probably knows now I was in the house last night and called the Sheriff. Bitch. She can't do this to me. But I sure can't stop here now.*

He again thought about talking to Jake, but again decided that wasn't a good idea. Instead, he drove to the golf course, had two beers and played poorly until it started to rain. He loaded his wet clubs into the trunk of his car and drove to the same restaurant as last night, where he flirted with the waitresses. One was particularly attractive and seemed receptive to his mood. He made a date with her for that evening.

TWENTY-TWO

Jake and Kendra returned from meeting the sheriff's deputy. As she unpacked and put away her things, he went to his study. After a while, she came into his study, barefoot and beautiful with a smile on her face. She stood next to him and touched his shoulder. "Are you working on something special?"

"No; just finishing up some loose ends."

"You didn't have any breakfast. May I fix you some lunch?"

"That would be great. Let's fix together. I need a break. My mind is elsewhere." He cocked his head, arched his brows and smiled conspiratorially at her. "Why do you think that is?"

"Hmm? Perhaps you could show me after lunch," she replied softly with a coy smile, a little surprised at her sauciness. *Kendra, you little hussy!* She smiled happily at her thought.

"Ah, titillation. It's good for the soul. I enjoy being titillated as much as the next person … maybe more."

"Titillated," she mused. "That's an interesting word—especially in this context."

They laughed.

As the rain began to gently fall outside, they made sandwiches and soup, and ate together sitting by the windows as they watched the steady fall of the rain and listened to the tympanic patter of raindrops. They cleared the table and placed their dishes into the dishwasher together.

He wasn't ready to go back to work, and she enjoyed being close to him. Jake poured two glasses of wine and they sat together, enjoying the soft sound of the rain drops. The rain intensified and soon the heavens were disgorging large, heavy raindrops that splattered the earth outside and splatted against the windows. Thunder rolled and echoed around them as serpentine tongues of jagged white lightning arched cross the sky. She instinctively pressed against Jake's shoulder and grasped his forearm as the strength of Nature overwhelmed the world outside, but not the emotions that ran through each of them.

It soon became apparent that their need needed to be fulfilled. They rose and went to Jake's bedroom where they undressed each other with slow, but eager anticipation, and took turns exploring the other's body as the rain slowed and became a gentle murmur outside. Kendra easily fell into Jake's rhythm and they finished together, wet with perspiration, and happy. They lay quietly together, listening to the patter of the rain, talking sporadically, cuddling and touching for several happy moments.

"Are you all right?" he asked quietly.

She paused briefly, then she giggled and whispered in his ear, "Oh, yes. I'm wonderful." Jake laughed.

They dressed and made the bed. She challenged him to a game of Scrabble as the rain continued to fall steadily outside. One game became three games, liberally sprinkled with some suggestive repartee. The word of the evening was sexcitement. Kendra challenged the word, but Jake told her it was a word in his vocabulary and he thought it should be in the dictionary. She laughed and agreed that it could be in their dictionary. They played Scrabble and teased until they decided it was time for dinner.

They prepared dinner together, talking, teasing and laughing easily. They ate, watched a movie and cuddled. When the movie ended, he turned the lights out and they walked hand in hand to his bed. Later, when they finally slipped apart, she sighed softly, nestling into him. He took her hand and she fell asleep immediately.

TWENTY-THREE

Walt went to Mitchell's, showered, dressed and drove to the girl's apartment. She looked great—short little black dress cut low, showing lots of tanned cleavage and lots of tanned legs. Walt smiled to himself. Tonight would be just what he needed—some drinks, some pussy. He could make it through the next week. He began flirting and making innuendos. He put his hand on her knee and stroked her leg as he drove.

He took her to dinner at an upscale restaurant that was very popular, and where he was known. He was greeted, exchanged pleasantries with the maître d', and asked for a booth. They were seated and ordered drinks. Walt immediately began telling her about his injury and the strenuous rehabilitation that he was going through to get ready for the coming season. Their drinks arrived. Walt drank his quickly, ordered another and began stroking her leg as he talked. She removed his hand.

"I read that you quit going to physical therapy and that you wouldn't be back this season," she said.

"No, that's not true. That was just written by some reporters who don't understand how hard this therapy is. It was a bad injury and initially I overdid the therapy, so we're taking a little break until my knee is ready to start again."

"So, you'll be back this season?"

"Sure. I have another surgery again in a few weeks that should fix me good as new," he lied blatantly, "and I'll be out there on the field again."

"That's wonderful. I like watching you play."

"Do you know much about football?"

"My brother plays for Oklahoma. My daddy coached high school here in Houston and in Oklahoma. Now, he is an assistant coach at Oklahoma. And my younger brother plays. He graduates next year and will probably get a scholarship to Oklahoma. I've dated some football players. I really like football."

Their waiter came and they ordered dinner and another round of drinks. Walt continued talking about himself. When she asked him what he was doing now, he again lied, telling her he played a lot of golf and was making public appearances for a young marketing company in order to help them out while he was out of the game.

"I didn't know you were a golfer," she said. "I love golf. I've played since I was a little girl and I'm on the U of H team."

"Are you any good?"

"I was junior amateur champion in Oklahoma. My last year in high school, I was ranked second in the state."

"Well, you know what they say about second place," Walt quipped thoughtlessly.

She was quiet for a moment, taken aback by his comment. "It was good enough to get me a scholarship," she replied evenly.

"Well, good for you," he replied carelessly. "Why are you working?"

"I don't have a benefactor yet and it helps with my living expenses. My parents aren't wealthy," she replied honestly.

Without hesitation, Walt told her he never had to work and resumed talking about himself. He described his successes in high school and told her that he was a high school All-American and that he went to college on a football scholarship … and on and on.

Dinner was served and Walt continued his self-aggrandizement through college and his first year in the NFL. He ordered a fourth drink. She declined another. She listened quietly and enjoyed her dinner, but not her date.

After dinner, she declined dessert, but Walt ordered dessert for himself and another drink. His speech was becoming thick, and he knocked over his water glass—narrowly missing her.

"I read that your wife filed for divorce. Is that true?"

"Yeah. She beat me to the courthouse, as they say. I was going to file, but she begged for a second chance. When I said yes and didn't file, she filed so that she would have the upper hand in court. She needs to go. She hasn't been supportive of me or my efforts to get back on the field. She only thinks about herself."

He put his hand on her knee, looked her in the eyes and said, "I need a woman who understands what I'm going through here. A woman who will be there for me when I need her." He ran his hand up her thigh, almost, but not quite touching her southern parts.

She moved his hand and replied, "I'm sure this has been difficult for you."

"You can't imagine." He again ran his hand back up her thigh as his dessert and drink arrived. She again moved his hand.

"Did you tell your girlfriends you had a date with Walt Williams tonight?"

"No; not yet," she said evenly. "I thought I'd see how the evening went before I told them."

"Ah, the evening is going to go great. It's going to be an evening you won't forget." He put his hand under her dress again.

This time, she jerked back and grabbed his hand. "Stop," she said with quiet anger in her voice.

He laughed.

"Stop it. Not here," she hissed as she again removed his hand and moved away from him.

"Sure," he said. "After we leave."

"I suppose you think we're going to your place," she replied incredulously, but her derisive tone was lost on him.

"Yeah, well. I'm kind of living with my brother right now. But we can go to your place. That's okay with me."

"I'm sure it is. Let me go to the ladies room and call my roommate." She rose, retrieved her purse and walked away. She returned after ten minutes.

"I thought you got lost," he said.

"No. I didn't," she said. She sat again, placing her purse between them and sitting out of reach of his hand. Neither spoke for a moment or two.

Walt broke the silence. "Did you talk to your roommate? Is everything good?"

"Yes, I did. Everything is going to be good."

"Great. Let me get the check and we'll head to your place," Walt said eagerly.

As he looked around for their waiter, her phone rang. She answered, listened and said, "Thanks. I'll be right there."

She dropped her phone into her purse, and quickly slid out of the booth. Looking directly at him, she said quietly, "I'm afraid you've misunderstood this evening. Thank you for dinner. My roommate is outside now and I'm going home. Perhaps you'll find someone more … agreeable after I'm gone." She turned and walked out.

"Bitch," Walt shouted as he tried to get out of the booth to go after her. In his efforts, he knocked over his water glass again and got stuck behind the table. Diners around him turned to stare as the maître d' hurried over. "Bitch," Walt said again under his breath. "Fucking little bitch."

"Mr. Williams, we cannot tolerate that kind of language or behavior. Please follow me and we will get your check for you," the maître d' admonished firmly. He stood quietly, waiting for Walt to rise.

Walt knew he had embarrassed himself and, fortunately for him, kept his mouth shut. *Shit,* he thought. *If this gets around and my boss hears of it, I'll probably lose my job. And it won't make that damned judge very happy, either.*

He paid his bill quietly, retrieved his Mercedes and drove carefully away.

TWENTY-FOUR

Walt drove to Kendra's home after his unsuccessful date, but the house was dark. He looked in the garage, but didn't see Kendra's car. He. He thought about driving to her parents' home, but that was a fifty-mile trip one-way—and it was late.

He was frustrated. He couldn't find Kendra. He drove around, but didn't see her car at Kelli's or Susan's, and he couldn't get into Jake's community. The date hadn't gone well; the little bitch had just been a tease, nothing more. And he had been certain he would get her between the sheets. *Fuckin' little bitch tease*. Now, he hadn't gotten laid and he had to spend the entire coming week out of town with his boss. He took two aspirins, a sedative and went to bed.

Walt slept fitfully Saturday night. He woke Sunday, tired, restless, angry and frustrated. It irritated him that he didn't know where Kendra was or who she was with. He had cheated on her when they were dating and more often while they were married, when being a star made women accessible. But he didn't think she had ever been unfaithful. She was too steeped in the church to commit adultery. Now, he wasn't sure—why else would she file for divorce? He was certain she couldn't do any better than him.

He had coffee with Mitchell. He complained about the little bitch, and complained about Kendra, and complained about that damned judge.

He dressed, packed, stopped for breakfast out, and met his boss at the airport. It was going to be a long week. It would be embarrassing when they took clients to lunch or dinner and he couldn't order a drink. And he wasn't going to be able to get a drink on the damned airplane, either.

TWENTY-FIVE

Jake awoke Sunday morning and rose quietly, letting Kendra sleep. He made coffee, showered, shaved and went to the patio as he usually did. Yesterday's rain was gone and the morning was bright and sunny, but more rain was predicted late in the day. He sat, enjoying the appealing view of his yard—lush, green and colorful from yesterday's rain. Although he had a service that mowed, edged and trimmed, Jake was his own gardener. He had planted virtually every tree, shrub, and flower in his yard, and was very proud of his work. He enjoyed tending his plants, and he took great satisfaction in simply sitting and enjoying the benefits of his labor.

Kendra woke and came sleepily to the patio, sat in his lap, kissed his cheek and quietly cuddled against him. She was warm and soft.

They shared breakfast, then lay in the sun by the pool for a while. Spring had come early this year and, until late in the day, the weather was predicted to be sunny and very warm. The sky was azure blue and clear, and the sun already dazzled hot and brightly. When they were sufficiently sunbaked, he followed her inside and they made love standing in the shower.

As they dried, Kendra gave Jake a long look of pure joy—and teased him with a coquettish wiggle of her naked body and a seductive thrust of her pelvis. They laughed until tears came to their eyes.

Kendra checked the airline flight status on her phone app and reported that Walt's flight had left on time. They both relaxed a bit with that news.

Later, Kelli called, and she and Kendra talked for a long time. Kendra brought Kelli up to date, explained about the intruder and told Kelli she was staying with Jake at her lawyer's suggestion. She didn't mention that she was sleeping in Jake's bed—and loving it. Kelli invited them to dinner and she accepted.

She told Jake she needed a quick trip to the mall. He offered to accompany her, but agreed that the trip should be safe in view of Walt's scheduled flight.

She had decided she needed new lingerie for Jake's benefit, and spent some time choosing. Additionally, she bought a vase that she thought complemented Jake's décor and stopped for flowers on the way back to his home. The rain started as she was getting into her car with the flowers. She called Jake and he opened the gate, then his garage door for her as she drove into his driveway.

Inside, she kissed him and offered the flowers and the vase. "A little something to brighten your home and say thank you for having me." He loved it.

"What a thoughtful thing to do. They're pretty and I really like that vase. Will you arrange them for me?"

His words and request made her happy. As she set about arranging the flowers, he asked what was in her other bag. She blushed as she noticed that the *Victoria's Secret* logo was in prominent view. "Maybe I'll show you later," she said with a coy smile.

"Ah, titillation again. I think you're trying to drive me crazy."

"Titillate," she mused. "You do seem to like that word."

They both laughed.

They dressed casually for dinner, and drove the short distance to Kelli and Scott's home. They quickly brought Scott up to date. Kendra and Jake tried hard to appear platonic, but she was sure Kelli had an inkling—their conversation at Timpano had certainly let the cat out of the bag. But Kendra didn't think Kelli suspected that things had progressed as far as they had in such a short time.

Dinner with Kelli and Scott was good for her. Kendra was now more comfortable with her decision to divorce Walt and with her new relationship with Jake. The rain returned on their way home. As they drove to Jake's, Kendra's phone rang. She looked at caller ID. "Walt's brother."

"Hello, Mitchell. How are you?"

"Hi, Kendra. I was just concerned for you and wanted to check to see if you are all right."

"I'm fine, thank you."

"I stopped by to see you last night, but there was no one home. Just concerned for you."

"My lawyer suggested I stay with friends until Walt left town."

"Where are you?"

"With friends. I should be home tomorrow. Thanks for checking on me. That was nice of you. I have to go now. Bye-bye."

She relayed the call to Jake. "That guy is ... strange. I've tried to be nice to him because he's Walt's brother, but he tries too hard to be nice."

"What do you mean that he tries too hard to be nice?"

"He's overly solicitous. He was always touching me and trying hard to get me to sit and talk with him. You've met him—big and strong like Walt, but not athletic and going to fat. And he is very smart. He likes to pose weird hypotheticals."

"Such as?"

"Umm ... I remember he once asked me what I'd do if someone kicked in our door in the middle of the night. Another time, he asked me what I would do if I were buried alive—that really scared me, and I told him so. He asked me if I liked the feel of Silly Putty. He asked me if snakes scared me. Just ... you know, strange things."

They arrived at Jake's home. When they were inside, he noticed a worried look on her face. "Are you okay?"

"Just a little unsettled, once again. Mitchell's call bothered me. I'm afraid he may be spying for Walt. He always looked out for Walt and righted Walt's wrongs." She gave a little what-can-one-do shrug and smiled at Jake. "May we just sit for a few minutes?"

He pulled her into his arms and she came to him eagerly, putting her arms around him tightly. She was pressed so closely to him that he could feel her heart beating like a drum. He kissed her temple.

"Sh. Slow down. Your heart is going a mile a minute—and I don't think it's because you're in my arms."

"I love being in your arms, but you're right. Mitchell upset me." She kissed him. "Help me relax."

"My pleasure, ma'am. Would you like a glass of wine?"

"That would be nice …" she paused thoughtfully, "but don't you have to work tomorrow?"

"I'm working from home this week—and I'm caught up for the moment. Nothing pressing this week, so I'm yours for a few days."

"Good. I like the sound of that." She kissed him.

"I'll pour if you'll find us some nice music."

She did and he did. They sat in two easy chairs and dropped their shoes. Kendra curled her legs beneath her. They relaxed, sipped and talked easily. Kendra laughed softly to herself, then chuckled aloud and said, "Kelli once told me she was glad she wasn't Scott's first. At the time, I didn't really understand what she meant. Someday, I'll have to tell her that I understand now. I didn't realize I was so naïve."

"I want this to be good for you, Kendra." His voice was soft and serious.

She nodded assuringly. "Thank you, Jake. It is. It's very good."

She smiled and stood. "Hold me, please." She nuzzled into the crook of his neck and he did as she asked.

She sighed, pulled his head to her and kissed him long and very slowly and very gently. She looked into his eyes and said softly, "Make love to me, Jake. Make love to me as though I hadn't talked my way into your bed." She looked earnestly into his eyes. "Make love to me as though it were last fall—the night of our first kiss."

Jake smiled as he picked her up in his arms, kissing her lips and her throat very gently as he silently carried her to his bedroom where they deftly undressed each other. They turned down the bed covers and lay together as Jake took her in his arms, slowly stroking her, kissing her everywhere. She sighed and lay quietly with her eyes closed, absorbed in the sensations of his warm breath, his hands and his mouth on her as he slowly caressed the length of her smooth, excited body, quelling any tension she may have had and making her tingle everywhere.

When he reached her toes, he asked softly, "Would you like to turn over and I'll rub your back?"

She gently squeezed his hand and, with a sentient and licentious smile, replied just as softly, "No. I think you should work your way back up."

He smiled and did so—skillfully, lovingly. His slow, gentle touch sent Kendra a message as old as time—she had never felt so aroused and ready. Every nerve hummed and she literally quivered inside. When he reached her intimate parts, she whispered, "Yes," so softly that she was barely audible. She moaned happily as she reached for him.

Kendra let herself go completely, moving involuntarily with Jake, so wholly lost in their lovemaking that she became anoetic—feeling nothing but rapidly spreading waves of pure, wanton emotion and physical sensation that flowed and cascaded everywhere within her. When she thought she would literally burst from the pleasure and desire that filled her, the first tremor broke, her nerve endings releasing like that of the plucked, taut strings of a fine instrument.

"Jake!" She cried out—startling herself. "Oh, my God, Jake," she again cried, shuddering and clinging tightly to him.

Kendra's nerves resonated like a precious instrument as Jake flawlessly played her to a breathless, resounding finale with the presence, skill and finesse of a consummate virtuoso. She whimpered and mewled with need. She trembled and quivered at his touch. She bounced and bucked and writhed against Jake. She moaned and keened and cried out as he took her higher and higher toward their crescendo. When the last tremulous chord was silent, their synergy sealing them as one person, Kendra took a sharp breath, exhaled softly and held Jake tightly to her. The perfectly tuned strings of her being were still, quiet. She wrapped her legs around him, clenching his warm length, not yet ready to release her hold on him.

Five years in the desert, she thought as a final shudder strayed languidly through her, *and I've found the oasis. I've found Paradise.* She slowly calmed and relaxed. *Oh, Jake. Don't ever leave me.*

She murmured with happiness, sighed and kissed him. Jake returned her kiss, stroked her head and gently rolled them onto their sides, holding her close to him. She was physically and emotionally spent, overcome with sexual torpor. Her breathing slowed. He took her hand and she slept.

Jake pulled the covers over them and kissed her forehead. He wasn't certain, but he thought he heard her say "don't ever leave me" just before she went to sleep, but her voice was so soft, he wasn't certain.

TWENTY-SIX

Walt and his boss arrived at their first destination, checked into the hotel and had a stiff, uncomfortable dinner together. He went to his room and watched a ball game, but it was dull. What he wanted to do was go to the bar, get a drink and look for a woman. Instead, he thought of Kendra and grew angry. It wasn't that he was upset at the thought of losing his wife; this just opened the door for him to see other women openly. But it was embarrassing that she had filed for divorce. And it was embarrassing that he couldn't drink and had to report to that damned judge. And that little bitch from the restaurant had embarrassed him.

He decided to check out the bar after all. As he entered, he saw a nice-looking woman at the end of the bar who was gathering some papers into a small briefcase. An almost empty wine glass sat on the counter in front of her.

He sauntered up to her and said, "You aren't leaving, are you?"

She looked up and smiled. "Yes. I just finished up some paperwork and was going to my room."

"Aww," Walt crooned. "Don't go so soon. Let me buy you another glass of wine. It would be nice to have some company."

She hesitated, evaluating Walt. "That would be nice," she replied as she moved her briefcase off the seat next to her.

Walt caught the eye of the bartender and pointed to her glass. He started to order a drink, but stopped short. "Club soda with a twist for me."

"Aren't you going to have a drink with me," she teased.

"Sure, but I have an early meeting tomorrow and I've already had a couple of drinks. Does that make you uncomfortable?"

"No. It's okay. I know about early meetings."

They introduced themselves and the drinks arrived. "Your name sounds familiar," she said.

"I play for the Texans in Houston. I'm on injured reserve right now, still trying to get a knee back in shape from a pretty bad injury. I'm here on business since I can't play right now."

"Right. I like football. I've seen you play. It was a pretty bad injury, wasn't it?"

They talked. Walt played up his injury. She was receptive. She agreed to another drink and Walt was soon running his hand up and down her thigh, and feeling optimistic. She finished her drink and said she needed to go to her room, but she laid her hand on his leg when she said it.

"Can I walk you to your room?"

"That would be nice."

In the elevator, Walt pulled her to him and they were quickly locked in a kiss as their hands began to explore. They reached her floor and hustled into her room where they excitedly began stripping off clothes. She dropped to her knees, happily taking Walt in her hands, then into her mouth. After a few seconds, he abruptly lifted her and tossed her into the center of the bed. He was immediately on her, spreading her legs and roughly forcing his way into her.

"Wait," she pleaded. "Not so fast."

But Walt ignored her. He drove into her, moving fast, pounding hard and deep until he quickly came with a resounding groan. He rolled off her, closed his eyes and was asleep.

Good God, she thought, *wham, bam and not even a thank you, ma'am. What a mistake. How am I going to get him out of here?*

She woke him. When he looked at her with sleepy eyes, she gently said, "Hey, big guy, time to wake up. You need to go to your room and get some sleep. You have an early meeting tomorrow."

"I'll just stay here," he mumbled.

"That would be nice, but you want to be sharp for your meeting tomorrow. Don't want to look sleepy in front of your client, do you?"

"Yeah, you're right," Walt replied. "Thanks." As he dressed, he asked, "Will you be here tomorrow night?"

"Oh, that would be nice, but no, I have to leave in the morning."

"Too bad. That was great."

"It was certainly unforgettable," she said sweetly as she escorted him to the door. She kissed his cheek and said, "Get some sleep tonight. You need to be fresh tomorrow morning."

When the door closed behind him, she sighed with relief and went to the shower. "What a disappointment that was," she vented.

Walt slept like a baby.

TWENTY-SEVEN

Kendra and Jake woke on Monday to a bright shaft of sunlight streaming into the bedroom. The rain was gone and the sun was shining. As Kendra was preparing to leave for her home, she received a call from the alarm company. The technician scheduled for her installation advised that the unit he intended to install was defective and he could not get a replacement until late that afternoon. She assured them she could wait until Tuesday. Actually, she was happy to have another day—and night, hopefully—with Jake.

She relayed the news. "Can you take me for one more day? I don't want to be in the way."

"Sure." He paused. "Unless, of course, you can stay longer," he replied with a broad smile.

She started to make a quip, but her memories of the last three days and nights suddenly overwhelmed her. "Until you tire of me," she said softly as she stepped to him, kissed him tenderly, and looked into his eyes.

"Jake, I've never in my life felt as I did last night. I'm not sure I can describe it, but it was as if I felt nothing but pure emotion and sensation. When I cried out, I startled myself. At first, I didn't know that sound came from me. I don't know how to describe it—surreal, metaphysical, otherworldly."

"Was it good for you?"

"Was it good? Oh, my God! It was the essence of the expression 'died and gone to Heaven.' It was incredible! You took me there … and you were there when I returned. You were right there and I was in your arms. I wish I could make you feel like that."

"I'm glad it was good for you. I want it to be good for you. I love making love with you, Kendra. I love it when you respond to me."

He pulled her to him and they stood quietly for a moment, just holding each other.

"So, the morning is now ours," Jake stated rhetorically and smiled as he slowly trailed the tip of one finger down her arm.

Kendra giggled, grinning happily as she took his hand. "All ours. Is there something you'd like to do?"

They eagerly returned to Jake's bed, where once wasn't enough.

Afterward, they fixed English muffins and took their breakfast to the patio. The morning was beautiful and they enjoyed the wonderful change of weather, despite the prediction of rain later.

"It's so nice to see the sun." She kissed him. "If you don't mind, I'd like to sit by the pool. Will you join me?"

"Give me time to run some things to my office. Then, I would love to join you."

While Jake ran his errand, she stood in the soothing, cool water for a long while, then settled herself on a chaise. She reclined, eyes closed, basking in the warm spring sun. Her mind was awhirl—exciting images of the two of them in bed, lifeless images of her and Walt in bed, conversations with Kelli and with Jake's sister, thoughts, questions, speculation all caromed in her head. She had called him and come to him because of his kiss last fall. It had stirred a primal need hidden deep inside her. Nevertheless, his sister's description of him certainly had played on her mind, as well. She hoped she hadn't embarrassed herself totally, but he seemed to be comfortable with her in his home and in his bed.

She didn't know where to go from here; she hadn't thought that far ahead. Part of her was excited about having her own home, but part of her was unsure of living alone. She knew she should move on soon; Jake had his own life to live and didn't seem to need a steady woman in it. She wondered if any of his sister's friends were bi-sexual—if he made love with them, or if he just serviced them when they needed it.

A vision of Anya suddenly filled her mind. Then, an ugly thought struck her—*is he just servicing me, just being kind?* After what she had experienced last night, the unnerving thought devastated her.

When Jake returned, he could see her through his window. She looked wonderfully fetching, and he felt the urge stir in him. He put on his swim trunks and joined her.

"Jake, I have to ask you something. It's none of my business, but … do you make love to any of your sister's friends?"

"In the past, I have. Yes," he replied honestly. "A couple of them also like men and we've occasionally spent a night together after an event. I've enjoyed their company, but it was just consensual sex. It wasn't amorous. With one exception, that hasn't happened for more than a year." He sat in the chaise next to her.

Her shoulders straightened and her lips tightened. She wanted to ask if the exception had been Anya, but she didn't want to know the answer. She sat quietly, looking away.

After a few minutes, Jake asked, "Kendra, what's the matter?"

"Nothing."

He could tell from her voice that wasn't true. Then it struck him. "If you're thinking this is like those women, don't. I was convenient for them; and they were convenient for me." His voice was firm.

"I've wanted you for months. Actually, I've wanted you since we first met. With our one exception, I would never have made an overture when you were married, but make no mistake—I've wanted you, wanted time with you and wanted to make love with you for a very long time. Quite frankly, I was overjoyed when you told me your plan and that we have the chance to finish what we started last fall. I'm glad you're here—very glad." He paused. "I hope I'm not just some boy toy for you to test with your new freedom."

She was taken aback by the serious look on his face and the strength of his response. The expression on her face and the tenor in her voice were tentative when she spoke. "Then … you weren't just being nice? Last night was real? And Saturday was real?"

He nodded and smiled. "And Friday. As real as it can get."

Relief flooded her. She looked at him, chagrinned, and stated, "Well, you've allayed my concerns and put me in my place all at the same time."

She smiled warmly. "Thank you, Jake. Thank you for your reassurance. I'm glad I'm here, as well. And I'm glad we've gotten to continue our kiss ..." she paused, and said softly, "and very glad we've made love."

She moved to sit next to him on his chaise and took his hand. "I'm sorry if I sounded bitchy." She paused. "This is all ... new to me ... I ..." Her words trailed off.

He nodded his head and smiled.

She kissed him and asked with mock guile, "Boy toy?"

Jake's responsive chuckle quickly became a full belly laugh.

The predicted rain came and went quickly. They spent the afternoon talking, reading, just being close. Once, she quietly touched Jake's cheek and kissed him gently, but the look in her eyes and her small act sent a palpable message.

She called Kelli and talked for a long time. When Kelli asked how she and Jake were doing, Kendra inhaled softly. "I have so much to tell you."

"Then, can I assume the kiss has progressed?"

"Oh, yes. Let's have lunch soon and I'll tell you. He's wonderful— unbelievably wonderful. Everything is wonderful."

"Oh, Kendra, I'm so happy for you. I can't wait to hear."

They didn't feel like cooking, so they ordered a pizza. When it arrived, they lit candles, and ate sitting cross-legged by the pool.

"Are you okay with everything? No regrets?" he asked.

"I should ask you that." She kissed him. "You've shown me more and treated me with more feeling in one weekend than I experienced in five years of being engaged and married."

"I'm fine. Having you here is wonderful."

"I'm afraid I'll wear my welcome thin."

"You're welcome here anytime. I kind'a like this."

"You are truly sweet. Thank you for your kind words. Right now, I'm suddenly feeling a bit awkward."

He looked at her quizzically.

"I think I've behaved like a trollop. It was pretty shameless of me to invite myself into your home and into your bed without a by your leave."

"Are you unhappy that you're here?"

"No. I'm selfishly very happy—but a little embarrassed—still working on the trollop part."

He took her hand. "I think I understand, but don't stress over anything that has to do with us. I've wanted you since we first met. If you need to back away, I understand. But if you're comfortable with us, then I'm a happy camper. You're welcome here for as long as you want and any time you want." He kissed her forehead. "Does that help you any?"

She leaned into him and laid her head on his chest. "Yes. More than you know. I care about you—and what you think of me. I'm a little confused right now, but yes—what you said helps me. I can't think of any person I'd rather be with right now."

She looked down, squeezed his hand gently and looked back into his eyes. "Thank you for the past days … and the past three nights. Thank you for your concern. Thank you for your reassurance. Thank you for allowing me to invite myself into your home and your life. I don't want to be a problem or a burden." Tears welled in her eyes and slipped down her cheeks.

"More than anything, thank you for your tenderness, your patience, your overwhelming care for me and concern for my feelings … and your understanding of what I needed."

He nodded quietly, waiting for her to continue.

"I thought telling you that I wanted intimacy with you was hard to do. It took me a week of internal struggle to work up the courage to do so. But this is harder."

She kissed his palm and swiped at the tears on her cheeks. "The last three days and nights you've given me the experience I've wanted, but never had. I don't know any other way to say it. For the past four years, I've felt cheated. I've known I never had the experience that I should have had as a bride or a new wife. Walt wasn't a loving and affectionate man. Every woman wants her first time to be special. That didn't happen for me and I was too naïve to know until months later.

"Walt took from me what he wanted, and gave nothing in return. You have unselfishly given to me what I wanted.

"For three days and nights, you have introduced me to a new world of tenderness and intimacy, and it has been wonderful. You taught me to walk on cloud nine. But last night, you took me back to the beginning, to the tenderness and gentleness that should be the beginning of a life of love. Last night was truly incredible. I will never forget last night. I will never forget this weekend, Jake. In this short time, I believe I've grown as a woman. You gave me what a woman wants early on from a man … and what I needed."

Her voice quivered and broke. Her tears came as though emptied from buckets. Kendra wept openly. "God bless you, Jake. You made me feel loved. You made me feel as though I were important to you."

Jake gathered her to him and held her quietly for a long time. When her tears stopped and she sighed quietly, he said softly, "You are loved. You're very important to me, Kendra."

She silently, gently kissed his lips and smiled inwardly. *Accept his words, Kendra. Don't push him. It's way too early to ask more of him.*

Jake yawned. She asked if he was tired and he said he was, but not too tired. They kissed, walked hand in hand to bed, and made love—sweet and gentle at first, but quickly followed by sudden, growing passion and need. Jake took her urgently, surprising her with his need, until his energy fueled her own passion and she took her pleasure from him with equal lustful greed, surprising herself. They finished as one, calmed and Jake took her hand as they drifted into sleep.

TWENTY-EIGHT

On Tuesday, Jake woke early, made coffee, and worked quietly in his study while she slept. He heard her before he saw her. She came into his study with a cup of coffee in her hand, wearing panties and a tank top. He stared. She laughed.

"What? You've seen me naked and you've made love to me." She bent and kissed him. "And you know much more about me than any other man."

"I know; memory and imagination are wonderful things. But the real woman is even better. You are truly beautiful."

"Thank you." She smiled warmly.

"Would you like to have coffee on the patio?'

"That would be nice. It's a pretty morning."

They went outside and sat with their feet in the pool where they talked and finished their coffee. He took her cup and returned with refills.

"Would you like breakfast?"

Yes, but I need to be home by nine o'clock to meet the security company's technician. Do you think it will take all day to install the system?"

"It took six hours to do my home. I imagine at least four, probably five hours for yours."

"Okay. Then I'll use the day to do things around the house and yard. Even if Walt didn't get on the plane, there will be someone there with me, so I should be okay." *Ask me to come back tonight, Jake. I want to hear that from you.*

"Good. Well, by tonight, you should feel much safer in your home. That makes me feel better."

"Thank you. I'm sure I will be. Well, I guess I'd better collect my things and head home." She stood, kissing him. "Thank you, Jake. Thank you for being tolerant with me all weekend." He smiled.

She kissed him quickly, then again, long and warm. *Please, Jake, don't tell me it's over.*

When she stepped away, he cocked his head, took her hand and looked at her. She thought he looked a little wistful.

"When you told me about wanting warmth and intimacy from a special person—was that something you wanted just for the weekend?"

She was momentarily taken aback until she saw his wry smile. She smiled, chuckled, then grinned broadly and laughed out loud. When she did, he chuckled, then laughed, and she saw the light in his eyes.

She hesitated. *Don't scare him. Don't say the wrong thing.* She looked him directly in the eyes.

"No," she said softly. "I was hopeful for the weekend and it has been wonderful. When it ends is up to you."

"Would you like to come back here tonight?"

Don't cry! She knuckled a tear from the corner of her eye, then a second. *Thank you, God.* She sighed.

"I would love to, but I've been gone for three days and I'll have a new toy at home. And Mitchell seems way too curious. Would you come to my home tonight and I'll fix dinner."

"Ah, a woman with a plan." He laughed. "Will that be awkward for you, having me there?"

"Maybe, a little. But I'd like to break the ice and exorcise some bad spirits. And, seriously, I want to get used to the alarm system before he comes back. Could we be there tonight?"

"Sure. What can I bring?"

"Your toothbrush."

She kissed him, collected what she needed to take with her and drove home wearing a huge smile.

He showered and wandered around the house. He tried to work, but couldn't keep his mind on what he was doing. He went to the gym, had a good workout, and thought of her the entire time, with constant visual memories. He was surprised at the turn of events in their lives. He was happy—for them both. She needed out of her bad marriage. He was elated to have her company.

He called his florist and ordered a dozen roses to be delivered. He went to the wine shop and bought two bottles of a wine that he knew she liked. He wanted to buy her a special gift. He thought about her to do list and made some phone calls.

TWENTY-NINE

Kendra left her car on the driveway and went inside to check for any sign that someone had been in the house since Saturday morning, but found nothing amiss. She met the security company technician, who explained the basic system and what he was going to install. He told her it would take about six hours, then he would walk her through setting and programming the system, and they would run through it until she was confident that she could operate the panel and the system.

She looked at her yard and decided she needed help. Coincidentally, her neighbors' son, Alan, was just getting their mower out of their garage. She walked across the street and asked if he would be interested in doing some yard work for her this week, and then mowing and edging on a weekly basis. He needed the money and readily agreed to the rate she offered. He would mow and edge today and would trim her hedges. Tomorrow, he would dig out space in the corner of the front yard and along the back fence for beds of flowers.

She asked if he had ever painted and he told her he had helped his parents paint every room in their house. He said he thought he was a pretty good painter, so Kendra also hired him to paint her bedroom on Thursday. It was obvious that time for projects was going to be slim now that she had Jake in her life—at least, in her life for the week.

She looked critically at her home as she walked back across the street.

It's my home for at least three months. I really do like the house and it's close to Kelli. Maybe I can find a way to buy Walt's share and stay here. But I need to make some changes. I can't live in Walt's house and be comfortable.

She checked with the security tech, but he didn't need her presence for a while. She quickly showered, dressed and drove to the mall where she shopped for bath linens, sheets and bed linens, covers and pillows. She found a beautiful duvet that cost more than she wanted to pay, but she loved it. She bought a pretty tablecloth and a nice set of everyday dinnerware and serving dishes, and new flatware, some attractive wine glasses and everyday glasses. And a new coffee pot—the old one should have been retired long ago.

She had her purchases sent to the shipping dock and wandered the mall, looking for ideas. An electronics store caught her eye. Their television and stereo system were what Walt had in college. They had once been state of the art, but were sorely outdated now. Walt wouldn't part with them, and between drinking and golf, he really didn't know how electronics had improved in more than five years.

She found a reasonably priced Smart TV. After the salesperson showed her how to set it up—and how to get digital music—she bought the television and a space efficient audio system that had excellent five-speaker surround sound. Someone from the store loaded her purchases into her SUV and she drove to the loading dock of the department store for the rest of her purchases. *Thank goodness. I have an SUV.*

She bought paint for her bedroom and bath, then hustled through the grocery for what she needed for the evening meal that she intended to prepare. She stopped for takeout lunch, and bought lunch for the security tech and Alan as well.

The security system was complete by three o'clock. The technician was a good teacher and she a good student. As he was gathering his tools, he noticed the new television and sound system. He asked if she needed help setting it up. After some embarrassed dissembling, she said yes, that would be nice, but she didn't want to trouble him. *It would be really nice to have it working before Jake arrives.*

"No trouble," he said. "You've been very nice to me and I have a special spot for teachers. And I have a little extra time today." In less than an hour, he had the audio and video systems in full operation and, once again, was a good teacher and she a good student.

All for the price of a burger and fries. It pays to be nice.

As he was leaving, a florist arrived with a dozen roses. The man from the security company grinned and gave her a thumbs up. "Looks like someone sure appreciates you. Hope you have a wonderful evening." She smiled and set the roses on the coffee table.

Jake called. She saw his name on caller ID and tried to sound calm when she answered.

"Hi. Do you still want company this evening?"

"Of course I do," she replied brightly. "What time shall I expect you and your toothbrush?"

"How soon do you want company?"

"Well, I want company right now, but I need a bath and a few minutes to make myself presentable. Is an hour okay?"

"I guess I can wait that long, but it's been a long day without you."

She laughed, and said softly, "Show me how long it's been when you get here."

Kendra bathed and applied her makeup. She examined herself and smiled with self-assurance. She dressed in white shorts and a pretty scoop-necked blouse, checked her make-up, added a dab of perfume and went to the kitchen to stuff pork chops and start dinner.

Jake arrived. He stepped inside, hesitated, and kissed her awkwardly. Kendra said softly, "I'm sorry if I made you uncomfortable this morning."

"You didn't," he lied. Jake was a good listener and women were comfortable with him. Many had opened up to him, but Kendra had opened her heart and her soul to him with complete trust in a way that appealed to Jake's protective nature—but it was a little overwhelming, in a wonderful way

She put her arms around his neck and kissed him warmly as he pulled her into him and returned her kiss.

"Thank you for the roses. They're beautiful. That was very thoughtful."

He smiled and kissed her. "I've thought of you all day."

She arranged the roses as he poured wine. He noticed the television and sound system, mostly because he realized that she had pleasant music playing in the background, which didn't happen when Walt was around.

He complimented her and she praised the technician who had set the system up for her.

She put the finishing touches on dinner. Just as they were seated, the doorbell rang. When she opened the door, Mitchell was on her doorstep.

"Hi, Kendra. I was just checking on you." He stepped inside without being invited. "I see you have a security company now. Why did you do that?"

"I'm here alone now, Mitchell. I thought it would be a wise thing to do."

"Are you going to give Walt the security code?"

"No. I think you know Walt has been ordered off the property."

"But, it's still his house."

Jake quietly stepped into the foyer behind Mitchell. "Isn't that a matter for the courts, Mitchell?"

Startled, Mitchell jumped and spun to face Jake. "Oh, it's you, Jake. I thought that was your car in the driveway. What are you doing here?"

Before Jake could speak, Kendra interjected, "I had to replace the old television. I promised Jake dinner if he would help me set the new one up."

"I could have done that for you," Mitchell responded self-importantly.

"I'm sure you could have," Kendra said evenly.

"Where did you get the roses?"

"A friend sent those to cheer me up." She paused. "Is there something you wanted?"

"I just wanted to check on you. You know, be sure you were all right."

"Thank you. I'm fine. Thanks for stopping by. But if you'll excuse us, dinner is getting cold." She opened the door for him. He stood awkwardly, then turned and left.

They watched him get into his car and drive off. He stopped a block away and sat for a minute, then continued.

"That guy gives me the creeps," she said quietly. "I'm sure he's spying for Walt. I'm sure Walt's ego tells him there is another man and that I didn't file just because of who he has become."

Jake wrapped her in his arms and kissed her head. She sighed and snuggled into him. "I'm glad you were here. Thank you." She kissed him. "Let's eat before everything is cold."

"Quick thinking," he complimented her as they ate. She smiled. "Did the other television give up the ghost?"

"No. I've wanted a new one, a bigger one with more features. So, I bought it. And that wonderful sound system, as well. I have decided I'm going to make some changes while I'm still here. If I'm going to stay here, I want to feel comfortable being here.

Alan, the young man across the street—you know Alan and his parents—he is going to mow and edge my yard weekly. And tomorrow, he's going to begin digging out flowerbeds for me. I'm going to paint the guest room and bath—my room for now—and put some personal touches here and there. I'm not ready to move back into the master bedroom yet."

Together, they cleared the table, then took key lime pie and coffee to the deck. She explained animatedly where she wanted the flowerbeds to be and talked about what she wanted to plant. He listened attentively, and at her invitation, made a suggestion she liked. He let her talk, enjoying her animation and the excitement in her voice. When she had exhausted her current plans, he asked if she had given any thought to the other undertakings she had mentioned.

"No. At least, not yet." She blushed. "You've taken care of the most important wish on my list."

He smiled. "I assure you, it was my sincere and absolute pleasure."

He kissed her and said, "I'll be right back." He went into the house and retrieved one small and three large envelopes he had surreptitiously placed on a side table when he came in. When he rejoined her, he handed the envelopes to her.

"What's this?"

"They're all for you. But open the small one last. You'll see."

Dusk was falling and Jake said, "Hopefully, there is still enough light for you to be able to read them."

She opened the first and found a reservation for the weekend four weeks hence at a resort in the hill country that offered individual cottages, hiking, rafting, tubing, horseback riding and zip lines.

She smiled wide eyed and he said, "I was hoping you might want company."

"Oh, Jake, thank you. This is wonderful." She moved to him, hugged him, kissed him, and said softly, "Of course, I want company. That would make the weekend perfect."

She looked at the other envelopes, raised her eyebrows and looked at him quizzically.

She opened another envelope and found two weekend admittance tickets to the Museum of Fine Arts and two tickets to the Museum of Fine Arts Ball the first Friday evening in May. "Oh, my," she said softly. "Thank you. But the ball is very formal, isn't it." He nodded.

"Like tuxes and ball gowns and expensive dresses kind of formal?" He nodded again.

"But Jake, I don't have anything like that to wear. I don't want to embarrass you. I guess I need to do some shopping."

"You could never embarrass me. You'll be the most beautiful woman there. But we'll talk about that in a minute. Open the other big envelope."

She did and found airline reservations and a reservation for two at a very nice, all-inclusive resort in the Cayman Islands in June, the week after her school closed for summer vacation. "Oh, this sounds like fun. What a wonderful way to relax after the school year. Thank you, Jake."

"Do you have a passport?"

"No, but I'll start on that this week. Thank you. But, Jake, you've spent a lot of money. I feel a little awkward. It's wonderful and very thoughtful, but it's so much."

"Shh. It's all right. My company does very well and this is something I want to do—for both of us. I'm going to be right there with you, having as much fun as I hope you do.

She hugged him and kissed him softly. "Thank you. Thank you so much. I'm so excited."

She held up the small envelope. "Good things and small packages," she said questioningly. He shrugged and smiled innocently. She opened the envelope and found a small card that read, *Good for one formal dress of your choice, with shoes.* She looked, up, distressed.

"Oh, Jake, dresses for something like that are expensive. I can't let you do that after everything else."

"Anything within reason is fine. I know you won't take advantage. What is reasonable for the kind of dress you'll need?"

She smiled appreciatively. "I can probably get a nice one for around two hundred to two hundred and fifty dollars, but that's still a lot of money." She looked questioningly at him. "Is that okay?"

"No."

Her heart sank.

"I was thinking the belle of the ball should have a bit more latitude than that. Do you think you could hold it to four or five hundred or so?"

"Oh, Jake; I'm not going to spend that kind of money on one dress."

"Let's see what we find. I want to see you in something that is as beautiful as you are, if that is even possible."

She threw her arms around his neck and hugged him. "Thank you," she said softly. "Thank you for caring. I'm so excited about everything. I can't wait to be with you."

Darkness fell and they went inside. She locked the doors and set the alarm, telling Jake what the arm and disarm codes were and how to operate the system. "I want you to know. No one else." He nodded.

She laughed, "But it's like yours, so I guess you already knew how to operate it."

He nodded again, paused for a long moment, and smiled.

"Sit with me for a minute." She did.

Jake kissed her gently, and spoke softly. "Last night, you opened your soul to me … and I was a little overwhelmed. All day I've thought about you and about all that you've said to me. This morning, you said you had been hopeful for the weekend, but when it ends is up to me." He looked directly at her.

"Only time will tell, but let's see where this takes us. I want you to be happy and to grow individually, but I like being with you. I think we know each other pretty well—we've certainly known each other long enough. I like who you are, and I like who I think we've become the past few days."

Kendra inhaled sharply and her breath quivered. Tears stung her eyes and she wept quietly. She pressed his hands flat in prayer inside hers, lifted them to her lips and kissed his fingertips. She looked into his eyes with tears streaming down her face and whispered, "Oh, Jake. Oh, my sweet man," as she folded herself around him.

He pulled her into him and they held each other until her sobs became sniffles, then sighs.

Kendra turned out the light, took his hand and led him to her bedroom. They made slow, gentle love. When she was calm, she whispered. "Just hold me until I go to sleep." He wrapped her in his arms. She kissed him gently, giggled and whispered, "If I die in my sleep, know that I died unbelievably happy."

She kissed him again when he took her hand. "Good night, sweet man."

THIRTY

Jake awoke early. He lay next to Kendra, replaying Tuesday night in his head, and it made him very happy. He stepped into his boxers and went to the kitchen. He found coffee and put it on to brew. He ran the dishwasher; and he washed, dried and stored the pots and pans from dinner the previous night. He took coffee to the deck and sat, visualizing the flower and plant beds Kendra had described. He thought today would be good therapy for her.

Kendra shuffled into the kitchen, sleepy-eyed and naked, as he was refilling his cup. She observed Jake, the empty sink and the coffee. "Thank you," she mumbled, nodding at the empty sink as she took Jake by the hand and led him back to bed.

"Hold me," she asked softly as she nestled against him. He did and she kissed his neck. She lay quietly against him and he thought she had gone back to sleep until she pressed herself against his thigh and whispered, "Get me ready."

She came into his arms and he stroked her until she was ready. As Jake moved to rise above her, she surprised him by rolling him onto his back; but she didn't move to straddle him, as he expected. Instead, she kissed his lips, then kissed her way down his torso and took him into her mouth until Jake couldn't stand the tension.

"God, that's incredible!" he growled breathlessly. "You're going to make me come if you don't stop."

She smiled inwardly. *Thank you, Kelli.*

He pulled her to him and they made love. When they were spent, they lay quietly until she sighed, kissed his lips and giggled self-consciously. When Jake looked at her, he saw an uncertain look in her eyes. He looked at her quizzically.

"I've never done that before. Was it okay?" she asked timidly.

Jake laughed aloud and pulled her into his arms. "It was wonderful. It was perfect. I loved it."

"Walt tried to force me once and he scared me. I wouldn't do it.

"He tried again another time, but I still wouldn't do it for him." She looked down disconsolately and, without looking at Jake, said softly, "That was the first time he hit me."

She didn't look up. Jake took her hand and gently stroked her cheek and her hair. He was furious with Walt.

"I've never done it." She looked up at Jake and said softly, "I wanted to do it with you."

Jake kissed her gently. "Thank you, sweetheart," he said quietly.

She smiled, happy that she had pleased him. And happy that she had learned a way to give Jake pleasure similar to that which he gave her.

They dressed and Alan arrived shortly. Alan and his parents lived next door to Jake when he lived in the neighborhood. Alan knew that Jake, Walt, and Kendra were good friends, so he asked no questions.

He told Kendra he thought it was going to take more time than they initially thought and volunteered a friend, Evan, to help him. She agreed readily. Evan arrived quickly and they strove to their task.

Alan had a small truck and he offered the use of it to Kendra while she and Jake went for compost and mulch.

They returned and the boys unloaded the truck. Jake left and Kendra took the truck for a second trip to purchase plants.

Kendra spent considerable time with the assistant manager of the nursery, asking questions and getting suggestions. She made wise choices and returned with an adequate supply of shrubs and flowering plants for the space she wanted to fill. The nurseryman jotted quick planting instructions for each of the various plants, recommended a bottle of root stimulator. He also recommended she rent a sod cutter, which she did. He loaded the equipment in the truck with her purchases and told her she could bring it back the next morning. She thanked him. On her way home, she stopped at a popular sporting goods store and purchased two gift certificates as an added reward for the boys.

Jake called during the afternoon to check progress. She said it was going well, but thought it would take longer than she had expected. She hoped to finish by five o'clock. "I'll take you out for dinner tonight because there is no way I'm going to have time to cook, if that's okay?

"Why don't you take a long, hot bath when you finish and I'll bring dinner. You can surprise me with the fruits of your labor. I'll plan on six-thirty unless I hear differently from you."

She thanked him and agreed. They paused and she said softly, "Jake, I miss being with you."

"I'm glad. After five days, I thought we might need a break from each other, but I miss you, too. I'm looking forward to seeing you this evening."

"Thank you," she said softly. "See you soon." She smiled to herself.

Kendra and the boys worked steadily, stopping only for a quick lunch. Thanks to the sod cutter, by four o'clock, all of her new plants were in the ground, nurtured by root stimulator and compost, and covered with fresh mulch. It was a nice transformation. Even the boys were enthusiastic in their praise of the new appearance. She and Walt had done little to add to the basic landscaping provided by the builder, and the enhanced appeal, especially of the back yard, was even more than she had expected. She couldn't wait to show Jake.

She poured cold drinks for the boys, and they relaxed and visited for a few minutes. Evan offered to help Alan with the painting on Thursday and Kendra agreed. A thought struck her and she asked if they thought they could paint the guest bedroom, the master, and both bathrooms, walls only, in one day. They agreed, but thought they would have to work into the evening or finish Friday. They settled on a price. She paid them for the day and put the gift cards aside for the next day.

Kendra brushed her hair, put on a clean blouse and made a quick trip to the area post office, where she was photographed for her passport picture and submitted her passport application.

Kendra bathed, slipped into lacy lingerie, shorts and a pretty top, and was ready to greet Jake when he arrived at six-thirty. He arrived with a very good champagne, a good pinot grigio that she liked, and dinner from a nearby oriental restaurant that had been a favorite when they were all together in the old neighborhood.

When she opened the door, he wore a huge grin and effused, "Wow, what a change! I can't wait to see the back yard."

She pulled him inside, closed the door and kissed him exuberantly. "Thank you. I can't wait to show it to you." She was proud of her day's effort and Jake's praise made it all the better. He opened the champagne and she handed him flutes. He poured and toasted her. "To hard work and just reward. Show me everything you've done."

She walked him around. The boys had trimmed the hedges in front of the house. The three of them added a line of day lilies in front of the hedge as well as a small bed of knockout roses in one front corner of the yard and a rose on either side of the front entrance, but the back yard was the most remarkable.

Kendra had planted deep-green pittosporum along the length of the back of the house and on each outer one-third of the yard along the back fence. In the center one-third, she had planted more knockout roses. She also planted a pigeon berry near the back door and begonias and impatiens on a shady side of the yard and added a trellis and star jasmine in a sunny spot.

It really was very well done, with the promise of much enjoyable beauty as the plants grew and matured. Jake expressed his surprise that she had accomplished so much in one day, but Kendra was quick to praise the boys, telling him they had worked like troopers all day. He complimented her several times and Kendra grinned from ear to ear like a child at her birthday party. *Oh, Jake, you don't know what your praise means to me.*

They refilled their glasses and sat, enjoying the view, with more compliments from Jake. She told Jake about her day and how hard the boys had worked, and she told him about her decision to paint both bedrooms and baths. He was happy that she seemed ready to keep the house.

They were hungry and went indoors, ready for dinner and quiet time together. After dinner, they went to her deck and enjoyed the evening. She told Jake she had applied for her passport. He grinned and winked conspiratorially. As darkness came, he asked if she was tired. She said she was.

"Why don't I go home and let you go to bed and get some rest," he offered.

"I'd rather you stayed here and took me to bed. I'm tired, but not that tired." She smiled and kissed him gently. "I've thought about you all day."

"That's a pleasant surprise," he said playfully.

She grinned just as playfully. "Good. I like surprising you. I like making love with you."

And they did, with great pleasure and satisfaction.

She kissed him and yawned. Jake took her hand and, as she always did, she quickly fell asleep in his arms.

THIRTY-ONE

On Thursday, they woke together early. She was still a little stiff and sore. Alan and Evan were due early, so they arose, made coffee. Jake offered to return the sod cutter, then stay the day and help. Kendra set out drop cloths, paintbrushes, rollers, tape and the paint she had purchased for the guest room. The boys arrived at eight a.m. and began moving furniture away from the walls while Jake went for more paint for the master bedroom and bath. Kendra left to shop for new linens for the master bedroom and bath. When she returned, she, too, joined in the painting efforts.

It was a long day for everyone, but the painting was completed by six o'clock. Jake and Kendra cleaned up and the boys carefully moved furniture back into place. They were pleased with the additional reward of the gift cards and offered to help Kendra any time she needed something done.

Jake had borrowed a ladder from a friend for the day, and left to return it. Just after Jake and the boys left, the doorbell rang. Kendra answered and found Mitchell at the door.

"I came by to check on you."

"Thank you, Mitchell, but I'm fine."

"Can I come in?" he asked as he started to walk past her into the house.

Kendra stepped in front of him, blocking his path. "This isn't a good time, Mitchell. I've been working hard this week and I need to get the house back in order."

"Yeah. I saw the plants." He sniffed. "And I smell paint. Are you painting?"

"Yes. I painted the bedrooms."

"Just painting Walt out of the picture while he's gone?" he asked, pointedly.

"No. We've done nothing to the house since we bought it. We needed more landscaping and the rooms need to be painted. With his drinking, I could never get Walt to agree or to help. So, now I'm doing some things that needed to be done."

"I guess you think you're getting the house," he stated churlishly.

"Nothing like that. But I will be here until the end of the school year and probably until the divorce is final. After that, it's up to the judge. I'm just doing things that needed to be done, as I said. If we sell the house, it will improve the sale price."

"And Jake has been helping."

"No. Actually Alan, the young man who lives across the street, and a friend of his have been helping me."

"Well, Jake sure seems to be here a lot."

I need to diffuse this, she thought. "The judge and my lawyer are concerned that I will be harassed. Jake, Kelli, Scott and some of the neighbors are watching out for me."

"You don't need them. I can look out for you, Kendra," he said, almost plaintively.

"Thank you, Mitchell. That's very kind of you, but I'm in good hands. And your help might be misinterpreted by the judge. But, now I need to get the house in order. It's been a long week, and I'm tired," she said with temerity, as she moved to close the door.

"But, you don't need them. I'll look out for you." His voice was firm and harsh.

"Thank you, but I'm fine," she said dismissively.

"What did you mean about the judge?"

"The judge may think you're trying to intercede on Walt's behalf and that could be misinterpreted as a violation of the protective order. I don't want you to get into trouble with the judge." *Thank you, Jake, for thinking of that.*

"Okay. Have it your way." His voice was hard and abrupt. He turned and stalked to his car, driving off much too fast.

Kendra saw Alan across the street, standing next to his truck. He came across the street and she waited for him, trying to smile as though nothing had happened.

"Are you okay, Mrs. Williams?" he asked. "I saw that guy and he looked mad. He's Mr. Williams's brother, isn't he?"

"I'm okay. Thank you, Alan." She smiled at him. "Yes, he is Walt's brother."

"Alan, are your parents at home?"

"Yes ma'am."

"Are they busy?"

"No, ma'am. Not really."

"If you have a few minutes, may I come over and talk to the three of you?"

"Sure. They would like to see you."

Kendra walked across the street with Alan to his home, where his parents greeted her warmly. They were good friends with Jake, as well as Kendra and Walt, and Scott and Kelli.

"I'd like to visit with you for a few minutes. I want to include you in some information before it becomes more widely known. I've filed for divorce from Walt. I know you're aware of his drinking problem. Since he learned that he can't return to the team, he has buried himself in the bottle to the point he has become unreasonable and intolerable. Two weeks ago, he struck me for the second time, and that was the straw that broke the camel's back.

"There is a restraining order that prevents him from coming to the house and from coming within one hundred fifty feet of me, but my lawyer and the judge are concerned that he will ignore the order. Walt's brother, Mitchell, has become a little overbearing and presumptuous since the order was issued. I'm not trying to prejudice you or plead my case, but Alan just observed a little of Mitchell's behavior and I want the three of you to know the circumstances in case you see any … umm … questionable or suspicious behavior, especially by Walt. Kelli, Scott and Jake know, and they are keeping an eye out for me and helping as much as they can. I want you all to know what's going on, just in case.

"Since Walt started drinking, the house hasn't had much proper care and I'm trying to do some things that need to be done. Alan and Evan have been a huge help. If they are willing, I will probably be hiring them to help me more from time to time. Right now, I don't know whether we will sell the house or what will happen, but I will be there at least until the divorce is final."

Alan's parents were well aware of Walt's drinking. They had been good friends until it became uncomfortable to be around Walt. They were sympathetic and supportive, thanking Kendra for sharing the circumstances with them, and promising to keep an eye out for her and to keep the information to themselves until Kendra told them otherwise. They visited for a few more minutes until Kendra saw Jake's car pull into her driveway and she trotted across the street to greet him.

She told him about Mitchell's behavior and thanked him for the suggestion of the gambit she had used. She happily proclaimed it had been a very productive day, but a long day for everyone.

"I assume there is still a smell of paint in your home?"

"Yes, there certainly is."

"May I offer you bed and board this evening?"

"You may and I readily accept, but I need a bath and clean clothes."

He suggested she lock up, bring her things to his home and bathe there in fresher air. She agreed.

They were clean and finally sat down to a simple dinner at nine o'clock. Kendra told Jake that she had explained the circumstances to Phil, Janice and Alan Purcell. After dinner, Kendra asked if Jake would just sit with her for a while. She leaned her head against his shoulder and sighed deeply.

"Are you okay?" he asked.

"Yes. Just confused, concerned, a million things zipping through my mind."

"Confused? Concerned?" He looked at her. "Anything you want to talk about?"

She nodded. "I know my behavior has been … umm, unusual … probably questionable. I'm sure our being together is also questionable—maybe even inadvisable. Have I gotten you into something with which you aren't comfortable? I don't want to cause problems for you."

It was obvious to Jake that her questions were objective and not driven by feelings of guilt or second thoughts.

"I agree. Our present circumstances may be unusual and maybe questionable. I suppose it might be advisable to back away from each other until the divorce is final—but you have justification for wanting the divorce, we really didn't cheat on Walt during your marriage, there are no children to consider, and I'm with the woman who stole my heart the day I first met her. If you want to back away, I'll understand. But I'm certainly not going to ask you to back away."

"Thank you, Jake. Right now, you're my anchor in all this. Thank you for being here. I like being together." She touched his hand. "I like it very much."

He nodded and they sat quietly, wrapped in their own thoughts for a long time. After a while, Kendra took his hand, kissed him and led him to bed. She fell asleep with her hand in his.

THIRTY-TWO

Walt returned mid-afternoon on Thursday, a day earlier than expected. He collected his baggage, said goodbye to his boss who told him to take Friday off, and went to the parking shuttle bus. He had been sober for most of a week and knew he should take advantage of the edge he had, but he was frustrated and angry. The sales trip had been fruitless. And he couldn't go home.

He retrieved his car and drove to Mitchell's home, dropped his bags and changed into comfortable clothes. Mitchell came in shortly afterward and was surprised to see Walt. "You're home early. Any problems?

"None," Walt replied, "except that I had no alcohol and we got no new business. We cut the trip short." Walt stretched and said plaintively, "I need to get away. I don't have to work tomorrow. I'm going to the deer lease. Do you want to come?"

Mitchell knew Walt would drink if he were there alone, so he agreed to go. "You drive," he told Walt, hoping that driving would keep him from drinking on the road. Their family had a deer lease more than a three-hour drive away in a heavily wooded area west of Johnson City, Texas. Walt groused about his boss, Kendra, the judge and his life in general the entire trip. They stopped for dinner on the way and arrived at the cabin around ten o'clock.

Walt dropped his bag in one bedroom and inspected the pantry as Mitchell went to the other bedroom with his gear. Just as he thought, there were several open fifths of liquor and a case of warm beer. He checked the fridge and found several cans of cold beer. He added a dozen of the warm beers to the fridge, took two cold beers, popped the tab of one and tossed the other to Mitchell.

"Not a good idea, Walt, "Mitchell said.

"Fuck it. I haven't had a drink in a week. One or two won't hurt. Let's go sit outside. I'm tired of being cooped up."

Mitchell followed him outside, popped the tab on his beer and sprawled in one of the two wooden rockers on the porch. There was only the last vestige of a waning moon, but the sky was studded with thousands of twinkling stars and the woods echoed with the tiny sounds of crickets and tree frogs, and the occasional hoot of an owl. Walt paced and drank. The first beer disappeared quickly and he went for another. Mitchell said nothing, just watched.

Walt paced and said with quiet frustration, "I can't believe this shit. I'm trying to get my career back on track, I'm stuck in this shit job, and my wife and my boss have no comprehension of what it's like for me. I wish I could make them both disappear. I can't work and get my knee in shape at the same time." He finished the beer and went for a third.

"Hey, man. Take it easy on the beer. You've made a good start on getting sober. Don't blow it," Mitchell cautioned.

"Fuck off, Mitch. I'm trying to get my life back in order here. I'm gonna quit that fuckin' job and concentrate on getting back in shape." He paused and starred into the darkness. "The house is paid for and Kendra makes enough to pay the bills right now. I deserve a chance to get back in the game."

"Great, bro. I'm all for you. But you can't do it if you keep drinking like you have been. You know that."

Walt bitched and pontificated and kidded himself for another hour and two more beers. Mitchell tried again. "C'mon Walt, forget the beer. Let's go to bed. We'll drive back to Houston tomorrow and you can talk to the team. Tell them your plan. Tell them you're going to concentrate full time on getting back. I'll bet Coach will get you on a program and make it happen."

"Yeah, good idea. They need me." He took a drink. "Man, I was good until that son of a bitch Morgan took my legs out and ruined my knee. It was a cheap shot. They should have thrown him out of the game and fined him." He finished his beer.

"I gotta pee. You want something?"

Mitchell shook his head.

Walt came back with two fresh beers and the resident deer rifle from the gun closet.

"Walt. Come on, man. Put it back and let's go to bed. We'll drive back tomorrow."

"Yeah, yeah. You go to bed. I need to blow off some steam." Saying that, Walt picked up the deer rifle and fired six rapid shots into the woods. All night sounds ceased immediately.

"Walt! Damn it! You'll have the sheriff out here. You can't just fire indiscriminately like that in the middle of the night."

"Sure we can, Bro. It's a hunting lease. We can fire anytime we want. We just can't kill a deer out of season." Walt laughed, went inside and came back with a box of shells. He popped the tab on a beer, and reloaded.

"Come on, Walt. Let's go to bed. You've blown off enough steam and you've had enough alcohol."

"Now you sound like Kendra. You're not my wife. Back off."

"Come on, Walt. You've lost your wife because of your drinking. And you'll never get rehabbed and back on the team if you keep drinking like this."

"Yeah?" Walt drained his beer. "You think I've lost Kendra and that makes you happy because you've always wanted her. But you were afraid to ask her out."

"I saw her first. That's true. You wanted her and you played your jock card before I could ask her out. You thought you could have anything you wanted just because you were a hotshot jock."

"You're just jealous. You wanted in her pants, but I got there first. Hell, you're the one who introduced us. You just can't take it. You didn't have the balls to play football and you didn't have the balls to go after the girls. Fuck you, Mitch."

Walt took a long drink of his beer and continued, "You may be smarter than me, but it never got you laid, did it?"

The barbs became more caustic and the argument sporadically bounced between heated and ballistic well into the early hours of the morning.

THIRTY-THREE

On Friday, Kendra and Jake woke early, shared coffee and breakfast on his patio and enjoyed a beautiful morning with the promise of a beautiful day to come. She told him she planned to put the two bedrooms back in order and asked if he had plans for the day. He said he didn't and offered to help however he could. She said it would be nice to have help hanging pictures and was open to suggestions from him. She hinted that there might still be some furniture to move.

They showered together, made love under the shower, playfully dried each other, and dressed. Jake followed her to her home.

As Kendra drove, she thought back over the past week. *How many times have we made love the past week? Too many to count ... and not nearly as many as I want. I was hoping to get a glimpse of what I've missed the past five years. I've certainly gotten more than a glimpse. What is it they say about learning a new language? The best way to learn is by full immersion. Thank you, Jake. I may not be fluent, but I think I'm learning to please you.*

Jake parked behind her in the driveway when they arrived. He walked to her and she silently took his hand. She smiled with all the warmth a woman can give and gently kissed him. "Thank you." He looked quizzical. "For everything," she said with another huge smile and a giggle.

During the course of the morning, two large box trucks arrived from which bedroom furniture for the master bedroom and living room furniture was offloaded. The deliverymen moved the old furniture into Walt's trophy room, set up a new bed in the master bedroom, positioned the other items and took the old mattress and box springs with them when they left. Kendra had found what she wanted on the internet based upon pictures and had arranged for expedited delivery, despite a substantial charge.

Kendra and Jake spent the day decorating and adding accessories—all to make the house her home. She needed to distance Walt from where she lived. Jake helped when asked or needed; otherwise, he stayed in the background—this was Kendra's project and he did not want to intrude. He knew it was important for her to know that she had made the changes on her own.

By mid-afternoon, the home looked fresh and new. Jake was impressed with the changes and complimented Kendra on her taste and the imaginative and creative changes. She took Jake by the hand and led him to the new club chairs.

"I'd like a small glass of wine. Would you?" He agreed and she poured. As she handed him his glass, she said, "I have a favor to ask.

"I need some time to … become comfortable here, comfortable with the changes … and to accustom myself to this being my home now. I've never lived alone or had my own home. I need to get my arms and my mind around this new step in my life. Would you mind giving me some time alone this afternoon?"

"No. I understand completely. Take all the time you need. Would you like to have a night alone in your new home?"

"No. I'd like a little time to become accustomed to the changes. Then, I would like to have my friend Jake come to dinner at my home this evening to share the newness with me. But I want my lover Jake to be here to share the night with me." She was quiet for a moment.

"I want to take advantage of you."

Jake grinned broadly and she poked him in the ribs.

"That, too. But I want to distance myself from old memories, from many unhappy memories. I want you to help me do that. If you don't mind staying here tonight, I want to wake tomorrow morning in my bed in my bedroom with you lying beside me."

"I understand. You get comfortable in your nest this afternoon. I'll be here this evening at whatever time you say, with my toothbrush. Actually, I would like to stay here tonight. What you've done, the changes you've made are very nice. I already feel more comfortable here than I ever have. You've done well."

She drew him into her embrace and kissed him warmly. "Thank you. Come at seven. Park in the garage tonight."

She kissed him again, and whispered softly to him, "It will be a special night."

Kendra bought what she needed for dinner together with some good wine and champagne, cheesecake for dessert, some fresh strawberries and sour cream. When she returned, she wandered through the house, enjoying the changes. She was excited—excited for herself, excited that she had Jake with whom to share this new adventure, excited that she literally felt the weight of the past easing from her shoulders. *This is good, Kendra. This is very good. Enjoy your new life, girl.*

Kendra prepared chicken breasts to bake in cranberry sauce, new potatoes, haricot verts, fresh sour dough bread, and apple salad. She stemmed and cut the strawberries and made cinnamon sour cream dip for the berries. She put a bottle of Krug champagne and a bottle of Ferrari Carano chardonnay in the fridge to chill.

She again wandered through the house. The changes were all positive and uplifting—and she was very glad she had decided to take back the master bedroom. It was a spacious room, bright and cheery with a vaulted ceiling and high, shuttered windows that accepted wonderful morning light when open. A large, en suite bath with a nice glass-walled walk-in shower and a spacious closet completed the area. The bedroom changes and the new furniture were complemented by a wonderful, large chaise lounge and a delightful lamp by the chaise for reading. The chaise had been her chair. She couldn't recall ever seeing Walt sit in it.

At five o'clock, she stepped into a warm bath, laden with oils, leaned back and relaxed, thinking ahead. Soon, she slipped into a robe, went to the kitchen and started the oven for the chicken and new potatoes.

Returning to the bedroom, she laid out on her new duvet the special purchases she had made with Jake in mind—a casual little black dress, petite black dress flats, a black lace bra and tiny black lace panties. She plucked her onyx bracelet, earrings and necklace from her jewelry box. She applied perfume to all the proper places. She smiled at the thought of Jake touching her there, and set about dressing.

Jake showered, shaved and dressed with her comment about a special evening in mind—nice slacks, a soft, linen shirt that fit him very well, and polished loafers. He gathered the new home card and the crystal vase that he had bought that afternoon for her, a boxed bouquet of fresh red roses, and a bottle of very good cabernet sauvignon. Arriving promptly at six o'clock, he took a moment to again take in the delightful changes Kendra had made to the yard, then rang the bell.

She opened the door and took his breath away.

It had been some time since he had seen Kendra dressed up and she looked stunning. He was looking forward to having a quiet evening alone with her, but a part of him wanted to be out with her on his arm. *My God, I had almost forgotten just how beautiful she is.*

"You look beautiful," he intoned seriously. He offered the flowers and gift bag containing the vase, saying, "A little something to warm your new home. And a little something for the palate on this special occasion."

"'Oh, thank you." She kissed him warmly. "Let's get these into water and on display," she said as she led him into the kitchen. "Will you open and pour, while I arrange?"

"Sure. What would you like?

"I think a glass of the special occasion cab would be perfect, if that's all right with you. Tonight is certainly a very special occasion for me."

She arranged the roses as he opened and poured. "They're beautiful. Let's put them on the table so we can enjoy them during dinner."

The carried their wine glasses through the house, enjoying the changes made by Kendra. As they walked and observed, Jake commented, and complimented her frequently.

When they entered the master bedroom, he was very pleasantly surprised. The king-sized bed was covered by a sumptuous and beautiful seafoam green duvet and large pillows in cream-colored shams that complemented the duvet. One corner of the bed was turned down displaying beautiful, smooth seafoam green sheets that looked soft and comfortable.

The room had truly become her room. It was light and airy and feminine and delightful. New lamps and a loose throw on the chaise gave the room a look of casual, comfortable elegance.

She took him into the bathroom and he noticed new towels and the new thick, soft rug that complimented and drew in the colors of the bedroom. Everything she had done in and outside the house the past week reflected her good taste and elegant beauty. He told her so and she was inwardly ecstatic at his approval.

"I overspent, but it was worth it. I've decided to keep the home, if I can buy Walt's share. And, I want you to be comfortable coming here."

"I am. What you've done is delightful. Your home is very inviting." He kissed her and overtly played his eyes over her. "And you're very inviting, as well."

She laughed. "Well, I certainly hope you'll accept that invitation."

"With pleasure," Jake replied as he drew her to him. They kissed, long and slow, their tongues exploring. Both were excited and eager.

She told him what she had prepared for dinner. "We have cheesecake for dessert."

"Any plans after that?"

Her voice was low and soft. "I thought we could do a little intimate exploring for a while. Then, I have champagne and strawberries, if that interests you." She smiled coquettishly as Jake nodded in emphatic approval.

A week ago, Kendra had been a sexual neophyte. Her exciting capacity to receive and give pleasure had been untested and unappreciated. In one week's time, she had become a sensual, exciting woman—a delightful lover who was eager to please and be pleased. And Jake loved it.

Kendra finished preparing dinner and they ate, cozy and happy in her dining room. They took dessert and coffee into the living room and enjoyed the new couch and furniture. She removed their dishes to the kitchen, returned with two flues of champagne, which they took to the patio, where they sipped and enjoyed the new look.

When their glasses were empty, she took his hand. Her hand shook.

"Are you all right?"

She smiled shyly. "I'm eager. I want to make new memories with you. I want you to want me as much as I want you."

"Kendra, you have no idea how much I want you. I hope I've shown that this week."

"You have. But I need you tonight," she said softly as she led him to her bedroom. "I need you to help me make this _my_ home."

She turned down the bed covers, came to Jake and simply stood before him. Taking his hands, she kissed him gently on his lips. She stepped out of her shoes and slowly shrugged off her dress, never taking her eyes from his. She laid the dress aside and turned back to face Jake.

"Beautiful," he said with admiration. He slowly finished undressing her. Then she undressed him. They lay together, exploring, touching, whispering seductively to each other. When they made love, it was a culmination of all the warmth and emotion that had grown between them for the past week.

"Yes, Jake," was all she said, but her voice was her message. It was a delightful amalgam of warm acceptance, heart-felt statement, gentle plea and joyful exultation spoken in that way that only a sensuous, sensitive woman can. It stroked Jake's heart, his spine, his face and his manhood simultaneously, as completely as if Kendra had physically touched him.

Afterward, Kendra rolled them onto their sides and they lay quietly for a time until she giggled. "I think it's time for champagne and strawberries. What do you think?" He smiled and nodded his agreement.

"Stay here." She slid out of bed and, to his delight, padded gracefully and superbly naked to her closet. She returned with two soft, oxford cloth robes, a black one with white stripes and a smaller one in white with black pin stripes. "I thought perhaps we could use these." She handed him the black robe as she slipped into the other and belted it. He did likewise with the black robe.

"Nice. I like these." He pulled her to him and they kissed.

They left the bed turned down and went to the kitchen where Jake retrieved the bottle of champagne while Kendra set out two fresh flutes, a bowl of cut strawberries and a bowl of cinnamon sour cream dip. They drank champagne and dipped strawberries, fed each other, kissed, teased and talked and touched.

For the past week, Jake had been completely enamored of Kendra, but tonight affected him profoundly. She had been eager and ardent from the first time they had made love, and her eagerness and response blossomed and matured each time, but tonight, there seemed to be an overriding desire in her—a desire to please him, a desire to find release and satisfaction—that was new. Jake was enthralled. Kendra was everything he thought she would be when he first met her, when he first kissed her—and more.

Kendra sighed softly. Tonight was what she thought she had wanted from the night of their first kiss, certainly what she had wanted when she came to Jake a week ago. Over the past week, he had shown her desire, respect and tenderness that she had never known. He listened to her, shared his thoughts with her, and made her laugh.

Unlike Walt, Jake treated her as an equal, a partner.

In the beginning, she believed Jake would please her and be attentive, but she was certain he would soon move on. Now—even though it had only been a week, she knew she wanted to hold on to what they were experiencing together, to hold on to the happiness and eagerness he instilled in her.

Tonight? Well, tonight was wonderful. Tonight she was making the new memories she desperately needed—and tonight she was filled with love for this wonderful man. She wanted to please him as he had pleased her every moment they had been together.

The strawberries and cream were gone. They poured the last of the champagne into their glasses and she led him back to her bed. Without a word, each knew that they had become more than just compatible lovers. Jake took her in his arms and she eagerly pressed against him. She uttered a low moan and her robe fell to the floor as she arched her breasts to him and rolled her hips up to meet the caress of his hand.

Cradling the back of his head in both hands, she drew his mouth to her, kissing him softly, and whispered, "Make love with me, Jake."

He aroused her slowly. She was eager and when she was ready, she pulled him to her warmth. They made love excitedly, murmuring to each other, reveling in the sensations each felt, lost in the warm touches they exchanged. Jake whispered to her and stroked her as they moved in excited unison until she cried out and quivered as she clung to him. They lay, once again spent and quiet, still joined as one.

Jake rolled onto his side, taking her with him. He brushed small tears from her cheek with a fingertip. "Are you all right?"

She nodded and whispered, "I'm fine. I'm wonderful. Oh, Jake, we're so good together," as she melded against him. *New life. New memories to keep me warm and happy. And a wonderful man.*

He nodded, kissing her. "Yes, we are. It's pretty incredible. It has been from the very first time."

Kendra now was not the timid, uncertain woman she had been a week ago. She moved with confidence in herself, in her ability to make love, and in her ability to convey her needs and satisfy his. She knew she had given Jake all that was deep within her—and that she would continue to do so as long as he wanted her.

She sighed, nestled against Jake as he took her hand, and they were asleep in seconds.

PART TWO

THIRTY-FOUR

They awoke in Kendra's bed to the sound of birds chirping happily. She felt Jake move to roll out of bed and whimpered softly, pulling his hand.

"Right back," he said quietly.

"Hurry," she whispered huskily. He returned, pulling her into his arms and she murmured happily, cuddling into him until she stirred, kissed him, then ran her tongue from his lips downward. "I like having you in my bed."

Jake pulled her to him and they made comfortable morning love, then lay quietly in each other's arms, reflecting. Kendra was thrilled. Jake was everything she had hoped he would be, believed he would be—and more. He was mature, intelligent, grounded, attentive, very handsome and very loving.

She rose on one elbow and looked down into his eyes as she rubbed the hair on his chest. Her hand moved lower as she continued looking into his eyes. Taking him in her hand, she smirked and asked incredulously, "Boy toy?"

They laughed and she tickled him. After a few minutes, she again rose on one elbow and asked, "Do you have things you need to do today?"

"I have some errands to run and I need to attend to the pool. Walt should be home by now. Hopefully, he has had a week to think and won't be a problem, but we don't know for sure. But I don't like leaving you alone. I want you to be safe."

"Thank you—you always make me feel safe." She kissed him. "I think I'll be okay. You do what you need to do. I'd like to just be in my home for a little while. I like what I've done. I want to take it in and enjoy it for a little while more. Then, it would be nice to lie by your pool and get some sun, if you don't mind?'

"Not at all. I'd like that. Anything special this evening?

"May I bring my toothbrush? I think I'd like to be in your bed tonight."

"You certainly may. I'd like that very much." He smiled, then looked serious. "Promise me you'll keep your phone with you. Call me or 911 if anything unusual happens or Walt appears. I really don't like leaving you alone."

"I'll keep my phone with me, and the Purcells are just across the street. I'll come over as soon as you're ready for me."

"Okay. Why don't you come over around two? I should be back home by then."

They rose. Kendra set soft music to play. They brewed coffee and took their cups to her deck. They talked and teased and touched. They made breakfast together and ate outside. They dressed and Jake left, reminding her to keep her phone close by. He wasn't comfortable leaving her, but on the other hand, he didn't want to frighten her.

Kendra decided she would forego a shower until after lying by the pool. She made the bed, poured another cup of coffee and wandered around her house, enjoying the changes. She made little adjustments here and there, and made mental notes of other changes she wanted to make. She refilled her cup and took it to the deck, taking in all the delightful changes and additions in her back yard. She was at peace with herself and her life at that moment. She sat, marveling at how quickly and easily she and Jake had melded. It had only been a week, but she knew that it could be good.

Her happiness was palpable. *Life is good, Kendra.*

As she sat, Kendra heard the sound of a car entering her driveway. It wouldn't be Jake and she wasn't expecting company. The doorbell rang. She went into the house, set her half-full cup on the counter as she picked up her phone, and went to the front door. She heard footsteps outside. Walt's car was in the driveway, but he wasn't at the door.

She looked outside, but didn't see him, which perplexed her. "*Oh, no. I don't want this today. I really don't want a confrontation with Walt today.* She scrolled to Jake's name in her contact list and pressed his number.

As his voice message was ending, Kendra was startled by a sound behind her. She sensed a presence behind her and a shiver ran up her spine. She started to turn, but a large hand roughly grabbed her by the upper arm. She screamed, "Jake, help!"

The intruder enclosed her neck in a three-point chokehold that pressed firmly against her carotid arteries, shutting off the flow of blood to her brain.

Her phone fell to the carpet as she struggled, grabbing for the arm around her throat. Fear overwhelmed her as she fought, trying to dislodge the tightening grip around her neck, until everything went dark as she collapsed against her attacker.

The large figure lowered her limp body to the floor, extended her arm and carefully injected her with the contents of a full hypodermic syringe. He closed the front door, then went to her linen closet from which he removed a flat bed sheet. He laid her on the sheet and rolled her inside it, snuggly wrapping the sheet around her body. He lifted her and carried her like a rolled carpet to the back seat of his car.

THIRTY-FIVE

Jake returned from his errands at one thirty. He mixed a pitcher of sangria, placed it in the fridge and went outside to attend to the pool. Two o'clock came and went. At two fifteen, he reached for his phone in order to check on Kendra. It wasn't in his pocket and he realized that he had forgotten to take it with him earlier. He went inside his home, retrieved his phone and saw that she had called him at ten thirty-seven. Jake tapped her message icon, tapped PLAY and went taut as he heard her scream and call his name. It had to be Walt.

Jake immediately called 911 and reported the message and circumstances. He gave the dispatcher Kendra's address and said he would meet the officers at Kendra's home.

As he drove, he called Kendra's father, Sam Clark. Over the years, Jake and Sam had become good friends. They often visited and discussed common interests when he Mei were in town. Sam had taught Jake's concealed handgun class and they shared a keen interest in American history and the American revolution. Jake succinctly explained the situation. Sam said that they would call her brother, and he and Mei would be in Houston in an hour. Jake told them to bring their bags and plan to stay with him as long as they wanted.

He arrived at Kendra's just ahead of the Sheriff's deputies. He knew enough not to wander about. He noticed the closed front door.

Two cars arrived. One deputy went to the house. The other came to him. Jake explained who he was, played Kendra's frantic call for the deputy and was told to wait. That deputy spoke with the other, and went to the back of the house while the other went to front door. They found the doors unlocked, entered, cleared the house, and exited.

"Is she inside," Jake asked hesitantly. Seeing his concern, the deputy who had first spoken with Jake came to him.

"No, sir. She isn't. Everything seems to be in order. No sign of a struggle, although we found her phone on the floor near the front door. The back door was open onto the deck. There was a half cup of cold coffee on the counter. A Lexus SUV is in the garage. Is that her car?" Jake nodded. "We were told she has a restraining order against her husband. What can you tell me about that?"

Jake summarized succinctly, emphasizing that it was alcohol that was the impetus for the divorce petition. He explained that he had been a neighbor until last year and that the three of them were close friends until Walt's drinking caused him to alienate his friends. He told the officer that he and Kelli Sinton had served as sounding boards for Kendra as she tried to deal with Walt's drinking. He gave the officer the name and number of Kendra's friends and her parents, telling the officer that he had advised her parents and they were on their way now to Houston. He said he believed Walt had been staying at Mitchell's house since the eviction, but didn't know Mitchell's correct address.

"This is my fault. I told her to call me if there was a problem; then, I laid my phone down and forgot to take it with me."

"Don't beat yourself up, Mr. Alder. Even if you had answered her call, by the time you got here, they would probably have been gone."

Soon, a detective and a small crime scene unit arrived. The Detective introduced himself as Detective Rodriguez. Officers were sent to canvas the neighborhood while the detective questioned Jake at length. As he was finishing, he took a phone call. "That was my partner. He has been speaking by phone with the friends you identified. No one has any information that can help us at the moment. If you're interested, they all seem to think very highly of you."

His phone rang again. He answered and listened. Looking at Jake, he said, "One of the neighbors saw a car on the drive around ten thirty this morning. I'm going across the street to talk to him." The officer gave Jake an appraising look and said, "Hang around. I'll let you know what I learn. Maybe you can add something to it."

He returned in fifteen minutes. "What does Mr. Williams drive?"

"White Mercedes E350

"Describe him for me."

"Six two, around two twenty, muscular but getting soft from the alcohol and lack of exercise. Played pro football, but blew out his knee and couldn't return. That was the reason for the drinking."

"I thought that name sounded familiar," Rodriquez said. "That coincides with what the neighbor boy saw this morning. He said that he was sure it was Williams' car and that he glimpsed a man fitting that description walk toward the back of the house. Do you think Williams could have done this?"

"If he had been drinking, yes. If sober, I'm not sure. Maybe. Walt was a good linebacker, but he often reacted faster than he thought. And he had a mean streak. That was good on the field, but not always off the field."

"It appears you were the last person to see Mrs. Williams. You were here this morning?"

"Yes. We had breakfast together."

"What was her mood?

"Very happy. She had been redecorating all week and was enjoying the changes in the home. She said she wanted to spend the morning enjoying the changes. She asked if she could lie by my pool this afternoon, which was fine with me. She was coming at two and we had planned to have dinner together."

"Anything there I need to know about?"

Without any guilty hesitation, Jake replied, "Her closest female friend and I have been her confidents for well over a year as she has dealt with his drinking. A week ago Friday, she called and asked if she could come over. She told me about filing for divorce, which I think was wise. She told me that Walt struck her on two occasions. Her lawyer suggested she stay the weekend with friends for safety reasons, so she stayed with me. I have a large house and a nice guest room. Kelli Sinton is aware that she was staying at my home.

"As the week progressed, we realized that we were attracted to each and the more we talked, we confided our attraction. Until this week, we were always just good friends. I was here last night."

"Thanks for being honest. I have to tell you, if it weren't for the phone message and what the neighbors saw, you would be high on the suspect list."

"I understand. But I'm just as worried about what has happened to her as her family and other friends. She's a very special person. If you get to meet her, you'll see that right off."

The detective's phone rang again. He listened and rang off. "My partner. They are at the brother's home. He wasn't home, but they had a warrant and entered. It appears that Mr. Williams has been staying there. My partner found a woman's ring and a pair of women's panties on the dresser in what appears to be his room."

"Right," Jake said. "Last Saturday, she went home for clothes and important items. When she returned, she told me that a ring that had been birthday present from Walt was missing, and she thought a new pair of black panties was missing also. She filed a report. I can't describe the ring, but Kelli Sinton can."

"Thanks. Do you have any idea where he could have taken her?"

"No. Nothing comes to mind."

"Okay. We have an all-points bulletin out on Williams' car. Hopefully, that will turn up something. I have your number. I'll call if we have any more questions. I understand you will see her parents." He gave Jake another of his cards. "Please give them my name and number. Ask them to call me."

Jake went home. Shortly after, Sam and Mei arrived. He brought them up to date and gave Detective Rodriguez's card to them. He explained that Kendra had stayed with him last weekend, and they stayed together during the week, at the suggestion of her lawyer for safety reasons.

Jake called Kelli and Scott and informed them of what had happened. Before she hung up, Kelli said to Jake, "Thanks for all you've done for Kendra. I know the two of you have become more than just friends. You're what she needs, Jake. I hope we find her and this works out for both of you."

Detective Rodriguez called Sam at seven o'clock. He apologized that he had no news for them.

Sam called Callen and brought him up to date. His wife was pregnant and due any day. Sam told him to stay where he was, that he couldn't do anymore if he were in Houston, and Callen agreed. Sam assured Callen he would keep him apprised of any news.

They had dinner and Jake got Sam and Mei settled into his guest room, but no one could sleep. He made coffee for him and Sam, and tea for Mei. They talked some, but sat silently most of the time, each of them with his or her own thoughts of Kendra. As the night wore on, they went to bed, one by one.

THIRTY-SIX

Kendra slowly came into consciousness. She was in total darkness. She lay on her back on something soft. It smelled musty and it felt like a mattress. Her mouth was dry. She was groggy and thirsty. She tried to move, but it was impossible to do more than roll her head a bit. It felt as though she were wrapped in something that held her arms tightly against her body and made her legs immobile.

She was disoriented and she was scared—very scared. The last thing she remembered was seeing Walt's car in her driveway and being accosted by someone from behind. She had a dim memory of being in a car and of a stinging sensation in her forearm, but the memory, if it even was a memory, was very vague and hazy.

Where am I? How did I get here—wherever this is? Why would Walt do this? She had no idea what time it was or how long she had been gone from her home.

"Jake," she said weakly. "Are you here, Jake? Where am I?"

An owl hooted and she jerked violently, startled until her mind recognized the sound. *There must be trees nearby, maybe woods.* She felt light-headed. She lay quietly and slowly became more alert. Soon she heard faint rustling and scraping sounds from outside. She listened intently, but couldn't identify the sounds. She turned her head as much as she could and looked around the still, ominous surroundings. She made out the very shadowy outlines of a small room with a window. The curtains appeared to be closed, but there was a slight gap between the edges. Kendra saw no moonlight through the narrow gap.

She heard a small skittering noise in one corner. *That sound must have been a mouse.* Turning her head as much as possible in the direction of the small sound, she saw a figure standing by the wall. She went rigid with fear.

"Walt?" she asked hesitantly. There was no answer and she felt a pang of despair.

"Who are you?" There was no answer. The figure stood silently as she began to tremble with even greater fear.

"Who are you? Where am I? Why are you doing this?" she asked desperately.

She stared intently, but the figure didn't move. *Don't panic! Don't go down that dark hole.* When the figure still did not move or speak, she stared intently at it until she finally realized that she was seeing the outline of a coat tree with a hat hanging above a long jacket. The heart stopping initial fear and the relief that followed sent her over the edge. Tears flowed freely as a feeling of complete and utter helplessness overwhelmed her.

Get control. Think, Kendra. She calmed herself. She knew she had to try to get free. She struggled, but could not loosen the cloying grip of whatever it was that held her. This frightened her even more. She felt it with her fingertips and surmised that she was wrapped tightly in a bed sheet. *How in the world did I get wrapped up in a bed sheet?* Her inability to move terrified her.

She was very thirsty and confused. Her arms and legs ached and were, ironically, at the same time, numb. The longer she lay like that, the more frightened she became. *Don't panic. Don't panic! Keep your wits about you.*

She again heard indiscernible sounds. After a moment, she realized that what she was hearing sounded like a shovel digging into the earth. *There has to be someone out there. What time is it? Is it as dark outside as it appears or is this just a dark room? There must to be someone working outside, but is it Walt or someone who could help me?*

The sound of the shovel stopped. She heard more indiscernible sounds, then a thump as if something heavy and wooden had been dropped. *I have to take the chance it is someone who can help me.*

She tried to call out, but her throat was too dry. When she had mustered enough saliva to wet her mouth and vocal cords, she screamed hoarsely for help as loudly as she could, several times. Immediately she heard a man's voice curse roughly.

A cold frisson of fear ran up her spine and she shivered. Through the window she saw a faint glow of light coming toward her and heard the sound of running feet. A door was thrown open and it banged loudly against the wall behind it. She jerked sharply at the sound and her body tensed as cold fear ran through her.

An electric light from somewhere outside the room came on suddenly and illuminated the outline of a door to the room in which she was imprisoned. She heard faint sounds from the other side of the door, then the door burst open and the silhouette of a large man filled the door frame. She screamed again as he rushed into the dark room. His face was indistinguishable, but a familiar voice said harshly, "It won't do any good to scream. There is no one within miles to hear you."

She was wide-eyed and went rigid as stark terror again overwhelmed her. She tried to scream, but this time, fear closed her throat and only a faint squeak emerged from her lips. *Oh, God. Will I ever see Jake again?*

She was overwhelmed with fear and desperation. The man reached for her, grabbing her sheet-covered arm. In complete panic, she tried to buck and turn away from him, but he held her arm firmly. She tried again to scream, but could only croak a dry plea, "No. Please, Walt—why?"

She felt a quick, sharp pain in her forearm as he again injected her, and the unrelenting terror overtook her mind. Mercifully, she fainted and her mind shut down as the liquid again invaded her body, rendering her stuporous and inert.

He stepped back, looking at the ersatz mummy that was Kendra. *Stay quiet and this will all be over soon and everything will be good. Just sleep a little longer.*

He took a cold beer from the refrigerator, opened it and sat at the kitchen table, reviewing his plan. It would work. He was sure it would work. When he explained everything to her, how it had all happened, what he had done, she would understand and everything would be good. Of course his account would be a fabrication, but she wouldn't know. She would never know. If she would just stay asleep for a little while longer.

He was tired. It had been a long, trying day and night. He hadn't slept since Thursday night, and only a little that night. He had been awake for the better part of more than forty-eight hours. He had to get some sleep. Morning would be here soon. But things had gone as he had planned.

He ate one of the fast food sandwiches he had bought along the road and finished his beer. He enjoyed the solitude of the woods and the cabin. He had always liked being out here at night. He checked on Kendra, but she was quiet and breathing very softly. She would be okay until morning. Then this would be over for her.

He closed all the curtains in the cabin, went into the other bedroom and pulled the blackout curtains in that room. He stripped to his underwear and rolled himself into a sleeping bag on the bed. He had no trouble going to sleep.

THIRTY-SEVEN

Jake slept fitfully Saturday night. He woke at six a.m., dressed and made his way into the kitchen where he found Sam seated at the table with a cup of coffee in front of him. Jake poured a cup for himself and sat opposite Sam.

"Did you get any sleep?"

"No." Sam shook his head. "Did you?"

"A little, off and on. How is Mei?"

"I think she finally went to sleep around three. Thankfully, she's still asleep."

Jake shook his head woefully. "I've never felt so helpless in my life. I'm not sure how to deal with all this."

"Be patient and don't let your imagination run wild," Sam advised. "Sometimes, no matter how bad things seem, you have to let them play out for a bit and watch for the handle to come into view. Think logically and never lose hope. Try to keep a normal routine; don't just sit and dwell on the problem."

Jake nodded. "Thanks. I'm glad you're here."

Sam rinsed his coffee cup and said, "I'm going to take a walk. I'll have my phone. If either of us hears anything, we call the other."

Jake nodded as Sam closed the door behind himself.

Mei came into the kitchen at seven o'clock. "Good Morning, Jake," she said as she made tea for herself. She sat where Sam had sat.

"Is Sam walking?" she asked.

"Yes."

"That's what he does every morning. He says it's good to have a routine to anchor the day."

"How are you doing?" Jake asked.

"I'm worried … and scared. But Sam always tells me not to jump to conclusions. And to keep busy." She patted Jake's hand. "Sam has been through some bad situations, so I usually take his advice. But's it's different when it's our daughter." Her voice broke and she said no more, but Jake could read the concern in her eyes and on her face. Just then, Sam returned and saw the concern on Mei's face. He took her into his embrace.

At eight o'clock, Detective Rodriquez called Sam. He told Sam that there was nothing to report and advised that the decision had been made not to notify the media of the facts of the kidnapping, except for the make, model and license number of Walt's car. The decision had been made to hold off for twenty-four hours in the hope that Walt would come to his senses and/or that Kendra could reason with him. In the meantime, there was an all-points bulletin out on the car.

He advised that both last night and at seven a.m., officers had gone to Mitchell's home. His car was there, but Mitchell was not at home. Rodriquez advised that he had tried to contact Walt's parents yesterday, but they were apparently on vacation somewhere on a ship and no one knew exactly where. And they were not answering their cell phone. He promised to stay in touch.

Sam relayed the information to Mei and Jake.

Sunday passed uneventfully. There was no news from Rodriquez. There were no communications from Walt. It was unnerving. Jake talked to Kelli and brought her up to date. Jake, Sam and Mei kept themselves occupied as well as they could. Mei made a casserole and they morosely ate supper together. Their spirits were waning as each became pensive and even more anxious. They finally, one by one, went to bed.

THIRTY-EIGHT

Jake eventually dozed off around two a.m. Monday morning. He hadn't been asleep long before he heard a knock on his door and Sam's voice softly calling his name. He opened the door. Sam, in jeans with coffee cup in hand, nodded his head toward the kitchen. Jake pulled on his jeans and shirt, and followed Sam down the hall.

He poured a cup of coffee and joined Sam at the table as Sam said, "I couldn't sleep. I've been racking my brain trying to figure out what Walt's plan is. Finally drifted off a little bit ago and was suddenly wide-awake. I may know where he took her."

Jake nodded encouragingly, and Sam continued. "Walt liked to hunt. Before he signed with the NFL, he and I hunted some together. His family had a lease near Johnson City. My guess is they still have it. It's been four or five years since we hunted there and I didn't think about that place at first, but the memory came to me."

"Now that you mention it, I remember Walt telling me that you and he had hunted together on the family lease," Jake replied. "The detective asked me if there was a place Walt might take her, but that never entered my mind either. You may be right. Do you know how to get there?"

"I might have some trouble finding it in the dark, but I can find it in daylight. I think it's worth a drive over there."

"I agree. Did you bring a handgun?"

"Always do."

They finished dressed quickly.

"Do you still carry your 1911?" Jake asked Sam, referring to the Colt model 1911 forty-five caliber semi-automatic pistol Sam had carried as a Special Forces Officer. Sam nodded.

Jake grabbed a box of shells for his nine-millimeter Beretta and a box of forty-five caliber for Sam. He clipped his carry holster and semi-automatic on, and pocketed two extra magazines. Sam filled a large thermos with coffee and gathered some bottles of water as Jake was getting his SUV out of the garage.

"Drive fast, but not too fast," Sam said. "No matter what his plan is, I know from experience that he's probably sleeping right now. Best time to catch bad guys sleeping is between three and five a.m. We should get there about the time he wakes, if that's where he is."

They talked sporadically. Jake blamed himself for not keeping his phone with him. Sam told him the same thing the deputy told him. Jake knew Sam was probably right, but it didn't lessen his guilt. After an hour, Jake thought about Detective Rodriguez.

"I think we should call Rodriguez and tell him our theory. I imagine they aren't going to appreciate us going up there alone without telling them."

Sam agreed. Jake dialed and got the dispatcher who advised that Rodriguez was off duty. Jake left him a message explaining their hunch and asked that he call when he got the message.

"Should we call anyone else? Texas Rangers? FBI since this is a kidnapping?"

"Not our place to do that and we'd probably step on a lot of toes. He should call you back soon."

Rodriguez called at five a.m. Jake explained their hunch and told Rodriguez that he and Sam were on their way and that they expected to reach the cabin around six a.m. When Rodriguez commented that he was concerned about civilians acting on their own, Jake explained that Sam was a retired Special Forces Field Officer with multiple tours in Iraq and Afghanistan. Since Jake could not give directions to the hunting cabin, Rodriquez said he would call ahead and have a sheriff from Blanco County meet them at the highway turn-off to Hye, a small town west of Johnson City.

"Don't go in there ahead of the sheriff," Rodriguez cautioned. "Get him to the area and let him take the lead." Jake agreed and relayed the instruction to Sam.

"Do you think Walt will be dangerous?" Jake asked Sam.

"Don't know. He always kept a pretty cool head on the field, but he has a mean streak. I've never seen him shoot or handle a pistol, but he knows long guns. If he's goofy enough to kidnap Kendra, then I think it's safe to assume his elevator isn't going to the top floor right now."

They met the deputy—Douglas, a stocky, florid man—a little before six a.m. at the turn-off to a macadam road, made introductions and explained their respective relationships to Kendra. Sam explained that the cabin had a front and back door, a raised, covered porch across the length of the front and a small back porch and roof over the back door, a double window on either side of the front door and two windows on each end of the rectangular cabin. He said there were two bedrooms on either end of the back side that flanked a kitchen and bathroom in the center and that there was a window on the back wall and the outside wall of each bedroom and a kitchen window in the center.

The cabin was a mile from the main road, down a rough, but reasonably good caliche road that ran past a field of oats and through an area heavily wooded with cedar, sycamore and live oak. Sam rode with the Deputy in order to guide him to the cabin and Jake followed in his SUV. The Sheriff asked the same question that Jake had asked about Walt and Sam gave him the same answer.

"It's a hunting cabin, so he probably has a rifle or two with a scope in there. He's a good shot.

"Have you done much of this kind of thing?" Sam asked.

"No. Been on the job for nearly thirty years and never had to draw my weapon. I go to the range quarterly and score okay. I was with a group that cornered an escaped con once, but the SWAT guys went in and got him out."

Sam was concerned, but all he said was, "Let me know how I can help."

Sam mistook one turn and they were forced to perform a three-point turn and back track down the rough road that was lined with beautiful dogwood and redbud trees, already blooming in the early spring weather. As they got themselves re-directed, they saw a tall, erect man wearing wire rim glasses and a worn fatigue jacket walking along the road with an old, white Labrador Retriever. Douglas lowered his window and greeted the man.

"Morning, Doc. You and Maisie out for your morning walk?

"Yup. Every morning it don't rain. What are you doing out here so early in the morning, Deputy."

"Got something to check out. Have you seen anyone come or go on this road lately?"

"White car went to the Williams lease Thursday evening. There Friday morning, but gone that evening. Back again Saturday afternoon and been there since."

"Did you see who was in it?"

"Nope. But I heard rifle shots Thursday night late—five or six close together around midnight, two spaced close together later in the morning. Could 'a been shooting at a coyote or boar. There's a few of them around."

"There are. See or hear anything else unusual?"

"Nope."

"Okay. Thanks. You and Maisie enjoy your walk."

"Thanks. We will. You take care now, Deputy."

As Douglas smoothly accelerated down the road, they heard the coo of doves from a thicket and the sharp scree of a red tail hawk in search of breakfast.

"That was Doc McDonald. Was a medic in Nam. Was awarded a Silver Star and a Purple Heart. Did two tours. He's a brave man. He's a retired professor from Texas A&M. Taught in the Vet School. Talks like plain folks, but that is one smart man. Comes from a family with a passel of kids, all of them smart as whips and every one of them has a least one advanced decree. But good, easy going folks. You'd like him a lot."

They continued down the road.

The wrong turn cost them about ten minutes, but Sam got Douglas to the cabin. The rustic structure was set on a patch of flat, wooded land, cleared roughly ten feet on all sides from the cabin. It sat below a low rise and about fifty yards from the crest at the end of a gravel drive. Sam had described the building well. A carport with a large storage room had been added behind and to the right side of the cabin since Sam's last visit. Woods, mostly cedar, live oak and sycamore, surrounded the cabin on three sides. Driving in, they could see Walt's Mercedes and a pair of mud-splattered four-wheelers under the carport, but no one was visible. They again heard the coo of doves and the call of the red tail hawk.

They stopped below the outside rim of the rise of the knoll facing the cabin. "How do you want to play this?" Sam asked.

"You get out here and wait with Mr. Alder and stay out of sight. I'll pull to the top of the rise, get out behind my door, and hail him. Let's see if he's in there." Sam exited the cruiser and the deputy pulled forward at a shallow angle to the cabin with the passenger side closest to the structure. Sam was glad to see he knew enough to protect himself from a shot at his feet or through the door when he got out.

THIRTY-NINE

He awoke slowly and looked at his watch. It read seven o'clock. *That can't be right.* He opened the curtain and realized he had slept until Sunday evening. He dressed quickly and went to check Kendra. She was breathing slowly and was very pale. He tried to get her to drink some water, but she was unresponsive. When he tried to pour a little water into her mouth, she gagged reflexively, and the water ran out the corners of her lips. She showed no other signs of consciousness or voluntary action. He tried to wake her without success.

Maybe the drug dose had been too strong this time. He hadn't been very precise when he hurried into the cabin last night and mixed the ingredients. Her screams had startled him and in his haste to quiet her, he couldn't remember how much powder he had used. He had done his research and was pretty sure it would have taken much more powder to be lethal, but he could have given her a pretty hefty dose.

He decided to stick with his plan, but to give her time to come out from under the influence of the drug he had given her. He had no idea how long that would be.

He waited two hours and tried again to wake her and give her some water, with no success. He tried again after another two hours with the same result. He tried again an hour later with no response from her. Her breathing had slowed, and her pulse was slow and weak, but felt steady.

He called to mind the Rule of Three—one can live three minutes without air, three hours without shelter, three days without water, three weeks without food, and three months without hope. How long had it been since she had water? It was getting close to thirty-six hours since he had taken her from her home.

Okay. Think. You can't call for an ambulance or carry her into an emergency room. If they revive her, how do you explain all this?

Think. It can still work, even if you do that … but it won't be the same. It will lose the effect you want.

Give it until morning, until the sun has been up for a little while and warmed things. If you can't wake her then, go to Plan B and you adjust the story. But get everything ready to go now.

It was time to move everything into place. If he had to abort Plan A, at least the stage would be set. He strode to the shed to prepare the last prop in his drama, then returned to the cabin.

He waited until six a.m. He gathered Kendra's inert body, still wrapped in the sheet, and carried her to the shed. He quickly laid her in place. As he did, he heard a car driving on the road toward the cabin. He looked carefully around the corner of the shed and saw a Sheriff's cruiser as it stopped on top of the knoll in front of the cabin. The driver parked with the passenger side facing the cabin.

"Shit," he cursed under his breath. *This is going to go to hell in a handbasket real quick. Unless he leaves, there is no way this is going to work now.*

He looked at Kendra where she lay motionless. He quickly, but quietly, covered her according to his plan as a lone deputy cautiously exited the cruiser and surveyed the area.

The only sound was the ticking of the now idle car engine as it cooled in the chilly morning air. The woods were silent. The deputy called to him using a bull horn. He furtively ran to the cabin and entered as quietly as the squeaky rear door would allow. Inside the dark interior, he picked up his rifle.

FORTY

The deputy unhooked the strap over his holster, extracted a small bull horn from a clip on the dash, exited behind his door and softly called to Sam that he could see a white Mercedes sedan in the carport.

"Mr. Williams," he called, "this is Deputy Douglas from the Blanco County Sheriff's Department. I'd like to talk with you, sir." There was no response.

Sam and Jake low crawled to a low patch of yaupon from behind which they could just see over the rise. As they looked over the ridge, a bulky figure ran from behind the storage shed of the carport to the back of the cabin. They heard a hinge squeak and the sound of the back door closing softly. They saw movement inside. There was silence for a moment, then a heavy wooden thud.

"He probably turned the table up on its side for added protection," Sam quietly said to Jake. "The deputy probably spooked him. He could probably have brazened this out, but now he's tipped his hand. Now, he has to decide what he's going to do about the deputy."

Douglas waited a minute and called again. "Mr. Williams, I'd like to talk with you, sir. Is Mrs. Williams in there with you?" There was no response.

Deputy Douglas waited a minute and called again. "Mr. Williams, I'd like to talk with you, sir. Is Mrs. Williams in there with you?" He paused. "I need to know where Mrs. Williams is, sir." No response.

Sam used the cover of the hill to run low to Douglas. "Keep talking. Keep his attention. I'm going to recon. I'll distract him right and go left." Before Douglas could protest, Sam flung a chunk of wood side-armed below the ridge. It landed with a harsh thud in the woods to their right of the cabin. As it struck the underbrush, they saw the figure inside look to his left. Sam said quietly, "Start talking and keep talking," as he moved out low to the left side staying below the hill.

Douglas keyed the bullhorn. "Mr. Williams, we have a report that Mrs. Williams is missing and her parents are very concerned, sir. If you know anything about where she is or what has happened, I would very much like to know." He continued talking, politely, in an even, nonthreatening voice.

He saw Sam moving low, slow and quietly into the underbrush, then into the tree line left of the cabin. "Mr. Williams, I don't want you to be surprised, but more officers are on the way here. It would be much better if you would talk to me now, just the two of us. Is Mrs. Williams in the cabin with you, sir?" He kept the chatter going well, seemingly purposeful, with no threat in his voice.

Jake moved under cover to the cruiser behind Douglas. A few minutes later, they heard a thump to their right. As they and the figure in the cabin turned to look in the direction of the noise, Sam materialized to their left without a sound, carrying a deer rifle equipped with a telescopic sight. Jake looked at Sam with admiration. *Damn, he's good. I guess we train our Special Forces guys well.*

"Where did you get that," Douglas asked.

"Back seat of the Mercedes. Six rounds in it." Sam squatted between Douglas and Jake. "There is a bulky form on the bed in the back left bedroom. I don't think it's Kendra. It looks more like a sleeping bag, but there wasn't enough light to be certain, so we can't fire in that direction until we know. He has upended the table by the window to our nine o'clock and is behind it with what looks like a thirty caliber rifle with a scope. I didn't see any handguns. He has a box of shells on the floor on his left side.

"My guess is he's going to get jumpy enough pretty soon to take a shot at you," he said to Douglas. "I can take a position in the trees to our left and get a shot at him using the scope with no threat to the back bedroom if he decides to shoot. Your call. His attention will be on you. He doesn't know about Jake and me, so he won't be looking that way."

"Can you get a shot at him through one of the back or side windows?"

"Maybe, but it means another trip to the structure. I'd prefer to use the scope from the left side."

"Let me call this in."

Douglas turned, reaching into the cruiser for the dashboard microphone. He grasped it, but the cord caught on the shift lever when he tried to pull it to him. He raised enough to free the cord and when he did, a shot rang out. A bullet shattered the front passenger window and tore through his shoulder. A second shot struck the edge of the doorframe next to his head.

Douglas swore, and Jake pulled Douglas down as Sam grabbed the mike, keyed it and without hesitation advised, "This is Deputy Douglas. Shots fired at the Williams deer lease. Officer down. Send two ambulances and back up ASAP." He gave directions to the location.

Sam sat Douglas on the ground, leaning him against the cruiser. He unsheathed the combat knife that he wore on his belt and cut Douglas's shirt sleeve at the shoulder seam. He quickly tore the sleeve off, wadded it and pressed it tightly against the bullet wound. "Hold this tight against your shoulder. Stay down behind the car. It isn't bad and we've got an ambulance coming." Douglas groaned and nodded affirmatively.

Sam reached into the cruiser and pulled the shotgun from its cradle, checked the load and racked a round into the chamber.

"With me. Stay low," Sam instructed Jake as he again moved out to the left. He guided Jake into a copse of yaupon and mature sweet gum. Handing Jake the rifle he had confiscated, he tapped the safety with his fingertip.

"Safety. Five rounds in the magazine, one round in the chamber. Bolt action. If Kendra is in there, we can't take a chance on him getting to her.

"My guess is that he probably thinks Douglas is alone, so his attention is going to be focused on the cruiser. He will probably hunker down behind that table and watch out the window. He has to be bat shit crazy to fire at a police officer the way he just did. So, be careful, Jake.

"Count off sixty seconds. Fire two shots into the wall of the cabin three feet left of the front door. That should put your shots into the table. Wait two seconds and fire two shots six inches to the left of the first two. I want to move him toward the other side of the room. Two seconds and two more shots where you fired the first two, unless you hear me call 'cease fire' first. Got it?"

Jake nodded and Sam disappeared into the underbrush.

Jake counted and fired the first two rounds. When he did, the figure in the cabin turned and fired two shots at Jake, narrowly missing him and striking the sweet gum tree six inches from his head. As the man fired at him, Jake heard a booming shot that came from the back left corner of the cabin. That sound could only have come from Sam's forty-five.

"Son of a bitch," the figure shouted as he turned toward the back of the cabin and fired in Sam's direction just as Jake fired the next two rounds. Once again, the man swore, "Son of a bitch!" He swung around and fired two more shots in Jake's direction.

Jake counted and heard the hinge on the back door squeak as he fired the last two rounds. He heard the crack of a rifle shot immediately followed by another deep blast from Sam's pistol, and the figure screamed in pain. Sam's voice called, "Cease fire. Enemy down. Jake, come in the front door with your pistol in your hand. Don't shoot me."

Jake charged the cabin. As he raced up the steps, carefully dropping the empty rifle to the porch, he noticed an irregular reddish stain on the weathered wood of the porch floor and what appeared to be a similar reddish partial footprint, both of which looked like relatively new blood stains that someone had smeared in an attempt to wipe them away. *Oh, no, he thought fearfully.*

He drew his pistol, thumbed the safety off and cocked the hammer. There was already a round in the chamber.

As he entered, he saw Sam standing over the shadowed form of a large man lying on the floor. The figure was holding his bloody left leg over a flesh wound obviously made by the shot from Sam's Colt. He was moaning in pain, covered with bloody splatters from the thighs down. When the man saw Jake, he tried to reach for the rifle next to him. Jake shot him in the hand and the man screamed, abandoning the rifle.

"Check the bedrooms," Sam instructed Jake as he kicked the man's rifle out of reach.

Jake rushed to the bedrooms. One was empty. In the other, he found only a rumpled sleeping bag covering a leather Gladstone bag that he recognized as Walt's, but no Kendra.

He came out to find Sam grasping the lapels of Mitchell's shirt, Sam's combat knife against Mitchell's throat. He was surprised. *Mitchell? Where the hell is Walt?*

"Where is Kendra, Mitchell? Where is my daughter," Sam calmly asked. "Tell me or I'll use the shotgun on you. Or I can just slit your throat and let you bleed out slowly and painfully right here."

Mitchell gritted his teeth and rasped, "Kendra is mine. I saw her first and Walt took her away from me. She's mine now. I came to save her."

Mitchell's statement stopped Jake in his tracks, but it didn't faze Sam. Instead of doing as he threatened, Sam purposefully struck Mitchell's bloody shinbone with the steel handle of the knife. Mitchell screamed in pain.

They heard sirens in the distance as handcuffs appeared in Sam's hand. *I didn't see him take those,* Jake thought, once again impressed by Sam. Sam handcuffed Mitchell to a support post nearby and stood. "Come with me. I think I know where she is." He quickly led Jake out the back door and around the back of the carport shed.

As he rounded the corner of the shed, Jake thought he would lose it right there. Fear for Kendra gripped him and turned his belly cold. Bile rose in his throat. Behind the storage shed was a low mound of freshly turned earth—a grave.

Oh, my God! He killed her and buried her body. "Oh, God," he moaned as he blinked back tears and a clear vision of a smiling Kendra in his arms flashed in his mind. His stomach heaved and bile again rose in his throat, but he managed to keep it down.

"Jake! Find a shovel," Sam instructed. "Look in that shed."

Jake did as he was told. As he did, he heard Sam calling Kendra's name. He hastily grabbed a shovel and rushed back hopefully. He was scared witless that Kendra was in that grave, but Sam's calm demeanor mollified his fear.

Sam pointed to a nub of garden hose protruding from the fresh earth. He was blowing into the hose. He looked up at Jake. "Trying to wake her. I found it when I reconned and blew into it then to ensure it was clear. She should be getting oxygen."

Sam took the shovel from Jake and began scraping its edge across the top of the mound, moving earth away without digging into it. When Sam had removed two inches of soil, they heard a rough scraping sound from beneath the shovel and wood appeared. They worked together quickly and unearthed a crude coffin. The short length of garden hose was inserted into a hole in the lid of the coffin. Jake and Sam tore the lid off the container and found Kendra inside, inert, eyes closed. She was wrapped tightly in a sheet. Her face was pallid, as pasty white as biscuit dough.

"Oh, Jesus," Jake moaned mournfully.

Sam checked her pulse and smiled at Jake. "Her pulse is shallow, but regular. Help me lift her. Get her feet." When Sam had his daughter's torso up, he lifted her in his arms and carried her into the cabin where he laid her on the empty bed, removed the sheet in which she was bound, checked her extremities and rubbed them to stimulate circulation. After a few minutes, he covered her with a blanket, telling Jake to bring some water. Sam elevated her feet, rubbed her arms and legs and wet her lips as he talked softly to her. He raised her eyelids and checked her pupils as he continued wetting her lips.

"I think she's seriously dehydrated and probably had the bejesus scared out of her. I think her mind has shut down out of fear and her body is shutting down due to dehydration. I imagine she'll come around as soon as the medics get an IV drip in her.

"Take some water back to Douglas and call in for another ambulance. Tell them we have Kendra and that we also have another gunshot victim with a leg wound. Tell them Kendra is unconscious, has a slow, regular pulse and appears to be in dehydration shock." Jake did as Sam instructed just as the first backup cruiser and two ambulances pulled next to Douglas. Within twenty minutes, the County Sheriff, Martin Taber, a lanky, grizzled man wearing cowboy boots and a military creased uniform, exited from a third cruiser as another ambulance pulled onto the scene.

Kendra was moved to the first ambulance where antibiotic and saline drips were started. She didn't stir. The sheriff moved everyone outside the cabin except the medics attending to Mitchell, telling his two deputies to search the area. He summoned Jake and Sam, who gave him a thorough briefing. Halfway through their briefing, one deputy returned.

"Sheriff, you need to see this, sir. And there's an empty grave with a crude wooden coffin in it behind the shed."

Sheriff Taber told Jake and Sam to remain on the porch, then followed his deputy to the storage shed under the carport where the doors were open revealing tools and a large chest freezer, lid open. He saw the grave and the coffin as he approached. The deputy pointed into the freezer and the sheriff looked.

"The lid was open and the freezer was turned off when we got here," the deputy said. The Sheriff turned and motioned for Sam who trotted to the shed. "You told me the guy in the cabin is the brother of your daughter's husband. Is that correct?" Sam nodded.

The sheriff pointed into the freezer. "Can you identify this man?"

Sam looked. He saw Walt, who appeared to have two bullet wounds— one to his chest and one to his head. His lifeless eyes stared myopically ahead. Sam nodded. "That about wraps it up, I guess. This is … was Walt Williams, my daughter's husband."

The Sheriff turned to his deputy. "Get the coroner and a crime scene unit out here." As he closed Walt's eyes, he looked at Sam. "Thanks. Let's go back to the porch and you can finish telling me what you know."

As Sam and Jake finished their account of the circumstances, one of the medics came to the Sheriff. "We need to get the lady and the guy with the wounds and your deputy to the hospital. We'll take them to Hill Country Memorial Hospital in Fredericksburg."

The sheriff nodded, looked at Sam and said, "You go with your daughter. I'll get in touch with you gentlemen later today. Thanks for taking care of my deputy."

FORTY-ONE

S am rode in the ambulance and Jake followed in his vehicle. On the road, Jake called Mei and Kelli, summarizing for them. Both were amazed that it had been Mitchell who had taken Kendra—and more amazed that Mitchell had apparently killed his brother. He arrived at the hospital and found Sam in the ER waiting room. As Jake entered, Sam looked up and nodded to the chair next to his.

"They said it will be about thirty minutes before anyone can speak with us, then we can probably see her. Thanks for calling Mei."

Jake nodded. "God, Sam. I was really scared when I saw that mound of dirt. I thought she was dead."

"Jake, you did well out there. I knew you would. I watched your face, especially when we were talking about Kendra and when we found her. Is there anything you want to tell me, son?"

Jake looked thoughtfully at Sam and was quiet for a moment.

"Yes Sir. But for the time being, I think it should stay between us." Sam nodded.

Jake succinctly and tactfully told Sam of the kiss and months that he and Kendra were constantly on each other's mind. He told Sam about the events of the past week and tactfully of the intimacy he and Kendra had shared.

"Just like you and Mei, I want Kendra to come out of this without any scars or nightmares or problems. She means a lot to me."

Sam listened quietly. "What if she comes out of this with problems?"

148

"I thought about that all the way to the hospital. In the last week, I think I've fallen in love with your daughter, Sam. I'll be there for her if she'll have me, regardless of what this does to her."

"I'm happy to hear that, Jake. Kendra called us last week, mid-week. She talked about you and told us how you've been there for her. Her voice said more to me than her words. I think she was hopeful the two of you could get to know each other enough to see if you fit together."

Sam stuck out his hand. "I appreciate what told me, and what you've done for our girl. Let's see where all this takes us." Jake took Sam's hand and nodded.

A doctor approached Sam, introduced herself as Dr. Moore, and led him into a private room. Sam nodded for Jake to follow. When the Dr. looked at Jake, Sam introduced him and said, "He's family. Whatever you have to tell me, you can talk in front of Jake. He was with me when we found her."

"Let me summarize quickly, then you can ask questions. We examined your daughter for physical or sexual abuse and found no evidence of either. We ran a blood test and it was positive for flunitrazepam, a central nervous system depressant that is commonly known as Rohypnol, or the date rape drug. There are two injection marks on her arm, so we surmise that he injected her at least twice with a strong solution of Rohypnol dissolved in water. We'll see what the lab work tells us. At the moment, she is dehydrated—not critically, but seriously to the extent that we are concerned and will keep her on fluids and antibiotic drips for another twenty-four hours, longer if we think she needs it.

"More importantly, and of primary concern to us, is that she appears to be in a trauma induced coma, possibly compounded by the drug. We have sedated her and will keep her sedated so that she can rest her limbs and her mind, and to give the effects of the drug time to wear off.

"I understand that she was in the process of a divorce when this all happened, that she was kidnapped from her home in Houston and transported to a deer lease near Hye, where she was buried in a wooden box for anywhere from a few hours to as many as thirty-six hours. I understand that her husband's body was discovered at the site, but we have no way to know whether she knows that or saw the body or the murder.

"Regardless, I believe her mind has shut down defensively. This could continue for a few hours, a few days, or a few weeks. If she knew or believed that her life was in danger, her condition may be a form of post-traumatic stress disorder. Belief or real fear of loss of life is a critical factor in a diagnosis of PTSD. If she has no memory of fearing for her life, then it is more likely a normal psychological escape from reality that she should overcome in time. Normally, individuals who were strong and of sound mind going into these situations come out all right. Occasionally, there can be long term or permanent memory loss and/or coma, but I don't think that will happen to her. We're going to keep her sedated overnight to let her hydrate, let her mind rest, and let the drugs wear off, as I said. We are optimistic she will wake tomorrow.

"Until this happened, how did you perceive her state of mind?"

Sam spoke first. "She has always been a well-adjusted woman with strong faith and good values. I know she has been unhappy in her marriage for three or four years. Her husband became an alcoholic three years ago after an injury that cut short his career. Two weeks ago, he struck her for the second time. That was her impetus for filing for divorce. Prior to that happening, her mother and I hadn't seen her for two weeks, but we talked regularly by phone. She seemed to be handling things well and seemed relieved that the marriage was ending without there being a child involved. She has a small circle of good friends who will be there for her in the times to come. Jake can probably tell you more about the past week."

The doctor looked at Jake. "She seemed to have embraced the idea of divorce well. Kendra is an associate professor at the University of Houston. Last week was Spring Break for her. She spent much of the week redecorating her home and yard. She said she wanted to make new memories to replace the old, unhappy ones. She seemed to be upbeat and handling things well."

The doctor asked, "Do you know when she last ate?"

"She had a full meal Friday evening and a light breakfast Saturday morning," Jake replied.

"Who is her family doctor?"

Neither man knew.

"Was she on any regular medications?"

"She has a hypothyroid condition and takes a daily pill," Sam replied. "I assume from what her mother has said that she is on birth control pills. To the best of my knowledge, she isn't allergic to any medications." He was thoughtful for a minute. "Let me call my wife. I think she knows who Kendra's primary doctor is."

While Sam called Mei, the doctor looked at Jake and said, "I understand you and her father rescued her?"

Jake nodded. "Sam is a retired Special Forces Officer. He took charge when the deputy was wounded. I've always had a lot of respect for him, but after today—well, he sure impressed the daylights out me. I was just along for the ride."

"It must have been very scary for you."

"Not really scary, just tense. Sam was in control and it was easy to follow his directions and his lead. But when I saw what looked like a grave out there, and I thought she was in it, it took all the life out of me. Kendra is … very special to me."

"That's understandable. How are you doing now?"

"I'm fine. Just very concerned about Kendra."

"Would you like to talk to a counselor?

"No. If she comes out of all this whole, then I can handle everything with no problem. If she doesn't—we'll see. But I'm an optimist.

Sam finished his call and gave the doctor the name, address and telephone number of Kendra's primary doctor. Mei packed a bag and left to join them right after she hung up from speaking with Sam. It would have taken a team of horses to keep her from coming to the hospital.

Dr. Moore said, "I'll contact her doctor. We'll keep her sedated tonight. She should wake tomorrow, but will be groggy and confused for a while. We'll keep her overnight tomorrow. If her cognitive functions appear normal, you can take her home Tuesday. At this time, I can't predict how much she will remember. Regardless, she will need an examination by a psychiatrist when you get her home. Treatment should begin immediately. And, she should be in her own home, in familiar surroundings.

"Best case scenario, two to six weeks with a good psychiatrist should have her back to normal, but that is only a very early suggestion. Expect that she will be uncomfortable in the dark and probably any time she feels trapped or confined. I imagine that will last for some time.

"Expect that there will be confusion and lapses in her memory, maybe large periods that she can't remember. Do not try to coax her memory by telling her things that happened that she should remember, or alluding to anything she hasn't acknowledged on her own. Her emotional recovery and her memory recovery must be solely on her own. There are some things that we will have to tell her, but, on the whole, cognition must come from her own mind and memory.

"My husband is a psychiatrist. I've asked him for a referral in Houston and he has given me two names of psychiatrists there that he respects." She handed Sam a slip of paper with the names and telephone numbers.

"For now, I suggest you get something to eat and get some sleep while she's sleeping. Her physical health is fine, and she'll sleep through the night. There is nothing for you to be concerned about while she's sedated. I will check her on my rounds at seven a.m. Try to be here at nine. She should be coming out of the sedative around that time."

They left the hospital around five p.m. to find a hotel. Sam called Mei to bring her up to date. Then, he called Callen and gave him a good synopsis of the situation. He again told Callen to stay with his wife and Callen agreed.

Jake and Sam found a hotel and checked in. Sam spoke with the detective who advised the home was still a crime scene, so it was sealed with police tape. He told Sam to call him an hour away from Houston and he would have it unsealed and all evidence of police presence removed before she arrived.

Jake called Kelli who said she would take the day off and she would be there when they arrived and she would come early enough to brighten things, put the house in order, and would bring some fresh flowers. Jake gave her the same admonition the doctor had given about prompting Kendra to remember.

Mei arrived at eight p.m., apprehensive, but calm. They found a restaurant that had been recommended. After they ordered, Sam and Jake answered Mei's questions and filled in what she didn't know. She handled everything well, as one would expect of the wife of a combat soldier, until Sam told her about the interment. She cried, as one would expect a mother to do when confronted with such an atrocity against her child.

Jake had difficulty sleeping. He finally got out of bed, made a cup of coffee and sat in the darkened room, thinking of Kendra. He thought of her reaction when he asked if she had told the special person her plan and he smiled. He thought of their first intimate contact, of making love with her that night and each night after. He marveled at how much he enjoyed making love with her, her touch and her harmonious movements with him. He laughed when he thought of "titillation." He thought of his four cards to her and hoped she would return to him in time to enjoy his arrangements for them.

And he thought about the depth of his feelings for her, thought about how she had become more important to him with each passing day, thought about her need to make new memories in her home. He thought of her efforts to make the home reflect her, not the past. It surprised him to think that they had only had a week together. And he smiled at how good the memories of that week were.

He thought about how good they were together, and about the possibility of an unhappy outcome for her as a result of Mitchell's heinous selfishness. He knew then that he would stay with Kendra to help her if she needed him. He finally drifted off to sleep and his last thoughts were of her.

FORTY-TWO

On Tuesday, they arrived at nine a.m., as instructed. The nurse advised that Kendra was awake, but groggy, and that Dr. Moore was with her. They were taken to an empty office down the hall to wait for the doctor, who came in forty-five minutes later.

Dr. Moore introduced herself to Mei and apologized for making them wait. "I was establishing a memory base with Kendra, establishing her last memories before the attack on her.

"The last clear memory she has is of calling you, Jake, and being invited to your home. I understand that was a week ago last Friday. She doesn't recall arriving there. She seems clear about events prior to that. She remembers filing for divorce and the hearing she attended. She remembers a conversation with the officer who removed her husband from the home. That's about it.

"I told her she was here because she had suffered an unfortunate incident, and that I was concerned that it may have affected her memory. I've told her that the last clear memory she recited to me was more than a week in the past.

"While she is here, she is sheltered. However, this event is going to be on the news and in the newspapers. Friends and neighbors will hear snippets and read accounts, some of which will be far from the truth. Before she leaves here, we are going to have to tell her as much as we can without harming her psychologically.

154

"I've told her that the only way for her to recover her memory is through her own efforts and some sessions with a psychiatrist. I've told her that you have been cautioned not to remember for her or describe incidents that she cannot remember. I've told her that she is not mentally ill, but is suffering a form of post-traumatic stress disorder as a result of the stress she has suffered. I've told her that, as her memory returns, she may experience some unpleasant, perhaps frightening memories, but that those memories will be of past events and that she is safe and has nothing to fear going forward. She knows she is in a hospital, but doesn't know where.

"Other than that, we are all going to have to be flexible and let her lead. By the time she leaves here, she will know the facts of what happened, but please don't cry or sympathize or bemoan anything that has happened to her while you are in her presence or within her hearing radius. She must work through this herself. Be happy to see her and talk of happy things. Give her no cause for any more concern than I have given her."

She rose. "You can see her now. She will remain here tonight and, barring anything unforeseen, you may take her home tomorrow. So, put on your happy faces and let's go see our young lady." She looked at Mei and nodded toward a bag she had in her hand.

"I presume you've brought her a robe and her own night clothes? And I see some pretty flowers." Mei nodded. "Good thinking. That will make her happy."

Kendra was in a bright, sunny private room. Jake hung back as they entered. It was obvious from her sleepy eyes that the sedative hadn't worn completely off, but she smiled and brightened when she saw Sam and Mei.

"Mother, Daddy. Oh, it's so good to see you."

They all hugged and Mei did a yeoman's job of fighting her obvious urge to break down and cry as she held her daughter. The three of them hugged again and chattered for a few minutes until Kendra looked up and saw Jake. He could see the surprise on her face.

"Jake. What a surprise to see you. It's so nice of you to come with Mother and Daddy."

Jake saw confusion on her face. He could tell that his presence surprised her, but not what else she was thinking. He hugged her and laughed.

"I couldn't pass up a chance to visit one of my favorite persons in the whole world, even if it meant a trip to the hospital to see her.

Kendra hugged him back, but had the strangest urge to pull him tightly to her and hold him. She recognized the urge, but it confused her, despite the fact that she remembered their kiss and her feelings for Jake in the months since the kiss.

"Can anybody tell me what's going on?" she asked the group in general.

"Before you leave here, we'll tell you as much as we can," explained Dr. Moore. "Until then, just relax and follow your thoughts. This past week has been pretty busy. When you remember things that happened, we'll fill in some of the related things that you don't know, but you have to remember on you own."

"Week?" asked Kendra, incredulously.

"Yes, but it will come back to you," Dr. Moore replied. "Just enjoy the company of your family, Kendra."

"Oh … goodness. I can't believe I can't remember a whole week of my life."

An aide came in with some Jell-O and a cup of orange juice for Kendra, who was advised by Dr. Moore to eat and drink, but to do so slowly.

"For some reason, I'm really hungry," Kendra responded. "Is there any chance of getting some ice cream and maybe a sandwich?"

Everyone laughed and Dr. Moore replied, "You can have all the ice cream you want. Let's see how you do with the Jell-O before we try solid food." The aid overheard and quickly fetched a small container of vanilla ice cream and another spoon.

As she ate, Kendra became more alert. "Okay," she laughed, "if I can't remember what I did last week, tell me what you all did last week."

Dr. Moore left them as Sam and Mei recounted their week in adequate detail. Sam told her some things he had done that made her laugh. Mei told her about some new bedding that she had bought for their guest room. They told her about a movie they had seen.

Kendra turned to Jake. She paused, looking at him curiously. *I get this strange feeling each time I look at Jake, and it makes no sense to me.*

"So, how was your week?"

"Pretty good. I worked from home all week. I did some chores around the house and yard. I had dinner with Kelli and Scott."

"How are they?"

"Good. Kelli is coming over when you get home. She's eager to see you."

"Does she know that I'm in a hospital?"

"Yes."

"Does she know why?"

"She knows a little bit about it."

Kendra laughed, but her eyes were wistful. "I guess I need to start remembering, don't I?"

"It will come, honey," replied Mei. "If you relax, it will come back faster than if you try to force it."

As Mei spoke, Dr. Moore entered the room. "We're going to let Kendra rest for a little bit now. Then the resident psychologist, Ellen Porter, is going to visit with her for a while. Give us a little time. Have lunch and come back around two p.m."

When they left, Kendra looked at Dr. Moore. "I get this strange feeling each time I look at Jake. Does he have anything to do with whatever happened last week?"

Dr. Moore thought for a minute. "Yes, he does, Kendra. I can't tell you what right now because my information is second hand, but I can tell you that Jake did you no harm and that you have nothing to fear from him. He wants to help you. Whatever you're feeling, don't try to analyze it or fight it. Does that help?"

"Yes …," she said cautiously. "I guess."

"Good. Close your eyes and try to rest a little. I'll be back later with Ellen Porter, the staff psychologist."

"Will I be addicted to that drug … or will it continue to affect me?"

"No. You didn't experience it for long enough and your body has forgotten its effects. That won't be a problem for you. Rest now."

Jake has something to do with last week. He didn't harm me and I have nothing to fear from him. And she wasn't surprised that I get a funny feeling when I look at him. That's all pretty interesting. And why would she say that Jake did me no harm? Did someone else harm me?

FORTY-THREE

Kendra rested, actually going to sleep soundly. Ellen Porter woke her and they visited congenially for a while. Ms. Porter asked many questions about her life and the time leading up to the telephone call to Jake, then took her back to her last memory, which was of calling Jake on Friday, a week before being kidnapped. Kendra had no memory of anything after the phone call to Jake that Friday afternoon. She recalled no bad dreams or nightmares and nothing of the time since the phone call. She had no memory of anything until she woke in the hospital.

She expressed surprise at seeing Jake. She articulated the unusual feelings that stirred when she saw Jake, but could only describe them as a warm feeling and that she felt a need to touch him. She explained that Jake and Kelli had been her closest friends and confidants during the many months when Walt was drinking heavily. Eventually, Porter told Kendra that the best thing she could do would be to let her mind and her body rest.

Porter told Kendra the same thing that Dr. Moore had told her about the feelings she experienced when she saw Jake—don't try to analyze it and don't fight it. She advised Kendra to let it happen and see if it sparked any memories or thoughts. As she left, she told Kendra she would discuss her observations with Dr. Moore.

At two p.m., Sam, Mei and Jake returned. They hugged her and Mei sat close to her bed. Shortly after they returned, Dr. Moore checked Kendra and said that Kendra could go to the cafeteria for dinner, if she wanted. Mei did some quick shopping and brought fresh clothes. Kendra's

IV tubes were removed; she changed into her fresh clothes, and they all left together.

Kendra asked if Callen knew and Mei assured her that he did. Mei reminded her that Callen's wife was due any time and they had advised him to stay with her.

At dinner, they talked about things before last week, about Callen and his wife and the expected baby, about Kelli and Scott, a little about the divorce and Kendra's lawyer. They returned to her room until the nurse shooed them out at nine o'clock. Kendra's tubes were reconnected with saline and a sedative drip. She had a peaceful night.

FORTY-FOUR

Kendra was discharged at ten o'clock the next morning with instructions and a prescription for a mild sedative if she needed it. Before she was discharged, Dr. Moore gave her a synopsis of what had transpired the past week. She briefly related the abduction, the drug injection, the interment, the death of Walt, and the rescue by Sam and Jake.

Kendra was dumfounded. She closed her eyes and cried, as Mei held her. "Mitchell buried me alive and Walt is dead?"

Kendra was understandably upset by the account, but Dr. Moore talked with her for a long while and suggested she get home to familiar surroundings, meet with a psychiatrist, and then ask her questions.

Kendra rode with her parents and Jake followed in his car. Sam gave her an accurate account of the abduction and her rescue, playing down his efforts and complimenting Jake highly. When they stopped along the way for a break and a quick sandwich, Kendra immediately went to Jake. The desire to touch him was overwhelming. She touched his arm and looked into his eyes, then hugged him. "Daddy told me it was you and he who found me. You're my heroes. Thank you, Jake, from the bottom of my heart." She kissed his cheek.

Jake kissed her cheek and whispered, with surprising passion and strength in his voice, "I'll never let anything bad happen to you again, Kendra. I let my guard down once. That will never happen again. Not for as long as I live." She looked questioningly at him until her mother called to her.

160

Kelli was at Kendra's home when they arrived. Kendra stepped from the car and hugged Kelli with relief. She looked around and saw the changes in her front yard. "Who did all this?" she asked. "It looks so pretty."

Kelli had been well briefed on how to respond to Kendra's need for knowledge and understanding. "It does look pretty, doesn't it," she replied easily.

When Kendra entered her home, she started to cry. "Oh, it's so pretty." She walked around the living room and dining room, taking in the changes, touching things. She saw the new couch, chairs, and television, and was surprised. Silently, she went to the guest room, where she had slept before the week she couldn't remember. She looked incredulously around her at the changes. "Oh, this is nice."

She hesitated, then walked into the master bedroom and tears came again. She looked at her mother and Kelli. "Did you do this to surprise me?"

Kelli and Mei looked silently at each other.

"Do you like it?" Kelli asked, without answering the question.

"Yes. It's perfect. It is exactly what I would have done. It's wonderful. Thank you. I can't believe you all did this."

Jake looked at her, wanting to wrap her in his arms and take away all her awkwardness and confusion. He decided that they couldn't go on forever parceling out information. *Someone has to go off the reservation— might as well be me.*

He stepped to her, taking her hand, and said softly, "You did all this, Kendra. Perhaps knowing that will help you a little. Walk around and get used to it. Take a look in your back yard, as well."

They all followed her as she wandered through the house and into the yard with little smiles and exclamations. Sam put his hand on Jake's shoulder and said softly, "Thanks, Jake. We can't treat her like a child. She deserves at least basic answers to her questions. We can't add to her confusion."

Jake nodded. "Thanks, Sam."

Mei and Kelli fixed iced tea for everyone. "Did you all help me do this?" Kendra asked.

Sam responded to her. "No, sweetheart. You mother and I were at home all week.

She looked at Kelli. "You?"

"No. I didn't know about it until I came over this morning to open the house for you. I had seen the front yard when I drove past, but that was all."

"You?" She looked at Jake.

Jake grinned at her. "Alan and his friend did most of the heaving lifting. It looks like what you would have done because you did it."

"Alan?"

"The Purcell's son from across the street. He and his friend, Evan, dug the beds and helped you plant the shrubs and flowers and spread mulch. You've hired him to mow and edge your lawn each week and to help you when needed. Alan and Evan did most the painting and moved furniture. I just helped you hang pictures and drapes."

Tears slipped down her cheeks. "I don't remember any of that at all. I feel so lost."

Mei and Kelli hugged her. "Shh," Mei said softly. "It will come. Give it some time. Maybe being home will help bring things back to you." Sam joined the hug.

Kendra looked at Jake wistfully. *My mind is trying to tell me something, but I don't know what.* She stepped to Jake and kissed his cheek. "Thank you. I'm sure I owe you more thanks than I will ever realize. I just don't remember doing any of this."

"You were a busy girl," Jake said with a laugh, "and the boys were terrific help. It was fun being with you and helping."

Jake went for Chinese carry out for dinner. Scott joined them and they had a very pleasant meal. It was a good evening for Kendra. Scott complimented Kendra on the changes and improvements to her home and yard.

During dinner, Sheriff Taber from Blanco County called Sam. "Just wanted to pass on to you and Jake some information.

"During questioning, Mitchell admitted to having an argument with Walt about Mrs. Williams. It seems that Mitchell met her first at church, but didn't have the nerve to ask her out. He told Walt about her. We're guessing Walt finally got tired of waiting for Mitchell to act and asked her out himself, then married her. It seems Mitchell has carried that grudge for years. When she filed for divorce, we think he saw this as his chance to take Walt's place. He says Walt made fun of him and told him he could never make her happy, and probably said some other ugly things. It got pretty heated. He says Walt threatened to kill Kendra and to beat him senseless. He says Walt came at him and he shot Walt in self-defense. But, all we have is his word for how it happened.

"Best guess from our staff parlor psychologist is that he buried Kendra with the intent of digging her up, telling her—and the authorities—that Walt kidnapped her and buried her, and that he had come to save her and he shot Walt in his effort to save her. He stored Walt in the freezer to slow decomposition in hopes we would think Walt died when Mitchell came to rescue Kendra, not Thursday night.

"When the deputy arrived, that threw a monkey wrench into Mitchell's plan. He couldn't change gears fast enough to make up a believable story, mostly because his brother was still partially frozen. So, he started shooting. Our guy says Mitchell is probably a psychopath, who has no conscience, rather than a sociopath, who has a weak conscience. And I think he's probably right. Mitchell has never expressed any regret over killing his brother.

"By the way, Douglas is doing fine and sends his thanks for taking care of him. He wants to buy you and Jake lunch or dinner if you're ever this way again. He told me you're a pretty handy man to have around in a tense situation. He likes you."

Sam thanked Taber and they finished dinner. Kelli and Scott left early. Sam took Jake aside and passed on what the Sheriff had told him. "Makes sense, considering the circumstances," Jake agreed.

Kendra was tired, but had questions. "How did Walt die?"

"Mitchell shot him," Sam replied. "The Sheriff said it was during an argument. Then Mitchell concocted the whole scenario. He believed you would think it was Walt who abducted you. Actually, the Sheriff thinks Mitchell was going to tell you that Walt abducted you. It was apparently his intent to save you after making it appear that Walt had taken you and buried you. He believed that you would then see him as your knight in shining armor. Mitchell was taken with you and believed your divorce was an invitation for him to take Walt's place."

Sam saw the look of distress on Kendra's face.

"You didn't give him that impression, honey. None of this is your fault. It appears he was infatuated with you long before you married Walt."

Tears ran down her cheeks. "Oh, my God. I didn't mean for any of this to happen. I think it was time for us to go our separate ways, but I never wished anything but good for him. This is so sad."

Mei hugged her. "It wasn't your fault, honey. Don't take on guilt for something you didn't cause. We're learning that Mitchell has probably been a little unbalanced and jealous of his brother for years."

"Murder and kidnapping and attempted murder of a police officer in two separate counties. He'll wither in prison for the rest of his life or in a hospital for the mentally ill, if he pleads insanity as a defense," Jake replied.

"How did you find me?"

Jake responded. "Alan saw Walt's car in the drive Saturday morning. Later, when we talked, Sam remembered the cabin at the hunting lease. He took us there and it was Sam who figured where and how Mitchell had hidden you."

"When was I kidnapped?"

Again, Jake responded, "Saturday morning. You dialed my cell number and left a message for help, but I didn't get the message for a few of hours. We were going to meet at two p.m.. When two fifteen came and went, I picked up my phone to call you and heard your message."

"What did I say?"

"You shouted, 'Jake, help.' Then you screamed. You were cut off before you could say any more."

He took her hand. "I'm sorry, Kendra. I shouldn't have forgotten my phone. I should have insisted you come with me that morning, but you seemed so happy in your new home and you wanted some time alone there. And I really didn't expect any problem—especially from Mitchell. We were all concerned about Walt."

"Jake, it's okay," she assured him. "I should have known better than to stay alone without you. I think you or Daddy said Walt wasn't due back until Friday evening, so I'm sure I didn't expect anything to happen Saturday morning. But, you and Daddy saved me and that's what counts.

"Did anything happen before Saturday morning?"

"It appears that Walt entered your house Friday evening, the eighteenth, while you were at my home talking with me. He took a ring and some underwear from your dresser."

"That's odd. Did anything else unusual happen?"

"Mitchell called you and came to the house, ostensibly checking to see that you were all right. But nothing odd or scary."

"What happened the week before I was … taken?"

"It was a quiet week," Jake replied. "Your lawyer recommended you stay with friends until Walt left town. You stayed at my home that weekend. The rest of the week, we alternated between your home and mine. You had an alarm system installed and you took on the redecorating project. You said you wanted to rid yourself of old unhappy memories and build new happy ones. You hired Alan and his friend to help you."

"You stayed with me all week?"

"Yes. We were uncertain of what to expect from Walt. The judge thought Walt would violate the protective order. I was concerned for your safety, even though we all assumed that he went out town and remained there all week with his boss."

Kendra moaned softly, a forlorn look on her face. "I'm so frustrated. I can't remember anything of last week"

"Honey, you've been through a lot." Mei said softly. "And the doctor said this is like PTSD. Just try to relax and give it some time. You have an appointment tomorrow with the psychiatrist. Let's see what he says."

They talked for a little while, until Kendra said she was tired. Jake hugged her and went home. When he put his arms around her, she had the same strange feeling of wanting to hold him tightly to her.

FORTY-FIVE

Jake left town for two days on business. He called each evening to check on Kendra. Thursday brought the first of many phone calls from the press, the curious and well-meaning friends. Kendra was news both because of her kidnapping and rescue, and because Walt had once been one of the city's football celebrities.

Sam quickly took telephone duty. He recorded a message on Kendra's phone that her number would be out of service until further notice. He gave Kelli, the doctors and the police his cell number, listened to messages on Kendra's phone twice daily and responded to those that were truly important. He called Detective Rodriguez and arranged for an officer to be assigned to Kendra for one week to keep reporters and the curious away from Kendra's home.

Somehow, a reporter got into Kendra's back yard and tried to force his way into the kitchen, but Sam quickly discouraged him. Sam's comment was, "I won't say the guy peed his pants ... but the guy peed his pants. I don't think he'll be back."

Kendra called her managing professor, who told her to take as long as she needed to recover. He said they had hired a substitute teacher for the remainder of the year if necessary, but assured Kendra her job was safe and that her students missed her.

Kendra met with the psychiatrist, Dr. Cohen, who was gentle and easy to talk to, but no memories came. He encouraged her to maintain a normal daily life and to let her mind wander when it wanted to. He encouraged her stay in her home and familiar surroundings and to try to remember backward from when she woke in the hospital and forward from when she called Jake on Friday, a week before she was taken.

He asked Kendra what her last clear memory was. She told him she remembered calling Jake because she wanted to tell him she had filed for divorce. She explained that Jake and Kelli were her closest friends. He asked about those friendships. In the course of talking about Jake and Kelli, Kendra related the evening that she and Jake had put Walt to bed and kissed.

He asked if she had feelings for Jake. She said she did, but she didn't know how Jake felt. He asked if it was possible her call to Jake had been an overture to test those feelings. She was thoughtful for a moment. *Yes; that's very possible. I know I wanted to see him as soon as the papers were filed. I do remember that.* She told Dr. Cohen of her thought. After learning that she and Jake were together most of the lost week, he encouraged her to spend time in Jake's company and not to resist feelings she experienced about Jake.

Alan and his parents came that evening to see Kendra and pay their respects. The three of them were very concerned for her and offered any help they could give. She hadn't known Alan very well before she hired him and was at a bit of a loss talking to him since she couldn't remember the time they had spent together the past week, but she was taken with how polite and concerned he was.

Friday was a quiet day. Kendra again met with Dr. Cohen, but her mind and her heart were heavy. She disconsolately confessed to him that she felt responsible for Walt's death. He worked with her on that issue. At the end of the session, she understood why she felt responsible and that she really wasn't, but she couldn't shake the feeling. He told her it was normal and she would overcome it with time. He explained survivor syndrome and told her she was experiencing a form of this syndrome. She had survived the events; Walt hadn't. So, she felt guilty. That made sense to her.

He asked about Jake and she said nothing had changed. She wondered if her feelings for him were simply because he had saved her. Dr. Cohen asked if she had strong feelings of attraction before the events of last week. She repeated the story of the kiss and said she frequently thought of Jake since that time. She acknowledged that he was her first thought after the divorce papers were filed. Dr. Cohen suggested she follow her heart. She told him that was strange advice, coming from a psychiatrist. He shook his head.

"Our heart feels what is hidden in our mind. Sometimes, it's best to let the mind tell us what it's thinking by speaking through our hearts. You weren't unfaithful to your husband. You had filed for divorce and were settled on your course of action. That one night was unresolved. It would be natural to want resolution, to experience what you had sublimated for so many months. Right now, you are filled with emotion, curiosity, and a need for resolution, closure—to the recent events, to an unhappy marriage, and to feelings for Jake. Ask your questions and listen to your heart."

Kendra asked Dr. Cohen if he thought she would be all right on her own. "You need to heal and you need company if you feel apprehensive. Don't rush into being alone. When you believe you will be comfortable on your own, then you should try it."

It was a beautiful day, sunny and balmy. Mei and Kendra did some shopping and bought groceries. Sam took them to lunch at Kendra's favorite deli. They talked easily, as they always had, and the day passed uneventfully and happily for Kendra. Jake returned home Friday evening and called, but didn't come over. Kendra was disappointed at not getting to see him.

On Saturday, the weather was again pleasant. Funeral services were held for Walt. Jake joined Kendra and her parents for the services—which were awkward, to say the least, but Kendra was gracious and sympathetic to the pain and discomfort of Walt's parents. She sat quietly with them for some time at the gravesite after interment, and that seemed to ease some of their turmoil.

Afterward, Jake joined Kendra, Sam and Mei for dinner at her home. They played Scrabble after dinner and shared some time on the deck, enjoying Kendra's attractive yard. Jake left at ten o'clock when Kendra said she was getting tired.

She walked him to the door and hugged him for a moment, then kissed his cheek and hugged him tighter. *Something inside me wants to hold him and never let go, but I need to know how he feels about me. I don't know what to do. I'm sure it all has something to do with his kiss the night we put Walt to bed. I'll never forget that night. The doctor said to follow my heart. Oh, I'm so confused.* They said good night and Jake left.

Callen called, as he had every evening. This time, he had news.

"Rachel gave birth to Samuel Jacob at 8:30 p.m. Baby and mother are doing fine. He is named in honor of Sam and Jake, who saved his aunt. And we're very thankful for what Jake has done for you, Kendra."

Callen was excited to be a new father and the news lifted Kendra's spirits. Kendra, Mei and Sam assured Callen they would be there to see the new young man as soon as they could.

As she prepared for bed, Kendra became melancholy and disconsolate. She cried herself to sleep that night, upset by the funeral, her uncertain feelings for Jake, and her frustration at all that she could not remember.

FORTY-SIX

Jake had offered to take Kendra, Sam and Mei to brunch on Sunday, after church services. She wanted to look nice, to get back some semblance of the old Kendra. As she dressed, she looked around her bedroom and smiled. She had done what she wanted to do with the room, even if she couldn't remember doing it. She was very pleased. She looked at the bed and a strange sensation warmed her inside, sending a tingle throughout her. *What? What is happening that I don't understand?*

She decided it was past time to remove her wedding ring. She opened her jewelry box in order to put the ring away and to get her good diamond stud earrings. When she lifted the lid, she found three envelopes and a smaller one in the case. She put the ring away, retrieved her earrings and took the envelopes to her bed, where she sat and opened them.

As she read the contents, one by one, she realized that they told her a story of the week she couldn't remember. *Oh, my! Something happened between us that week and I don't know what. Now what do I do? How do I handle this?* She was confused by the contents of the envelopes.

She also noticed that her birthday ring was missing, but remembered that Jake told her Walt had come into her home and taken the ring. When Jake's words came to her, she had a vision of opening the case before the envelopes were in it and seeing that the birthday ring was gone. *That had to have occurred that week.*

Brunch went well with no mention that it had only been a week since Kendra had been abducted and the subject wasn't raised. Talk was comfortable and she was becoming more at ease with herself, but she couldn't keep her eyes off Jake. The envelopes begged a question that she didn't want to ask in front of her parents.

Jake invited her for dinner at his home the next evening and she accepted with the encouragement of Sam and Mei.

FORTY-SEVEN

After Sunday brunch and with no small reluctance and with repeated assurances from Kendra, Sam and Mei returned to their home. They hugged Kendra as if they were going to the far corners of the earth for an extended period of time. She promised to call every day and give a progress report. Their plan was to return in a week.

Kendra spent the day in her home and yard, enjoying the changes. She put fresh linens on the guest bed and laid out fresh towels in the guest bath. She tried to relax, but her mind whirled like a merry-go-round, populated with thoughts Jake, of the changes to her home, the envelopes and the Museum of Fine Arts Ball and a weekend resort and an island vacation. She tried to imagine what had transpired during the lost week. Thoughts ran rampant, from the benign to the erotic.

Why would Jake make plans like that? I had to have done something to cause him to do that, and the nature of the cards paints a pretty obvious picture. But I can't believe I just jumped into bed with Jake without a lot of hesitation and forethought.

She pondered for a moment. *Kendra, get real. You're not that naïve. You wanted intimacy with Jake. You know it and Kelli knows it. You wanted closure to what happened the night of the kiss. You're not really concerned that you might have slept with Jake. You're concerned that, if you did, you don't remember what it was like.*

She pondered again. *And the simple fact that you can think like that probably means that you changed during that week. But this is frustrating.*

You're back where you were before you called Jake—just wondering what it would be like to really be in his arms. Kendra, you need to get your memory back. This is so frustrating.

She finally couldn't stand the uncertainty any longer. At three o'clock, she called Jake. When he answered, she said softly, "Hi. What are you doing?" The moment she said those words, a frisson ran up her spine, but she didn't know why. The coincidence wasn't lost on Jake.

"Sitting by the pool, waiting for you to call. If you didn't call by four, I was going to call you. Would you still like dinner?"

"Yes. Very much," she said softly. When she realized that she had unconsciously lowered her voice, she knew she was very eager to see him. "What time would like me to come?"

"Anytime. What's good for you?" He didn't want to appear too eager. She probably wouldn't understand how much he wanted to have her with him.

"Is four too early?"

"Not at all. Four is good. Bring your suit if you want to get in the pool. I'm looking forward to seeing you."

Another frisson ran up her spine. "See you then," she said softly.

She arrived, looking cheerful and beautiful, hair in a ponytail, dressed in shorts that were almost, but not quite, short shorts, and a soft tank top. She carried a bag containing her swim suit and the four envelopes.

He kissed her cheek and she his, but she held him tightly for just a few wonderful seconds. *Listen to your heart, Kendra. That's what the doctor said.*

"Inside or out?"

"Out."

Jake opened a bottle of Kendra's favorite white wine and put the bottle in a chiller. She took the glasses and they settled in the shade by the pool. The day was balmy, and she enjoyed the sight of Jake's beautiful yard. Seeing his yard made her proud of the changes she had made in her own yard.

"How are you today?" His voice was gentle and friendly, but there was concern below the surface.

"I'm happy that I'm an aunt. I can't wait to meet little Samuel. That was so sweet to name him after daddy and you. He has some big shoes to fill." She paused.

"I'm very confused. Except for the void in my memory and sleeping with a night light, I feel like my old self. There is a lot going on in my head that is disconcerting, but I'm good."

"Are you all right being around me?"

"Of course! My goodness, why would you think I might not be?"

"You've been through a lot. I don't want my presence to remind you of things you want to forget."

"Jake, you and Daddy saved me. You're my hero. You're my best friend and have been for a long time. You remind me only of good things. I'm just very confused when I'm around you. I have … feelings that I don't understand."

"What kind of feelings?"

She looked in his eyes. "It's hard to explain. I remember our kiss five months ago. I remember wanting to see you after the divorce papers were filed. I just want to be close to you. I have this very strong feeling that something has happened between us that I should remember. I don't know a better way to explain it."

"Do you want to talk about it?"

"Yes. I want to talk about everything that happened since my last memory. But first, I want to understand everything that happened when I was … abducted. Will you help me?"

"Let me tell you what I think I understand happened. If I have misunderstood something, please tell me. I need to understand everything in order to deal with all this. Walt is dead. Mitchell was shot and is in jail. Mother and Daddy walk on eggshells around me. I can tell Kelli fights the urge to hug me and cry when we're together. Walt's parents are devastated. And I have this sense that you're walking on eggshells, as well. I'm sure you and Daddy have told me everything, but I need to know that I understand what you told me."

That makes sense to me," Jake said. "Go ahead."

Kendra began and recounted the facts of her abduction, Walt's car having been on her driveway, the phone call to Jake for help, the search for her and her rescue. She repeated what she had been told about Mitchell's motivation and the death of Walt. She clearly understood her activities the week before the abduction with regard to improving her yard and redecorating her home.

All in all, she had a good grasp of the overall facts, and Jake confirmed what she had described.

"Do you know where Walt was when he was killed?"

"The Sheriff said blood stains and fluids indicate that Mitchell shot Walt on the porch of the cabin. Apparently, Walt got home a day early and they went to the deer lease Thursday night. Mitchell said that he and Walt argued most of the night. Mitchell shot Walt, then hid Walt's body in the freezer. He came back to Houston on Friday, after he shot Walt. He told the Sheriff he planned to abduct you Friday night, but didn't because I was at your home. So, he waited until Saturday morning."

She nodded and touched his arm gently and asked, "You were with me Friday night?"

He nodded. He looked directly into her eyes, not avoiding what he thought would be her next question.

She saw the honesty on his face and in his eyes. She started to ask, but shook her head and said softly, as if to herself, "Not now." She didn't ask for elaboration.

"What actually happened the morning you found me?"

Jake recounted the trip to the deer lease, meeting the deputy, and the shots fired by Mitchell.

"Sam took charge. He called for backup and an ambulance, and we went into the cabin. Sam went in the back door and shot Mitchell in the leg when Mitchell turned his rifle on him. Sam called me to come in the front door. Mitchell reached for his rifle as I opened the door, so I shot him in the hand.

"Mitchell had buried you in a wooden box behind the carport."

Kendra shivered and Jake paused until she nodded for him to continue.

"When Sam reconnoitered, he saw the fresh earth." Jake stopped and watched her, but she seemed to be handling the information adequately. "When I saw that mound of earth, my heart jumped into my throat. I thought the worst."

Jake described unearthing the coffin and bringing Kendra into the house, and the arrival of the medic team. There were tears in her eyes, but she didn't break down. After several quiet minutes, she looked at Jake.

"Mitchell actually buried me alive?"

He nodded.

"Thank God, I was unconscious. That would have scared me witless," Kendra said disconsolately.

"Does anyone know why?"

Jake repeated what Sam had told him. "One of the forensic guys in Blanco County speculates that his plan was to kidnap you and bury you, then to rescue you and tell you that Walt had kidnapped you. They believe he was going to tell you he had saved you, but had to kill Walt to do so. They think he believed you would see him as your knight in shining armor. Why he chose to bury you, we don't know."

"I know why. Mitchell knew that would really scare me. I once told him that the thought of being buried alive scared me." Tears formed in the corners of her eyes and she shook her head. "That was cruel. That was so cruel."

"We don't know for sure, but that all seems to be a logical scenario, given his infatuation with you."

"Oh, no," she said softly. "God forgive me if I've caused all this."

Jake put his arms around her and held her gently, remembering what he had been told about making her feel trapped. "Shh. Don't think that way, Kendra. You have nothing to feel guilty about. Talk to the Dr. Cohen. He'll tell you the same thing and he'll help you deal with this."

She cried into his shoulder and nodded her head. "I know, but I can't help how I feel right now. Oh, Jake." Jake held her and let her cry herself out.

When she was calm, she sat quietly, looking alternately out into space and at Jake. Finally, she straightened her back and spoke. "I have an appointment with Dr. Cohen tomorrow morning. Then I have to meet with someone in the District Attorney's office to talk about Mitchell. Tomorrow afternoon, I have a telephone conference with someone in the District Attorney's office in Blanco County. Right now, I think it's best that you don't tell me anymore than you have until after I've spoken with them."

She decided not to ask about the four cards until after tomorrow.

Jake nodded. "I've already talked to lawyers in the DA's office in Blanco County several times. I've been asked to meet with our District Attorney's representative tomorrow as well. I'm scheduled right after you. Why don't we go together?"

"You're always there when I need you, aren't you?" She kissed his cheek, but she wanted to be wrapped in his arms.

"Whatever you need, I'll be here for you."

They prepared dinner together and ate outside. They played Scrabble and she beat him three games to one. She called Callen for an update on mother and nephew. Darkness had fallen and Jake could tell that she was becoming uneasy.

"Is everything all right?" he asked.

"Yes. No. I don't know. I know I should go home, but I don't want to be alone. I'm sure that something happened between us, and I don't know what it is. I'm upset because I don't remember a whole week of my life." She paused.

"I remember your kiss last fall and … it makes me anxious. I want to ask you if we were … intimate that week, but if we were, I don't want to know until after tomorrow. I think I'm becoming a basket case, Jake. I don't know what to do."

Jake gathered her in his arms. "Does it frighten you when I hold you?"

"Goodness, no. Why do you ask that?"

"Dr. Moore said you might feel trapped if we hugged you too tightly or held you too close."

She looked into his eyes. "I guess I understand that, but I don't remember being taken or confined or buried, so I guess that's why it doesn't scare me to be held. You don't scare me, Jake. I feel safe when you hold me."

"I want you to feel safe. You don't have to go home tonight. You can stay here. The guest room is clean and open for business."

She laughed. "Thank you. I'd like that. I guess it will be like you taking care of me the week I can't remember.

Jake nodded.

"May I borrow a T-shirt to sleep in?"

Jake locked up and turned off the lights. He led her to the guest room. "There is a night light in the bathroom. If you want another in the bedroom, I have one. Would you like a mild sleeping pill?"

"Yes. Please."

She waited at the door while he went for the night light, sedative and a T-shirt. When he returned, she took the items and asked softly, "Hold me, Jake. Just hold me for a minute, please."

He did and they stood together like that for several minutes. Kendra raised her head and kissed him tentatively on the lips. "I've never forgotten your kiss," she said softly as she laid her head against his chest and thought, *Oh, God. I wish he could just hold me in his arms all night. I wish he would just give me an indication of what happened between us that week.*

Jake didn't know what to do. He wanted to pull her to him and kiss her, but was uncertain. She stepped back, kissed his cheek and said good night.

FORTY-EIGHT

As usual, Jake woke first. He showered, dressed in shorts and a soft polo shirt, went to the kitchen and made coffee. He thought of Kendra and hoped fervently that she would get some relief from her confusion soon, even if it meant that he would lose her. It was upsetting to watch her float aimlessly and confused.

She came into the kitchen, dressed and smiling. "Good morning. Did you sleep well?" she asked.

"Sure did. And you?"

"Eventually. I think your little blue pill helped. I feel rested." She kissed his cheek and asked, "May I help myself to coffee?"

"Of course. *Mi casa es su casa*," Jake replied—and Kendra froze. A tremor ran up her spine and she quivered. She turned to look at him, pensive and intent.

"Jake … I have this sense of déjà vu. You've said that to me recently. Or, I think you have."

"I did. Do you have any memory of when or where?"

"I think I was here, in your home, when you said it. I don't remember specifically but I think it must have been that week. But nothing else comes to mind. Did that happen last week?"

"Yes." Jake nodded. "You're right. It was here." He grinned happily. "The first baby steps in the return of your memory. This is a good thing."

"Yes."

She looked pensive.

"Don't try too hard. Just relax. Things will come back. Maybe not as quickly as you would like, but I think this is a good sign." He took her hand. "How about some breakfast?"

They settled on scrambled eggs, bacon and English muffins. When they had eaten, Jake said, "You go get dressed and I'll come for you. I'll take you to the doctor and the DA's office. Then we'll get some lunch. Does that work for you?"

"That would be wonderful, if you're sure you have the time." *Oh, Jake, I don't know what I'm going to do when you aren't here to look after me.*

She drove home, showered and dressed. Little sounds made her jump, but she got through the time alone. Jake arrived and she breathed a sigh of relief. They arrived just in time for her appointment.

Kendra told Dr. Cohen about noticing her birthday ring was gone and of the little memory snippet that had returned. And she told him about the memory sparked by *mi casa*. He was pleased. She mentioned that Jake had brought her and they were to see the DA's lawyers when they left the doctor. She talked of how she felt when she was with Jake.

It was evident that she was dealing with the trauma—except for being startled by little noises and uncomfortable in the dark—better than with her confusion regarding Jake. Time would smooth out the first concerns. He suggested, as he had before, that she spend time with Jake and accept what she was feeling.

He observed that, unlike many trauma cases, there was virtually no chance of a repeat. The bad guy was going to prison, she was surrounded by good people, and the stress of going through a divorce was removed. *That's right. I had almost forgotten about the divorce. I need to ask my attorney if she can do the probate.* He reiterated that the small memories that had surfaced were a good sign and said he believed she would start seeing some progress in the days to come.

"Some things have happened that make me think Jake and I made love the week that I can't remember," she said. "I don't know what to do about that."

'What do you mean."

"I don't know whether to simply ask Jake or wait for my memory to return. Do you think it would help me to ask him and know?"

"If his answer is no, how do you think that will make you feel?"

"It would contradict a lot of what I think and feel right now, but at least I would know."

"Would you like to make love with Jake?"

She was quiet for a moment. "Yes. I see no reason why I couldn't ... or shouldn't. We were obviously attracted to each other before this. And my mind is a turmoil of feelings for and about him right now."

"If you have made love with him, how would that make you feel?"

"Uncomfortable. Not because of the fact that we had made love, but because I can't remember. If we had made love, I would hope that he would want to make love again, but I think it would be awkward, knowing that he had memories of us together and I had none."

"I think whether you ask or don't ask is a question you have to decide. I don't think it will hurt you to ask and know; it might be helpful. I don't think it will harm you if you wait to ask that question."

He looked at the clock, confirmed her next appointment on Wednesday, and asked her to introduce him to Jake. When they were introduced, he asked Kendra to excuse them for a minute and invited Jake into his office. "Jake, I'm going to step out of line a bit, if you will allow me." Jake nodded.

"I like Kendra. I just like some patients from the beginning. She is one of those. She's a bird with a broken wing—a woman who is understandably more confused by her lack of memory and her relationship with you than the trauma she has been through. But she can heal. I can't tell you what she and I have discussed, but I have a question. Do you have strong feelings for her?"

"Yes. More than I would have imagined."

"She told me about the kiss last fall. And she told me about the shortcomings of her marriage. She wants the fairy tale. And you seem to be an important part of that in her mind. If that isn't what you want, you should let her down gently and soon. If it is, be patient with her."

He extended his hand. "I've probably said more than I should have, but, as I said, I like Kendra. And I'm sure she is going to recover from this quite well. It was good to meet you."

As they walked to his car, Kendra asked, "What did you two talk about?"

"He told me that your prognosis was very favorable. And that he likes you as a person. He said he was glad to have met me." He took her hand. "I like you as a person, too. Very much."

Kendra laughed. "I like you, too."

They arrived at the office of the District Attorney. They were introduced to an attorney who took Kendra, then Jake, into a large conference room. He asked a prepared set of questions about the events leading up to the abduction and rescue. Kendra could remember nothing. Jake answered everything he could honestly.

They had a quiet lunch, both thoughtful of what had been said the past three hours. They returned to her home. She called her parents and brought them up to date, then called the attorney in Blanco County. Jake wandered about as she listened and responded to the attorney.

When she was finished, Jake suggested she call her attorney about the divorce and the probate. She did and her attorney told Kendra that she would have the divorce action dismissed that day and suggested Kendra get the probate action started. When Kendra assured her she knew where Walt's Will was, the attorney stated that she would file the probate action as soon as she had the original will in her possession, instructing Kendra to bring the original Will to her office the next day.

Jake asked if she wanted company that night. She smiled and said yes. He asked where she wanted to be and she asked if he would stay at her home.

"I'll have to go home and get clothes and my materials for the next two days. If you don't mind, I need an hour or two this evening to prepare for tomorrow."

She looked abject. "Oh, Jake. I'm taking advantage of you. I'll be okay tonight. I'm going to have to do without you tomorrow and Wednesday. There's no reason why you have to be here tonight. I need to get used to being alone."

He gathered her into his arms and kissed her forehead. "You aren't taking advantage of me. I'm here for you. Just give me a little time tonight to work. I'll call you both nights I'm gone. Maybe your mother would come for a couple of days?"

She snuggled against him. "No. I need to do this. I'll be fine Tuesday and Wednesday. It would be wonderful if you were here tonight ... if that doesn't make you uncomfortable."

Jake just smiled and shook his head.

He went home, gathered his things, and returned. They went out for dinner and talked easily. "I want to talk about the lost week, but you need to work tonight and I need to digest what Dr. Cohen told me today and ruminate on things that are going through my mind. May we talk when you return?"

"Sure." He smiled at her. "Ruminate. That's an interesting word."

When he said that, she started and looked thoughtful.

"Did you have a memory?"

"No. Yes. I'm not sure. But ... something seemed familiar and I don't know what."

They returned to her home and Jake spread his materials out on her kitchen table. As he worked, she called Callen for an update on Samuel and Rachel, then went to her bedroom and retrieved the four envelopes. She re-read each and thought about each. It was becoming an interesting exercise in logic.

She enjoyed the Museum of Fine Arts and recalled that she had planned to visit the museum over her spring break. Logically, she must have said something to Jake that prompted him to get the tickets to the museum and the ball. And to make the offer of a ball gown. She thought about the cost of a nice dress and got a little mental tingle—not anything definite, but it seemed she had talked about the cost of such a dress. But why would Jake go to all that trouble for her? Surely, there were other women he would prefer to take to an event such as that? There had always been a pretty woman in Jake's life.

She looked at the resort brochure. The first time she saw it, she had noticed that zip lining and horseback riding were highlighted in yellow. Those were also two things she recalled thinking she would try to do during spring break. At some time, she had obviously mentioned that to Jake and he had acted with her in mind.

The brochure for the Cayman Islands was a surprise. She had always wanted to visit the Caribbean Islands, but she didn't recall specific plans to go. But she had intended to ask Jake if she could use his pool, lie in the sun and read a book. *Hmmm.*

She thought about the house and it sparked a memory that she had planned to make some beds in the yard, and wanted to plant roses. So, she had apparently acted on that thought.

She looked around, and in her closet and her drawers. There was a pretty, new outfit in her closet. And there were two new soft oxford cloth robes—a man's black robe and a woman's smaller robe, white with black pinstripes—and some very sexy new lingerie in her drawer. She didn't remember buying the outfit, or the lingerie or the robes, so logic indicated they were purchased the week of spring break. Logic also dictated that they were probably purchased with someone in mind. She didn't buy lingerie like that for every day wear.

It certainly wasn't for Walt, so who was it for? It had to be Jake.

Kendra was pleased. If she continued to think logically, she was sure her memory would return and the lost week would be revealed. *This could be interesting. It has to be Jake. Had the memory of their kiss prompted him to act? Her? Them?*

She heard Jake coming down the hall and quickly stored the envelopes and the lingerie away. *Suddenly, I have a lot to think about. Now, all I need is a memory to go with those thoughts.*

He stuck his head around the doorframe and grinned. "All done. How about a glass of wine?"

She agreed. Kendra, the proud aunt, gave Jake an update on her nephew. They finished their wine. Kendra turned out the lights except for a small lamp, and set the house alarm, as Jake had shown her the first night she returned home, when was surprised by the unfamiliar lock and realized she didn't know the procedure or the pass code.

She walked him to the guest room and put her arms around him. When he embraced her, she kissed him gently on the lips, and laid her head against his chest. He quietly held her close to him, stroking her hair gently with his fingertips and returned her kiss. A tingle ran through her and she again kissed his lips and he returned her kiss. When he did, another tingle and warmth filled her intimate parts. *I need to know and I need to know soon.*

She stepped back and whispered, "Sleep well. Will you be here when I wake?

He shook his head. "Probably not. I need to be on the road by eight."

She nodded and said "Good night." She hesitated, then kissed him again and went to her room.

Jake brushed his teeth and went to bed. The house was dark and quiet. Sometime during the night, he was awakened by a soft sound and he felt a weight upon the bed next to him. He opened his eyes to find Kendra sitting on the edge of the bed in a short cotton nightgown.

"Are you all right?"

She shook her head.

"I'm sorry if I woke you. I'm having a rough time. I spent the time when you were working trying to think logically about some clues I've gathered about the lost week. I think, in the process, I triggered my imagination. When I close my eyes, I picture the grave you described and the box. Although I don't think I ever saw it, I can picture it vividly. She laughed subtly, and said, "Active imagination."

Jake sat up in bed and took her hand.

"And I had a strange … memory, I guess, run through my head. I think I remember being in a dark room. I think I was wrapped in a bed sheet and couldn't move. Just the thought of that scares me. I heard a sound like shoveling dirt, and I think I screamed for help. The next thing I knew, someone burst into the room. I tried to scream, but no sound came out. He grabbed my arm. I felt a sting. It scared me silly at the time and the memory—if that's what it was—scared me again.

"You were wrapped in a bed sheet," Jake affirmed. "We had to unwrap you as soon as we got you into the cabin."

She nodded. "I must have fainted or gone unconscious because I don't remember anything else. I suppose he injected me again. But now that I have that small memory, I think I remember feeling a sting the Saturday morning I was taken."

He moved over and pulled her to him, wrapping her in his warm embrace. "You're okay. I'm not going to let anything happen to you."

"I know, Jake. I know you won't. Will you just hold me for a little while?" She snuggled in close to him, sighed, and whispered, "This is better than being alone. Thank you."

He gently squeezed her to him. After a few minutes, she yawned, again kissed his cheek and said softly, pragmatically, "Logic tells me we've made love. I'm not quite ready for that right now. May I just sleep next to you tonight?"

Jake nodded, pulled her to him, took her hand and she nestled close. She murmured a soft, "Umm," and was asleep.

Like a *Tale of Two Cities*, it was the best of times and the worst of times for Jake. A beautiful, nearly naked woman who he ached to have was lying in bed close against him. He was aroused and could do nothing about it—knew better than to try to arouse her, despite her prescient deduction. It was too soon. It was a long night, but he finally drifted off to sleep with the soft smell of her shampoo and perfume teasing his mind.

Jake awoke early, rose, showered and dressed as quietly as he could. As he was picking up his briefcase, she came down the hall, hair tousled and rubbing sleep from her eyes. "Are you leaving?" she mumbled.

He nodded. She kissed his cheek and whispered, "Be careful. Call me." She hesitated, then stepped to him and kissed him on the lips. "I'll miss you while you're gone."

He reset the alarm system and closed the door behind him.

PART THREE

FORTY-NINE

Mitchell woke Tuesday morning to a warm, sunny day filled with the sounds of birds and the smell of new mown grass. He was scheduled for his first mental health examination that day. That morning, he was issued a gray cotton twill jumpsuit rather than the standard prisoner orange. The change had been allowed because he would be in a public facility and the sheriff didn't want to unduly alarm the public by emphasizing Mitchell's status as a prisoner. The authorities were not too concerned about Mitchel's behavior that day because he had been a docile and complacent prisoner during his tenure in the jail. Notwithstanding his good behavior, the deputy encircled Mitchell's waist with a chain, which he ran through the smaller chain connecting the handcuffs on Mitchell's wrists, then locked the ends of the chain together. He escorted Mitchell to his cruiser and helped him into the back seat.

When they arrived at the county medical health facility, Mitchell and the deputy were led to the proper wing and seated outside an office while his paperwork was checked and signed by an attendant. The attendant buzzed the doctor using the desk phone, announced Mitchell, then left. The office door opened and the County Psychiatrist, Dr. Sijaoti, introduced himself to Mitchell and escorted him into the office as he reminded the deputy that the session was private.

Mitchell sat in an upholstered chair as Dr. Sijaoti began a recitation of the purpose of the visit and various instructions and admonitions. As he recited, Mitchell squirmed in the chair and repeatedly turned, looking down at the seat behind him.

"Is there something wrong?" Dr. Sijaoti asked.

"Yes. Something is sticking me, but I can't see anything." Mitchell again turned, squirmed, then stood and bent to look closer at the seat cushion. He ran his hand over the fabric of the cushion. "I can't find whatever it is. Would you have a look?"

Sijaoti approached cautiously, then bent and looked. When he did, Mitchell awkwardly enclosed Sijaoti's head inside the joint of his right elbow, slid his arm down and tightened it into the same three-point chokehold he had used on Kendra. Sijaoti grunted and struggled, but Mitchell quickly pulled Sijaoti backward into him to keep Sijaoti as immobile as possible and increased the pressure on his artery until he quietly blacked out. Mitchell removed Sijaoti's belt and bound his hands with it, then removed his tie and stuffed it into the unconscious man's mouth. He struck Sijaoti sharply on the temple with the side of his fist, then drug Sijaoti behind his desk, He turned and looked around the room.

On Sijaoti's desk was a bronze bust of Sigmund Freud. Mitchell squirmed and pulled on the waist chain until he had wriggled it just below his armpits. He hefted the bust, then took it in both hands and stepped to the side of the door next to the knob, flattening himself against the wall.

"Deputy," he said in his best imitation of Sijaoti's voice, "would you come in here, please?"

The deputy opened the door and stepped across the threshold. As he did, Mitchell spun into him and brought the bust of Freud down and into the deputy's temple with great force. The deputy's knees buckled and he dropped to his hands and knees. Mitchell struck him again just behind his ear and he collapsed, unconscious.

Mitchell pulled the deputy into the room and closed the door. He quickly found the keys to the shackles and handcuffs in the deputy's pocket and freed himself. He handcuffed the deputy's hands behind him and chained his ankles together. He searched the deputy's pockets, removing a wallet, a handkerchief and a pocketknife, then stuffed the handkerchief in the deputy's mouth, counted the bills in the wallet—sixty-three dollars—and stuffed the wallet and the knife into his own pocket.

He pulled the wallet from Sijaoti and found another one hundred and twenty-eight dollars, which he added to the deputy's wallet. He went through the desk drawers and removed a black marking pen, a sturdy ballpoint pen, a pair of sun glasses, a cell phone and a small bottle of Ibuprofen, all of which he pocketed. He lifted each man under the arms and drug him to a closet, struck each sharply on the temple again and shoved them roughly into the closet together.

Mitchell donned a windbreaker that was hanging in the closet, slipped the sunglasses on and calmly walked out of the facility without attracting attention. As he left the entrance, he exaggerated the limp caused by his leg wound. He hobbled to the parking lot, saw a man walking toward a pickup truck and hailed him.

When the man turned, Mitchell gave him a good old boy smile and drawled, "Mornin'. I gotta meet my brother at the Dairy Queen out by the highway and my knee is botherin' me somethin' fierce. I was wonderin' if I could get a ride from you. Be happy to pay you."

The man turned and looked at him. "Sure. I'm going that way. Hop in."

Mitchell limped to the truck and awkwardly mounted onto the passenger seat. When the driver was seated, Mitchell turned and stuck out his good hand. "I'm Mitch. Much obliged to you."

They shook hands. "Alton. Good to meet you." Alton looked at Walt's injured hand and commented. "Looks like a bad one."

"Yeah. Fell on an old board and ran a three-inch nail through my hand. Hurt, but it's gettin' better."

Alton nodded sympathetically, then nodded again in the direction of the building. "Got someone in there?"

Mitchell nodded. "My mother's bein' examined for dementia. They're gonna keep her for observation for a couple of days. It's sad to see how her memory has gone downhill lately."

"Me, too. Except it's my daddy. Sad to watch him."

They drove to the Dairy Queen, which was only ten minutes away. Mitchell reached for his wallet and awkwardly extracted a five-dollar bill, offering it to Alton. "Thanks. This'll help some with the gas."

Alton waved his offer off. "Happy to do it. Is your brother here?

Mitchell looked around the parking lot. "Not yet, but he'll be along shortly. Thanks for your kindness," he said as he depressed the door handle and awkwardly dismounted. He waved as Alton drove off.

Mitchell hobbled inside and ordered an ice cream cone. He sat outside, convincingly rubbing his leg as he calmly ate his ice cream. He disposed of his napkin, then hobbled around the building to the dumpster behind it.

He found what he sought—an empty cardboard box with a clean, blank side approximately sixteen inches square. He cut it neatly along the creases with the pocketknife and, using the magic marker, lettered FAMILY EMERGENCY—HOUSTON. NEED A RIDE in large letters. He hobbled down the high berm of the road until he was out of sight of the Dairy Queen, then began walking as rapidly as his injuries would allow to an intersection of two highways a mile down the road. He knew there were four-way stop signs at the intersection. He was optimistic that someone would eventually stop and help him.

He positioned himself on the Houston bound side of the intersection and held his sign against his chest. Within ten minutes, an eighteen-wheel tanker truck rolled to a stop for oncoming traffic. Mitchell held his sign up and removed his sunglasses, as he smiled imploringly at the driver. The driver leaned to his right across the seat, opened the door and yelled, "Hop in before this break in traffic closes."

Mitchell awkwardly boarded and they were their way, down the highway toward Houston. He thanked the driver, introduced himself and told the driver his brother had suffered a heart attack and was in the hospital in Cypress, just outside Houston. The driver told Mitchell he could get him as far as Hempstead, but had to turn there toward College Station.

Two miles down the road, they saw two Texas Ranger cruisers with lights ablaze coming toward them from the east. Mitch turned in his seat and watched them cross the median of the highway just behind the truck in which he was riding. In the side mirror, he could see them block the eastbound lanes as they were joined by two Sheriff's cruisers. The driver looked in his mirror and commented, "Road block. Wonder what's going on? Something must be coming this way."

"Yeah," Mitchell replied, watching the driver carefully, as he imperceptibly prepared to act. He began to sweat and felt wet rivulets slide down his back and chest.

"Sure glad we're ahead of them. I'm running twenty minutes late and a stop would have been a real problem for me."

"Yeah, me too. I need to get to my brother as quick as I can. Thanks for your help. It sure means a lot to me and the family."

"Glad to help. Sit back and relax. We're making good time."

Mitchell breathed a sigh of relief. He knew he had just dodged a big bullet.

At Hempstead, forty miles from his home, Mitchell repeated his efforts and was offered a ride by two men in a large, four-door dually truck advertising paving and construction services on its doors. That ride got him to a mall within five miles of his home. He thanked the men and walked to the mall, where he bought a disposable cell phone, comfortable shoes, and conventional clothes.

He changed in the restroom, and discarded the jump suit and Sijaoti's phone. He walked to a hotel at the edge of the mall, paid cash and booked a room. He showered, dressed and walked to a nearby restaurant where he ordered dinner and enjoyed his meal. He returned, watched the news, but there was no mention of him, and he slept the night.

FIFTY

On Tuesday, Kendra retrieved Walt's will and drove to her attorney's office. When her attorney reviewed the Will, she explained that, as of now, at least unofficially, the house and all Walt's property and his share of the community property were Kendra's, to be official when the Will was admitted to probate, which would take two weeks. She told Kendra to start gathering information on assets and personal property, all bank and investment accounts, retirement accounts, insurance policies and trusts, if any, that pertained to either of them.

Kendra was surprised. It hadn't been immediately obvious to her that Walt's death changed the complexion of her life so radically. And, despite the unhappy and unfortunate circumstances, she was pleased that the home she had just redecorated would be hers now.

She returned home, enjoyed the changes and tried to relax. She continued to think logically, but had no new thoughts. She re-read the contents of the four envelopes and reviewed the prior conclusions she had reached, but had nothing to add to them. She was, however, more convinced that she and Jake had become intimate, during the lost week. It was a logical deduction based upon the contents of the four envelopes. It was either logical or Jake was a very presumptuous man.

She called her managing professor and they talked about her returning to work. They agreed she would return on the twenty-fifth of the month when her medical leave expired. She retrieved her briefcase and tried to figure where her classes would be in the semester curriculum by then.

Sheriff Taber called Sam at two o'clock that day. When Sam answered, Taber quickly said, "Sam, I have some disturbing news. My deputy took Mitchell Williams to his appointment with the County Mental Health Examiner this morning. Somehow, Williams overpowered both the deputy and the doctor, struck them repeatedly in the head, unlocked his handcuffs and escaped. The deputy is critical. He has a cracked skull with internal bleeding. Right now, we have no leads. We think Williams must have made his way to the highway and hitched a ride.

"We have a statewide APB out on him, but it's anybody's guess where he is headed. Our guess is he is headed either to Mexico or to Houston. I wanted you to know. I'll update you when I have something, but meantime, you might want to keep a close eye on your daughter. I have notified the Sheriff in Harris County and he'll keep an eye on Mitchell's home and Kendra's home. Call him if you see anything suspicious."

"Thanks, Sheriff. Her mother and I will leave for her house right away. Jake has been taking good care of her, but he's out of town for two days. Would you ask the Sheriff in Harris County to send someone to her house until we get there? She's alone right now."

Taber assured Sam he would do that. Sam and Mei immediately packed and set out for Houston. When they were on the road, Sam called Kendra and Jake. He conveyed the news, then called Callen, who was understandably concerned for his sister.

Jake called late Tuesday. He apologized and explained that they had been out to a late dinner with clients that had run long. They talked briefly. She told him she missed him and he replied that he missed her, as well.

Kendra put Sam on the phone and he updated Jake. When Jake offered to come home, Sam told him things were under control and there was no need to cut his business trip short. Jake agreed, knowing that Sam was fully capable of protecting Kendra.

Throughout the day, snippets of the memory in the cabin had flashed through Kendra's mind—perhaps sparked by the news of Mitchell's escape. The memories upset her and frightened her. Tuesday night was trying. Her mind would not shut down. She took a sleeping pill before going went to bed. Three hours later, she was consumed with a nightmare. She was in the dark, unable to move, and a man burst into her room. She woke in a cold sweat, screaming and shaking. She shook and sobbed until Sam and

Mei came running into her room. Mei held her and they comforted her. It took a long time before she calmed enough to think reasonably.

She wanted so much to call Jake, to hear his reassuring voice, but it was the middle of the night and he had business tomorrow. *Will this never end? I wish Jake were here.* She sent her parents back to bed and sat in the chaise, covering herself with a comforter, and fitfully dozed off and on until dawn.

Jake couldn't sleep that night. He was worried for Kendra, and thoughts of the grave at the deer lease flashed thought his mind. He knew Sam would take care of Kendra, but that didn't ease his concern for her. He kept his appointments the next day, but he was tired and it was a long day for him.

FIFTY-ONE

At eight o'clock Wednesday morning, Kendra called Dr. Cohen. She related the nightmare and told him of Mitchell's escape. He told her to come at ten a.m. She arrived promptly and recounted the nightmare. Dr. Cohen asked for permission to hypnotize her. She agreed and he took her back to the events beginning that Saturday morning.

Most importantly, he wanted to know if she had been harmed in any physical or emotional way about which he, her doctor, or the authorities needed to know. When she reached the frightening part of that night, he calmed her, listened to her recount of the night, and instructed her that whenever that dream—or any frightening dream—recurred, to tell herself it was just a dream and to wake up. He reassured her as he brought her out of hypnosis, explained to her what had transpired and told her he planted the suggestion that she had permission to wake herself when a bad dream recurred, and to reassure herself that it was just a dream when she woke. He told her to think of safe times with Jake or her parents when she woke.

She was hopeful, but skeptical. She voiced her skepticism. He told her that it might take another session or two to get to the point where she could control the dream, but that her mind was sound and she had Jake and her parents and her friends to keep her safe and support her, so he was optimistic it would work.

He didn't ask whether she had talked to Jake about their relationship, and she didn't mention the subject.

She had lunch with Kelli that day. She told Kelli of Mitchell's escape—which was disconcerting to Kelli—and of Dr. Cohen's comments. She explained her exercise in logic, enumerating each of the conclusions she had reached. Kelli agreed with Kendra's assessment.

"Do you think we've slept together and I just can't remember it? I mean, apparently we were together, alone, every night that week. I had never slept with anyone but Walt, but I know how I felt the night Jake kissed me and how much I wanted to be with him. So, why wouldn't I have slept with him that week … except that it went against all my upbringing." She sighed deeply. "I am so confused, Kelli."

"I think the operative questions are why did you call Jake that Friday and did you want to sleep with him before your memory failed? I know how much you care for him. Maybe you did."

"If I didn't and I jump in bed with him when he gets back from Dallas, what will he think of me? And if I did and I won't make love with him, what will he think of me?"

"Kendra, the man cares for you. Scott and I can see that just from the way he looks at you and treats you. He knows you have no memory of that week, and Jake is no fool. He isn't going to push you just because you made love with him, but don't remember it. Remember what his sister told you. Jake is considerate and comfortable with women. He isn't going to force you into bed under these circumstances."

"I know. You're right. But I'm so confused. I know I care very much for him and have since the night he kissed me—maybe even before that. If I could only remember what happened that week, I would know how to act. I can handle what happened to me, and what happened to Walt because I know all the details. But I can't handle not knowing and feeling awkward with Jake. I've put off asking him directly until after we talked to the DA and I had some more time with Dr. Cohen. I needed some time to digest all that has happened. But, I know I need to do something. I can't continue to simply tread water. Jake will eventually grow weary."

She told Kelli about the four envelopes and the plans Jake had made for them. "I don't think he would have spent the money he has spent and made the accommodation reservations he has made if we hadn't slept together. I don't think Jake would be that … um … presumptuous."

Kelli agreed. "I agree. That makes logical sense to me, as well."

"I keep waiting for a memory to appear and answer the question, but it doesn't seem that will happen. And I need to know. When he gets home Thursday, I'm going to ask him straight out to tell me everything about that week. I have to ask him for my own sanity."

Jake called Wednesday after dinner, but much earlier than he had Tuesday night. He told her he had a successful day and asked her to celebrate with him when he returned. She was excited for him and readily agreed to dinner. She told him about the dream and the session with Dr. Cohen. Jake was concerned for her, but happy that Sam and Mei were with her. She agreed that her parents helped, but said eventually she would have to try it alone again and see what happened.

She said that she was more confused than ever. When he asked what confused her, she sighed. "Everything. I don't know whether I'm coming or going. I miss you, Jake. I want so much from you and I'm scared to give back. I don't know how to behave. I don't want to drive you away or ruin our friendship. I think constantly of your kiss last fall."

"I think about that, too. All the time. I'll be home tomorrow evening. We'll have dinner and we can talk all night if you want. I'll try to help you as much as I can."

"Thank you. I needed to hear that. Hurry home and be safe." *I think I'm in love with you, Jake, and I'm scared to say it.*

She had difficulty going to sleep, but it was because she couldn't stop thinking of Jake, and not because of the tragic weekend. She again took a sedative and slept.

The nightmare recurred, but—miraculously—her dream self told her sleeping self to wake up, that it was just a dream—and she woke without waking her parents. *Bless you, Dr. Cohen. I can't believe it was that easy. The mind truly is a wonderful thing.*

FIFTY-TWO

Wednesday morning, Mitchell availed himself of a complimentary breakfast at his hotel, called the front desk, asked for a late checkout, and stayed in the hotel until three o'clock, watching the news. His picture was displayed on various news reports and he learned that the deputy was in critical condition from the blows he had inflicted. *Shit happens. But, I can't check out at the desk now.*

At three o'clock, he left the room key on the dresser, locked the door behind him, put on the sunglasses, and walked to the mall where bought a floppy boonie hat and pulled it low on his forehead. In the food court, he ate a sandwich in a corner and watched the persons around him carefully. He went to the adjacent theater, bought a movie ticket, watched a movie, then sneaked into another. When he calculated it was sufficiently dark, he left the theater, bought two sandwiches in the food court, and called Uber for a ride. He was met at the mall entrance and driven to an address one block from his home.

With his sack of sandwiches in hand, Mitchell calmly surveyed the neighborhood, but saw nothing suspicious. He walked down the street and past his home. He noticed nothing unusual and no person or vehicle that aroused his suspicion. He returned, walked up his driveway, entered his back yard and located the spare key he kept hidden beneath a patio table. He cautiously approached the back door and looked inside. Seeing nothing that aroused his suspicion, he inserted the key and entered without a problem. *Lock the door behind you, Mitch. An unlocked door would be a dead giveaway.* He locked the door.

When he left the morning that he abducted Kendra, he had closed all the shutters, blinds and curtains; and they appeared undisturbed. In what dim light was available, he could see that his home had obviously been searched, but not ransacked. He carefully made his way to his office where he found a flashlight and a work light that one wore in the manner of a miner's headlamp.

Mitchell went to the kitchen, poured a cold drink, retrieved his sandwiches and returned to his office. He ate at his desk, refilled his drink in the darkness of the kitchen, returned to his office, put his feet up on the corner of his desk and thought about his circumstances.

I was lucky. Although it was surprisingly easy to escape and get home, I was still incredibly lucky that the Law of Murphy didn't dump me in the soup somewhere along the line. Now what do I do? This isn't like the movies or books—I have no false identification and no idea how to go about obtaining false ID.

Mitchell laughed to himself because he had once thought he would investigate how to obtain false identification, simply for the sake of knowing how to do so. And now, unfortunately for him, it was too late.

I have ten thousand dollars in cash in my safe. I have more than twenty thousand in my investment account, but I probably can't get money out of that without attracting attention. Maybe one time, but certainly not more than once. And it will take more than one day to get it in my hands.

I can't just go back to work and I can't live here as if nothing had ever happened. So, I have only three realistic options. I can become a street person and live off the grid. I can make my way to Mexico and see what kind of life I can establish with thirty thousand dollars. Or I can go to Canada and do the same.

I could probably live off the grid, but I'd be cleaner, safer and better fed if I just gave myself up and went to prison. I hate being cold, so I really don't want to go to Canada. So ... turn myself in or go to Mexico.

Damn Kendra! Damn her to hell! This is all her fault. She shouldn't have ignored me when we were back in college. She shouldn't have married my fucking brother. I'm smart. I had a good job. I could have made her happy. But Jake had to come along. First Walt, then Jake.

I can't just leave and let things go. She has to go. And Jake has to go. This is all their fault and they have to pay for what they've done to me.

Okay, think about this. Mexico makes the most sense. Crossing the border on foot or in a car is going to be difficult. Passport, border guards, Mexican cartels and bandits. What do I do in Mexico with a car sporting U.S. plates? So … what makes sense?

He went to the bathroom, then to the kitchen where he refilled his drink and returned. As he sat, he heard a car pull into the driveway. *Shit. Well, you figured they would be checking your home. And they are. Sit quietly. It will be okay unless they try to come in. The house is dark. No reason for them to be suspicious.* He checked the clock. *Ten p.m.. They will probably check once a shift, but not more than twice.*

He sat quietly, eyes closed so that he could hear better. A car door closed quietly. Footsteps approached the house. He heard the front door knob rattle, then footsteps and the accompanying glow of a flashlight moving around the house. The rattle of the back door came from the kitchen and the glow of the flashlight shined through the back door. More footsteps, then he heard the garage side door being opened, then closed. The footsteps and glow of the flashlight receded. He heard the car start and back down the driveway, then change gear and move down the street.

Okay. Back to important matters. How do I get to Mexico and what do I do once I'm there? Mitchell thought, mulled over various options and finally came to a conclusion. *Boat. I get there by boat. I'm going to have to buy a boat.*

Okay. I have ten thousand in cash. I have twenty-three thousand something in my investment account. It will take at least two days to get that out in cash. I'll need money for living. What kind of boat can I get and still have money left to live on?

Mitchell was tired and confused. His hand ached from Jake shooting him and his leg ached from Sam shooting him. *Sam has to go, too. That son-of-a-bitch didn't have to shoot me and neither did Jake.* He sat for hours, thinking, drifting into sleep, only to wake and ponder again. At two thirty a.m. he again heard a car in the drive. He heard the footsteps, followed them and the glow of the flashlight as the house doors and the garage were checked. The car left. *Okay. Roughly, every four hours. Probably twice each shift.* He slept intermittently and fitfully, and again heard a car arrive at six thirty a.m. The car left and Mitchell again pondered and slept intermittently.

At nine a.m., he ate breakfast. He retrieved his spare car keys, and took ten thousand dollars and a short-barrel three-eighty caliber semi-automatic handgun from his safe. He had arrived at a conclusion. He waited for the next inspection, which came at ten-thirty a.m.. When the officer was gone, Mitchell showered, shaved and dressed in clean clothes. He called his broker and made arrangements to close his account. He was advised that his broker could only get the money to Mitchell quickly by wire transfer and that it would be available after two p.m. Friday. He had decided— Jake, Sam and Kendra had to go. After that, he would enjoy himself until the money was gone, and he would find a way to obtain false identification so he could get a job. *I'm not going to prison, and I'm not going to live under a bridge. Life as I know it is over.*

Mitchell waited for the next inspection. When no one came by two forty-five p.m., he grew impatient and drove to Jake's home. He knew Jake worked from home and guessed he would be there on a Thursday. The officer came at two fifty p.m.

When he arrived at Jake's gated community, the gates were closed, as usual. Irritated, he sat across the street waiting to follow someone in. Just as he was about to give up, a FedEx truck pulled to the key pad and the gates opened. Mitchell quickly started his car, put it into gear, pulled onto the street and followed the truck through the gates. He parked in front of Jake's house, took his handgun from the seat beside him and racked a round into the chamber. He stepped out of the car and stood, using the door as cover, as he slipped the gun into his pocket. He closed the car door and strode up the walk to the front door.

Good-bye, Jake, old buddy. Can't say it was nice knowing you. You should have stayed out of this. You shouldn't have tried to steal my girl.

Mitchell rang the bell and waited. There was no answer. He rang the bell again, still with no answer. He walked around the house and into the back yard. He peered through the kitchen and the den windows, but saw no sign of Jake. As he was returning to his car, a pretty woman walking a large standard poodle passed by the end of Jake's drive.

"Hi. Do you know Jake Alder?" he asked.

"Yes."

"Do you know if he is home?"

"No, but I haven't seen his car for a couple of days."

Mitchell thanked her, looked back at the house, shook his head and got into his car.

Damn it, Jake. You were supposed to be here. I guess I'll have to find Kendra first and then come back for you. He pondered a moment. *She is either at home or at her parents. My guess is that she is seeing a shrink and he has told her to stay in familiar surroundings. My money is on her being at home. If not, I know where Sam lives.*

I'm going to have to be careful. Sam will have a gun. Gun or no gun, I can't take Sam by myself. Not unless I surprise him. I'm going to have to come up with a way to surprise him.

He drove within the speed limit to Kendra's home.

FIFTY-THREE

On that same day, Jake departed Dallas after having lunch with his client. He called Kendra from the road, told her that he should be home by five thirty, and they made plans for the evening. He asked where she wanted to be.

"I want to be in your home; I think the chances of jogging my memory are better there; but Mother and Daddy won't leave until you're here, so we'll have to wait until later tonight. I want to be where everything happened. After dinner, I want to talk. If we can recreate that first night, maybe we can shake some cobwebs loose. I ran that by Dr. Cohen and he thinks it's a good idea.

"If we can't jog my memory, then I want you to tell me everything and relieve my frustration at not knowing."

"Makes sense to me. I'll come straight to your house, and the four of us will go to dinner. Talk to Sam and Mei and see what they are in the mood for.

"How has the trip been," she asked.

"Great," he enthused. We're going to celebrate tonight. Where would you like to go?"

"Some place quiet where we can talk. You choose—this is your celebration. And you haven't even told me what we're celebrating."

"I'll tell you when we get to the restaurant. Carmelo's or Johnny Ross? Which would you prefer?"

"Carmelo's would be nice. That way, we can dress more casually."

"Sounds great. Let me talk to Sam for a minute, please." When Sam answered, Jake asked if there was any news.

"Nothing at this end. I haven't heard anything from the local sheriff, but don't expect to unless they actually spot Mitchell in Houston."

"Makes sense. Okay, I will see you in four hours. We're all going to dinner to celebrate. This has been a successful trip."

"That's good news, but there is no need for us to intrude. I know Kendra wants to see you."

"No, no. I want to see you and Mei. And I'd feel better if you were with us—at least, until we know where Mitchell is. We can talk about it at dinner."

Sam agreed and said they would decide at dinner about returning to their home.

"Okay. I'll give you a call when I'm about five or ten minutes out."

No news from the Sheriff. In this case, no news is not necessarily a good thing.

As Jake drove, he pondered on what Mitchell could be doing and where he could be. Mitchell was extremely intelligent, but allowing circumstances to get to this point didn't seem particularly smart.

What makes sense for him to do in his situation? The smart thing to do would be to get out of the country. He could easily slip into Mexico and disappear, assuming he has access to funds. But, why had he kidnapped Kendra at the beginning? That doesn't make sense, even if he was infatuated with her. And it certainly wouldn't make sense to make a second attempt to do so. Not when he was wanted for murder and being sought by the authorities.

The only reason he would have headed to Houston would be for Kendra—unless he had a large cache of money at his home. That would be the only reason that would make sense. The smart move would have been to get to a safer location outside Houston and outside Texas.

Jake drove and thought—about Mitchell, about Kendra, about Kendra's rescue and his conversations with Sam. He felt sure that Sam was good with his relationship with Kendra. He liked Sam and Mei. He looked forward to seeing more of them under happier circumstances. He was really looking forward to seeing Kendra this evening, and to dinner at Carmelo's.

He stopped for a restroom and a cold drink in Madisonville, and was quickly on his way again. He was making good time until he was caught in construction traffic north of Conroe, about thirty miles north and east of his home, and came to dead stop for nearly ten minutes. He grew anxious, but he had no word from Sam that there was any reason for concern, so he sat as patiently as he could, listening to music. He knew Sam was more than capable of handling Mitchell, but he would feel better when he was there with Kendra and Sam.

FIFTY-FOUR

Three hours after Jake's call, Sam's phone rang as Kendra went through the kitchen and into the mud room. "I have to get something from my car," she said as she walked into the garage.

"Wait, Kendra," Sam called as he answered the phone.

"Mr. Carter, this is Sergeant Mallory at the Precinct Four Sheriff's Office. My man just did his drive by of the Williams home and reported that Williams' car was in the garage at the earlier check, but is missing now. I wanted to give you a heads up, just in case. By the way, the deputy Williams struck in the head died this morning. I thought you should know. This guy is dangerous."

Sam thanked the Deputy. As he was debating whether to call Jake, and tell Kendra and Mei, he heard a tapping at the door leading into the garage. *Did Kendra lock herself out?* Sam looked, but the door into the garage stood open. He called to Kendra, but there was no response from her. He cautiously pulled his handgun out of his holster and stepped into the mudroom toward the open door into the garage. When he did, Mitchell stepped into view before him, pulling Kendra with him at his side. His bandaged left hand pressed hard against Kendra's throat. In his right hand, he held a compact semi-automatic pistol to her temple.

"Hello, Sam," Mitchell said nonchalantly. "Drop your magazine on the floor, clear your weapon, and put it in your holster, Sam. We need to talk." He pressed the muzzle of his gun tighter against Kendra's head.

"I'm sorry, Daddy," she moaned.

"Sh. It's okay," Sam said as he did as he was instructed.

"Step back," Mitchell instructed, "and sit at the table with your wife."

Again, Sam did as instructed and Mitchell limped through the doorway, pushing Kendra ahead of him.

"Everyone have a seat at the table," he said congenially, "and put both hands on the table in front of you."

They did as instructed and Mitchell leaned back against the kitchen counter, pointing his gun at them. "If you move your hands without asking, I'll shoot you. Understood?"

Everyone nodded.

"Let me hear you," he instructed contumaciously. "Understood?"

One by one, each said, "Yes."

Looking at Sam, Mitchell said, "I guess it was you who figured out we were at the cabin? I don't think Jake knew about the deer lease."

"It was me. It has been a while since I was there, but it came to me in my sleep."

"I guess it was you who told Jake to fire into the table while you moved behind me."

Sam nodded, never taking his eyes from Mitchell.

"You shouldn't have shot me."

"You shouldn't have pointed that rifle at me," Sam replied, calmly.

"Don't get smart, Sam," Mitchell replied angrily. "You're in no position to get smart with me right now."

Sam shrugged.

"This would have been so easy, if only you had stayed away. I could have saved Kendra and taken Walt's place. He never knew how to treat her right. And I saw her first."

"So you knew how to treat her right, did you?" Sam asked.

"Better than Walt did."

"So that's why you drugged her, scared the living daylights out of her and buried her alive—because you know how to treat her right?"

"That was the only way to get her to realize that I loved her and was better for her than Walt," Mitchell responded angrily.

Kendra laughed out loud. "Love? Neither of you had any idea of what love is. I was just something that Walt possessed—and that's all you wanted. You just wanted me as a possession."

"Well, it doesn't matter now. I figured it out. All this time, you wanted Jake. Walt was so damned dumb, he never figured it out, but I knew. All this time, you were at Jake's house, fucking him. Did you bring him here for kicks when Walt was out of town?"

Kendra looked at Mitchell for a long moment, then quietly said, "You're mistaken, Mitchell. I was never intimate with Jake. I was never unfaithful with Jake, or anyone. I talked with him and Kelli about Walt's drinking. That's all. I was trying to get Walt sober. I didn't cheat on him."

"Why not? He cheated on you plenty of times?"

"I don't believe you."

"It's true. All the girls in college wanted to fuck him. And it got even easier when he became a hotshot NFL star. You were just arm candy for him. He told me you didn't even know what to do in bed."

To Kendra's credit, she maintained her composure, but little tears slid down her cheeks. Mei reached to touch her, to comfort her, but Mitchell waved his gun at her.

"Uh uh—don't move your hands. No more warnings." Mei quickly pulled her hand back.

"Our parents always thought you were such a perfect little church girl, but I know different. After today, everyone will know the truth."

Sam cleared his throat to shift Mitchell's attention to him and away from Kendra. "How so?" he asked.

"Because I'm going to tell them. I just wanted you to know before I kill you that I know. You should have left everything at the cabin alone. I shot Walt so that Kendra could be my girlfriend again. He threatened me and he threatened Kendra. I would have saved her. Then Kendra would have wanted me and you wouldn't have to die. But now, everyone will know about Jake, and you all have to die."

"What are you going to accomplish by killing us? It didn't do you any good to kill your brother?"

"My brother was an ungrateful, conceited piece of shit," Mitchell shouted.

"Same question. It didn't do you any good to kill your brother. What good will it do you to kill us?"

"Not just you three. I'm going to find Jake and kill him, too. Jake is supercilious and arrogant. He doesn't deserve Kendra. Actually, I went to his house first, but he wasn't home. I was going to kill him, then come and tell you about it before I killed you. But, it will be okay this way. Either way, you'll all be dead.

"Besides, you and Jake shot me. Now, it's my turn to shoot you. That's fair, isn't it?" he asked with a sophomoric grin.

"What did my mother ever do to you?" cried Kendra. "She has always been nice to you,"

"You're right. She was always nice to me. Killing her is one way to get even with you and Sam."

Sam stood quickly. Mitchell pointed his gun at him and screamed, "Sit down and put your hands on the table!"

"Mitchell, this isn't getting you anywhere. Let's go into the other room and talk. There is no need to upset Kendra and Mei. They aren't your enemy." Sam spoke evenly, even paternally, and held Mitchell's gaze.

"I said sit down," Mitchell shouted, pointing his gun at Sam. "If you don't, I'm going to shoot Mei in the head." He wildly swung his aim to point his weapon at Mei's head.

As Sam sat, Mitchell launched into a long, vitriolic diatribe describing how it was he who looked after Walt, who encouraged him to play football, who helped him cram for exams so that he could get C's and remain on the team. Mitchell told how it was he who apologized for Walt when Walt angered others or insulted girls. It was he who proudly introduced Walt to Kendra, never suspecting that Walt would steal his girlfriend. He complained that Walt was his parents' favorite and they never appreciated him. He went on for more than thirty minutes without pause, recounting episodes, ranting and applauding himself for being the consummate big brother and deserving son; and telling Kendra that it was he, and not Walt, who really wanted her.

He was still going strong when Sam's phone, which was lying on the table, rang. Sam looked. "It's Jake. He's coming here later. If I don't answer, he'll think something is wrong."

"Okay, but watch what you say."

Sam answered and Jake said, "Hey, it's me. I'm five minutes out."

"Put it on speaker," Mitchell mouthed as Jake asked, "What are you doing?"

"I'm putting you on speaker so the ladies can hear." Sam did so. "We're just sitting around the kitchen table talking."

"Well, enjoy. I'm looking forward to dinner—"

Before he could continue, Sam interrupted, "Me, too. But I'm used to doing it a little earlier. I think between three and five is the best time. Guess it will be a little later today."

Jake paused briefly, then said matter-of-factly, "Yeah. I remember that about you, three to five. I guess you'll just have to wait until I get there this time. See you in about thirty minutes."

"Okay," Sam replied. "See you when you get here."

Mitchell looked hard at Sam, but didn't say anything.

FIFTY-FIVE

J ake ended the call and pondered Sam's words. *Three to five is when bad guys are asleep. Isn't that what Sam said on the way to the cabin? I'm guessing he is telling me that there is a bad guy there. So, Mitchell has them in the kitchen around the table. And Mitchell now thinks I'm thirty minutes away. And he either has a gun or a bomb; otherwise, Sam would have taken him by now. And my money is on a gun.*

Jake quickly dialed 911. When the operator came on the line, he succinctly explained that Mitchell Williams was holding Kendra Williams and her parent's hostage in her home at gunpoint. He gave the address, and stated emphatically that there should be no sirens and no noise.

He drove into the subdivision from a direction that wouldn't take him in front of Kendra's home. He parked in front of Kelli and Scott's home—coincidentally, behind Mitchell's car. He tried to calculate how long it would take the Sheriff's men to arrive.

A vision of the shallow grave behind the shed filled his mind. And it scared him. *I can't just sit here and wait for them. Mitchell is unstable and he obviously has a weapon. Hopefully, the deputies will arrive in time, but Kendra and her parents are in danger and I can't wait for help. I have to do something to protect them.*

Jake took his Beretta from the glove box. He checked the load in his gun—one in the chamber and a full magazine. He clipped his holster over his belt and checked to ensure it was secure. He reached into the back seat for a windbreaker and a golf hat. It was all he had for a disguise. He put them on, pulling the brim of the cap low and stepped out of his car.

Kendra's kitchen was at the back of the house. It overlooked her back yard and the side yard. The only view from the kitchen out to the front of the house was through the front door. If they were sitting around the table, it was unlikely that Mitchell could see his approach from the front. If he could, Jake hoped the jacket and hat would sufficiently disguise him.

Jake calmly walked into the neighbor's yard, carefully watching Kendra's house. He took cover behind a large white oak tree that was already filled with new, shiny green leaves. The tree was next to Kendra's driveway. He looked from behind the thick trunk of the tree and could see through the side window over Kendra's sink. He saw what looked like Mitchell's head, back and right shoulder. He appeared to be leaning against the counter, talking animatedly. Jake saw Sam and Mei across from Mitchell at the table. The view of where Kendra sat was blocked.

Jake drew his Beretta, quickly thumbing the safety off. Keeping Mitchell's back to him, he cautiously advanced across the driveway and into Kendra's yard, moving quickly to the side of the house where he crouched below the kitchen window. He could hear Mitchell's words— ranting, berating his parents for favoring Walt's athletic skills over his intelligence. Then, he heard Mitchell switch his attention to Kendra.

"And you were just like my parents, Kendra. Walt was as dumb as a post, but you chose him over me."

"Mitchell, I didn't choose Walt over you. I didn't even know you were interested in me until all of this happened. You never asked me out."

"You should have known," he whined. "I was always nice to you. I always saved you a seat next to me in church on Sunday mornings."

"You did," Kendra agreed. "But I just thought you were being nice. I didn't know you were interested in me. Why didn't you ask me out?"

"You never gave me a chance!" Mitchell retorted angrily. He was agitated and it showed in his voice. "You were just interested in Walt because he was a big football star," he shouted.

"Mitchell, you met me first. It was you who introduced me to Walt. If you were interested, why didn't you ask me out instead of introducing me to your brother?"

"You never gave me a chance," Mitchell shouted again.

"Mitchell," Kendra replied evenly, "Walt asked me out two weeks after you introduced me to him. You had plenty of time to ask if you had really been interested." Kendra looked him in the eyes and said calmly, evenly, "Wouldn't that have been better than kidnapping and drugging me?"

"You never gave me a chance," Mitchell shouted a third time. "I had to save you so you would know that I loved you."

Jake heard Sam say, "Mitchell, think about what you're saying," but Mitchell cut him off.

"Shut up, Sam. This is between Kendra and me."

Jake heard a long silence, and then Kendra spoke. "Mitchell, I'm confused. What is it you want?"

"I want you."

"But why?"

"Because I love you. I want you to love me," he said petulantly.

There was another silence until Kendra said, evenly, "If I go with you, will you leave my mother and father and Jake alone? You won't try to kill them?"

Mitchell was silent for a moment, then mumbled something.

"I'm sorry," Kendra said. "I didn't understand what you said."

"You don't love me."

"You're right, Mitchell. I don't love you, and I won't try to convince you that I do. You're too smart for me to try to do that."

"Yeah," Mitchell gloated. "I'm too smart to fall for that."

"Mitchell, I don't want you to kill my parents and Jake. If I go with you, maybe I'll learn to understand you better and maybe I will grow to love you."

"You'll go with me?"

"If that's what you want."

Mitchell was again silent for a long moment. "Where would we go?"

"I don't know, Mitchell. I suppose that is up to you. Where do you want to go?"

He paused thoughtfully, then again spoke petulantly. "Some place far away from Jake. I think you love Jake."

"We're talking about you and me, now. Where do you want to go?"

"Far away, where we can be alone."

"Where would that be?"

Mitchell pondered her question. "Mexico." He paused. "No. Australia. I've always wanted to go to Australia."

"That would be good. I'd like to go to Australia, too. And you're smart. You could get a good job there."

"I could. I'm really smart."

"You are," Kendra agreed. "We'll have to get airline tickets. Do you want me to make the reservations?"

Mitchell thought for a moment. "Yes."

"All right. Do you have a passport?"

Mitchell hesitated. "No."

"Well, you'll have to have a passport to travel to another country. Do you want me to get you a passport application?"

"How long will it take to get a passport?"

"Probably a couple of weeks."

Mitchell was quiet again. "You'll really go with me?"

"If that's what you want, but you have to promise me you won't kill Mother and Daddy and Jake. I'll only go if you'll promise me that?"

Again, Mitchell was silent for a while.

Then, he shook his head. "I don't think this is going to work. The cops won't let me go. I think I'd better stick with my plan." He mused for a moment. "But I'm going to take you with me."

"What do you mean?"

"I'm going to kill them, but not you. You're going to come with me," he replied perfunctorily

Jake knew he had to act. He knew Mitchell's attention was on Kendra right then. He surveyed the situation. If the small door to the garage was open, he could get into the garage undetected, then he could get into the kitchen. Or at least have a line of fire at Mitchell. He would be coming in from behind Kendra, so he had to distract Mitchell from her.

Jake knew the floor plan of Kendra's home. He checked the change in his pocket—three quarters and two pennies. If he could get to the mud room door, and if the door into the kitchen were open, he could flip a quarter into the kitchen away from Kendra and Mitchell. The sound should catch Mitchell's attention and cause him to look away from the mud room.

Jake thumbed the hammer back, cocking the Beretta with a soft, metallic click. He rose carefully and quietly until he was looking through the window into the room, his weapon pointed at Mitchell's back. He saw that the mud room door was open. He also saw Kendra across the table from Mei—and she saw him.

Jake quickly put his finger to his lips and shook his head, but it was too late. When Jake's face appeared in the window behind Mitchell, Kendra saw him and involuntarily gasped.

When Kendra gasped, four things happened in split second succession. Mitchell saw where she was looking and spun around, saw Jake, swore, brought his gun up and fired through the window. When Jake saw Mitchell's gun come up, he fired at Mitchell and snapped his head sideways. Sam stood and threw a saltshaker at Mitchell's head, and the SWAT van and a Sheriff's cruiser pulled to a stop in front of Kendra's home.

When Mitchell fired at Jake, Kendra saw Jake's hat fly off as he limply fell backward and lay motionless. Wide-eyed, she screamed, "Jake! Oh, God—no," immediately followed by Mei screaming Sam's name.

Jake's bullet struck Mitchell just as the shaker struck Mitchell at the back of his head. Mitchell lurched against the counter, turned awkwardly, almost involuntarily, and fired once at Sam as he crumpled to the floor. Mitchell's bullet struck Sam just above his beltline on his left side. Sam grunted with pain, clutched the bloody wound on his side, and dropped to his knees.

Two SWAT officers raced to Jake who lay inert on his back, unconscious, his face turned against his left shoulder. The right side of his head, his neck and his shirt were blood soaked. One officer dropped to Jake's left side, identified the location of the wound, tore open a compression pack and quickly pressed it to the wound to stanch the bleeding while the second officer checked for a pulse and other wounds. A third officer sprinted to the scene and pointed his weapon directly at the kitchen window where Mitchell had been.

Sam called loudly, "He's down; doors are unlocked." Two SWAT officers burst through the front door and two more burst through the back door. Three of those officers encircled Mitchell where he lay on the floor as the fourth officer and Mei went to Sam. That officer applied a compression pack to Sam's wound as Mei cradled his head against her, tears streaming down her cheeks. Sam groaned and looked up at Kendra, who stood transfixed, staring out the window, sobbing.

"Go to Jake. See how he is."

She remained motionless, eyes glazed until Sam repeated himself in a stern voice, "Kendra! Go to Jake. See how he is."

She came alert and looked at Sam. "Oh, Daddy! You're hurt!"

I'll be okay," Sam assured her. "Go to Jake!"

Sam's words registered in her mind and she rushed to the door. As Kendra passed Mitchell, she heard him cough, gurgle and saw blood spill from his mouth. She raced outside. When she saw Jake's blood-soaked head, she screamed his name a second time and dropped to her knees on his right side, reaching for him and pressing her face against his.

"Give me a little room here, ma'am. Let's see what we've got." The deputy attending Jake quickly raised a corner of the compression pack, checked Jake's wound, and pressed the pack back against the wound.

He patted Kendra's shoulder and said quietly, "It isn't as bad as it looks. The bullet grazed his head, cut a good furrow in his skull and took a big chunk of scalp and hair, but doesn't appear to have penetrated. I don't think it did any internal damage. He is bleeding freely because there are a lot of blood vessels in the scalp. The pain and impact must have knocked him unconscious. We need to get him to a hospital."

Kendra nodded her understanding. She took Jake's hand and whispered softly, "Thank you, God. I'm not going to lose him."

The officer again patted her shoulder and said reassuringly, "No, ma'am. You aren't going to lose him. My guess is he'll be okay. How is everyone inside?"

"My Daddy was shot on his left side at his waist. He's bloody, but was coherent when he told me to come out here and check on Jake. Mother is okay, just scared for Daddy. Mitchell was bleeding from his mouth and coughing up blood."

"Sounds like Williams was hit in a lung. Not a good thing. Glad your dad is coherent. Sounds like a flesh wound. Probably painful and will require some surgery, but not life-threatening." As it turned out, the deputy was right on all counts.

Three ambulances screamed up the street with full sirens and blazing lights. They stopped abruptly at Kendra's driveway. They were followed by three more Sheriff's cruisers. EMTs quickly went to work, checking Jake, Sam and Mitchell, then placing them on gurneys. As they were loading Mitchell, one of the EMTs attending him looked at his partner and said, "No rush now. He's gone." They covered Mitchell's face, slid the gurney holding his body into the ambulance and departed without haste.

FIFTY-SIX

Jake and Sam were loaded into separate ambulances. Kendra and Mei both wanted to go with them, but the deputy in charge said he needed some information before anyone could leave. Kendra watched sadly as the EMTs loaded Jake. She said she would stay if Mei could go with Sam, and the deputy agreed. Mei boarded the ambulance with Sam and it raced to the hospital behind the ambulance carrying Jake. She wanted so much to be with him.

She still didn't know what had occurred during the forgotten week, but she knew that her feelings for Jake had grown enormously over the past days and knew that her feelings had to have some valid basis. Thoughts of Anya played in her mind and she knew how they had upset her when Anya was with Jake. She thought of her dinner conversation with Kelli. She realized then the source of all her uncertainty now about Jake. The problem was that she didn't know if Jake had reciprocal feelings for her. But she knew then that a part of her would have died if Jake's wound had been fatal.

Kendra gave a tearful and quick, but accurate, account of the afternoon and the events that occurred. She told the deputy she needed to go to the hospital and that she would come to them tomorrow to give any additional information they needed. She asked where Jake had been taken. The deputy in charge called another deputy over, told Kendra that Jake had been taken to the Methodist Hospital Emergency Center near her home, and instructed the deputy to take Kendra there and to ensure that she found Jake. He told Kendra that Sam and Mei would be at the same emergency center.

As she entered the deputy's car, Kendra felt blood on her face and saw that her hands and her blouse were bloody from when she had hugged Jake to her, frightened that he was going to die. She slid onto the passenger seat as the officer handed her a plastic container of wet wipes. "Looks like you can use these, ma'am."

By the time she had herself cleaned up as well as possible, they were at the ER. The deputy quickly escorted her to where Jake was being examined and learned where Sam and Mei were. He told Kendra, and returned to the scene of the shootings.

After the surprised ER nurse quickly verified that the blood on Kendra's face, hair and blouse was not hers and she was not injured, Kendra was told that Jake's vital signs were excellent and he was being prepped for an X-ray and MRI of his skull. The nurse told her it would probably take an hour before she could see him or speak with him.

Kendra found her mother, who gasped, inhaled sharply, and went wide-eyed when she saw the blood on Kendra. Kendra quickly calmed Mei, told her what she had been told about Jake, and learned that Sam was in surgery and would probably be there for at least two hours, but that his vital signs were also excellent.

She called Kelli and tearfully relayed the events of the day and their current situation. Twenty minutes later, Kelli and Scott arrived. After tearful hugs all around, they sat together, talking intermittently, but often just sat, quietly concerned.

After an hour, Kendra was told by a nurse that Jake was still unconscious and had been transferred to intensive care so that he could be monitored and watched. The nurse assured Kendra that this should not be misinterpreted, but was necessary until Jake was conscious, at which time he might be transferred to a room.

Two hours later, Mei was told that Sam's surgery went well and that he was in recovery and would be there for about forty-five minutes, then would be transferred to a room, where Mei and Kendra could see him briefly.

Kelli and Kendra went to the cafeteria for coffee. Kelli squeezed Kendra's hand and asked how she was doing. When she did, Kendra couldn't hold it in any longer. She slumped against Kelli and cried and shook. Between sobs, she moaned and her words rushed out, filled with raw emotion.

"Oh, God, Kelli. I thought I had lost him. I watched Mitchell shoot him. I was literally petrified when I saw Mitchell shoot him. He fell backward and all I could think was that he was dead. I was scared out of my mind that I had lost him." Kelli hugged Kendra and didn't ask questions. Kendra's heart—not her damaged memory—had just told Kelli everything she needed to know about Kendra's relationship with Jake during the lost week. And she was happy for Kendra.

When Kendra calmed, Kelli asked if she had remembered any more of the missing week. "No, but I know that something inside me was scared beyond reason that Jake was dead—something inside me knows much more than I do, and I need to know. My heart stopped when I saw his bloody head."

"I'm sure you're right. I wish I knew something I could tell you that would help. I can only tell you that, when you and Jake were with us that week, you beamed. I have never seen you so happy. You looked at Jake with puppy dog eyes. And he looked at you the same way. Scott and I both agreed that there was something very strong going on between the two of you."

"I'm sure there was," Kendra agreed, "and I wish I knew what. Something inside me knows." Kelli smiled quietly.

A little before ten o'clock, two doctors entered the waiting room and introduced themselves respectively as the surgeon who had operated on Sam and the neurologist who was treating Jake.

Dr. Ryan, who was Sam's surgeon, told them that Sam's wound had been a through and through, meaning that the bullet entered and exited. He said that the bullet was obviously a hollow point, which had flattened and tumbled upon contact and had, consequently, caused some internal damage that was of concern, but not life-threatening. He said that, fortunately, it was a smaller three-eighty caliber round and that no organs had been struck. He said Sam would be in the hospital for at least two more days and should heal rapidly, but would experience some pain for a week or so. He said that they could see Sam for ten minutes, then he would receive a strong pain-killer and they could see him tomorrow at nine a.m.

Dr. Sanchez told them that, although Jake's wound was very bloody, it did not appear to have caused internal damage. He emphasized that Jake did have a concussion and needed to be monitored closely for twenty-four hours, and would probably remain in the intensive care unit until Saturday morning. He said Kendra could see him then.

The doctors emphasized that, considering the areas where Sam and Jake had been struck, both men were very lucky their injuries hadn't been much more serious. Both doctors told Kendra they were aware of what had previously happened to her and asked how she was doing. She told them that she was fine physically, but working on the mental part. She told them she couldn't remember anything of that week of her life, and they sympathized with her.

Kendra and Mei visited Sam briefly, but he was still groggy from the surgery and anesthetics. His nurse suggested they go home and rest until tomorrow morning.

Scott and Kelli drove Kendra and Mei to Kendra's home. Being practical women, and needing something to take their minds off Jake and Sam, they immediately set about cleaning the blood and damage in the kitchen. They talked as they worked. Mei asked if there was anything between Jake and Kendra.

"I wish I knew. I tingle when I see him and I have this strong urge to touch him. When I saw Mitchell shoot him, I was so scared. And when I ran out the door and saw him lying on the ground with all that blood on his head, I felt like a piece of me had died. When the deputy told me it wasn't as serious as it looked, I was overjoyed. There are little clues that something happened between us the week before Mitchell abducted me, but I can't remember anything."

She didn't tell her mother of the quick image that had flitted through her mind when she saw Jake lying on the ground outside her home—an image of them, bare from the waist up, holding each other in bed.

Mei reminded Kendra of what Dr. Moore and Dr. Cohen had told her. "It will come to you in time. Don't get discouraged—especially now. Jake and your father need you right now."

"Thanks, Mother. That means a lot. I'm just so confused."

"I know. We want you to get your memory back, then see what happens. If there is something between you and Jake, I think you know that Sam and I think very highly of him. No disrespect meant toward Walt, God rest his soul, but your daddy and I would like to see you with Jake … or someone like him. We love you, sweetheart … and we want you to be happy. We know you haven't been happy for a long time now."

Kendra quietly hugged her mother as tears trickled down her cheek.

Kendra slept fitfully that night. The bad dream of the cabin recurred, but she woke herself. *Thank you again, Dr. Cohen.* She went back to sleep and dreamed of seeing Jake lying outside, blood on his head. She rose and made a cup of tea. It calmed her. She returned to bed and slept peacefully until morning.

FIFTY-SEVEN

Kendra and Mei arrived at the hospital at nine a.m. Sam was awake, alert and in good spirits. He kissed each of them and asked Kendra about Jake. She kissed Sam, told him what she knew, and went to Intensive Care to check on Jake.

Kendra checked in with the desk nurse, who told her Jake was being examined and she could see him in a few minutes. Soon, the doctor left Jake, closing the curtain behind him. The nurse nodded toward Kendra and he took her hand. "You must be Kendra. Your husband is a little disoriented and confused, but I've heard your name a dozen times in the past fifteen minutes. He's doing fine and, absent something unexpected, I'll probably send him upstairs after lunch. He's a very lucky man. You can see him, if you would like, but he's pretty fuzzy from the injury and the painkillers at the moment. He'll be more alert by this afternoon." Kendra didn't correct his perception of her relationship to Jake.

Kendra slipped between the curtains. Jake's eyes were closed and his face looked pained. She took his hand and kissed his cheek. His eyes fluttered open and he looked at her blankly, then she saw recognition in his eyes and he mumbled, "Kendra," with quiet relief.

"I'm here, Jake." She gently kissed his lips. "You gave me quite a scare. How do you feel?'

He groaned and spoke slowly. "Whopping headache. Get a little queasy off and on. What happened? Doc said I was shot, but I don't remember much."

"Welcome to my world," replied Kendra softly and Jake looked at her with confusion, then closed his eyes and was silent. He seemed to have gone to sleep. She went back to the Desk Nurse, asked and was told that he would probably drift in and out of sleep for two or three more hours, but she expected he would be moved to a room after lunch.

Kendra returned to Sam's room where she brought him and Mei current. The three of them visited for an hour until the nurse suggested Sam should lie back and rest for a while. They told him they would be back after lunch. Sam asked Mei to bring him a book and a candy bar. She hugged him, kissed him and said she would. Kendra hugged him, kissed his cheek and said softly, "Oh, Daddy; I'm so sorry. This is all because of me."

Sam pulled her to him and shushed her, assuring her that he was fine. "Mitchell caused all this, honey, not you. Don't you think any differently."

FIFTY-EIGHT

Kendra called the sheriff's office. The detective handling the case said he could meet with her as soon as she could get there. She told him where she was, and she and Mei arrived twenty minutes later. They gave a brief account of the background, which the detective knew, and a succinct but thorough account of what transpired Thursday afternoon. The detective asked about Jake and Sam. Kendra brought him current on their respective conditions.

"Well, from what the officers told me, I'd say they are both extremely lucky that they weren't injured more seriously or killed. I'm happy for you that it wasn't worse."

He thanked them and asked if they had questions. Kendra asked how Mitchell got free and was told as much as the detective knew about events in Blanco County. Apparently, the jailers had let Mitchell wear a gray trustee's jumpsuit instead of the well-known orange prisoner suit to the evaluation, where he escaped. He said there were no reports of a carjacking or a stolen car, so the best guess was that Mitchell somehow got one or more rides that got him back to Houston, where he went to his home, retrieved a pistol and his car, and set out to find Kendra.

"I know Mitchell is dead, but how did it happen?"

"I'm not supposed to talk about an ongoing case, but this case is basically closing itself and you will know as soon as I talk to Mr. Alder, so …" He looked at Kendra and Mei, "Simply put, based on what you told us yesterday and this morning, coupled now with what the medical

226

examiner has found or deduced, we believe your gasp alerted Williams to Jake's presence. He followed your eyes, turned in that direction, saw Jake and fired at him. Jake apparently either fired simultaneously or returned fire as he jerked his head to one side. The Medical Examiner believes Williams' bullet struck Jake as Jake fired and that's the position we are taking. That takes any allegation of liability away from Jake. Our position is that his shot was purely self-defense.

"The M.E.—the Medical Examiner—says Jake's shot pierced Williams' right lung, which caused his death. The M.E. believes that he lurched against the counter when the shot struck him, then turned involuntarily toward Sam. Based on what you told me, he may have turned when he was hit by the salt shaker."

The detective laughed. "That was an interesting wrinkle. Don't know that I've ever heard of a salt shaker being used as a weapon. Anyway, it's anybody's guess whether he intended to fire at Sam or just jerked the trigger involuntarily as he was going down. He's dead, so it really doesn't matter much—the shot was fired in the commission of a crime, so it doesn't matter what caused the shot. The sad part is that all this must be causing more terrible grief and suffering for his parents."

FIFTY-NINE

They left, had a quiet lunch, and returned to the hospital. Jake was in a room now. Mei visited for a few minutes and left to see Sam. Jake was still thinking a little slowly due to the painkillers, but he was coherent.

"What happened?" I think I remember bits and pieces, but my last clear memory is of being in your neighbor's yard behind an oak tree."

Kendra told him about Mitchell appearing as she came into the garage. She related the events of which she had knowledge and what the detective had told her. She told Jake he had called while Mitchell was holding them at gunpoint around the breakfast room table and said that she thought Sam had given Jake a cryptic message, but she couldn't understand what it was.

She related the events in good, sequential order, including her gasp and Mitchell shooting Jake, then Sam.

"How is Sam?"

Kendra told him.

Jake looked thoughtfully at her. "I guess we both have a memory problem now. Has anything come back to you since I left for Dallas?"

"Only one thing. When I ran out of the house and saw you lying on the ground with your head covered in blood, a very brief glimpse of you holding me flashed through my mind." She didn't tell him they were naked and in bed in that quick memory. "It came and went in a split second and I was so upset, thinking you were dead, that I didn't give it any thought until much later. No other memory has developed from it, so I'm basically where I was when you left."

"It will all come back to you. I'm sure I will remember yesterday soon, as well." He squeezed her hand. "Aren't we a pair." He chuckled.

"I'd sure like to see Sam." He pressed the call button and asked the nurse if he could travel to Sam's room.

"Umm … it might be a little early for that. We're not sure of your balance. If you rest this afternoon, we'll see if you can sit and stand after supper. If you have no balance problems, I imagine you can go visiting as long as you stay in a wheelchair."

They talked for a while until Jake grew drowsy. Kendra let him sleep and went to see Sam.

As she travelled to Sam's room, she recalled the fleeting image that had rushed through her mind. There was something about it that troubled her. She tried to remember the image, and got it into her mind. She saw Jake's face and their arms around each other. She saw his bare chest and the tops of her naked breasts … and it struck her. In the image, they lay on seafoam green sheets. Kendra had seafoam green sheets in her redecorated bedroom. *Oh, my. Is that just a coincidence or a fact?*

She was perplexed as she entered the room, kissed Sam and stood beside his bed.

Sam took her hand. "Baby, that was a brave thing you did, offering to go with Mitchell. That was resourceful. You slowed him down and gave Jake time to get to us. I'm very proud of you."

"It was all I could think of to do." Sam squeezed her hand.

"Your mother told me what the detective told you two. Thank God for Jake's aim. If he hadn't taken Mitchell out, all three of us—and maybe even Jake, as well—would be dead and not enjoying life together."

Kendra was quiet for a few seconds as Sam's words sank in. "Oh, my God, Daddy! My mind has been on you and Jake. I haven't thought that far past what happened. Jake would have been lying unconscious outside the house and Mitchell would have turned his gun on us."

Tears began to roll down her cheeks and she spoke in a quavering voice. "Jake saved our lives. There is no doubt about that. Jake saved our lives."

She pulled Mei to the bed and hugged her parents tightly as tears continued to run down her face. Mei cried and Sam knuckled the corners of his eyes, as well. When the tears stopped, Kendra looked at her parents. "The two of you like Jake, don't you? I mean, not just because of what he did yesterday and in the past weeks. You liked him before all this, didn't you?"

Both Sam and Mei paused for a second, then said simultaneously, "Yes. We like Jake very much." Mei added, "We have always thought very highly of Jake." Kendra smiled from ear to ear.

Sam thought of Jake's words to him at the hospital in Kerrville. He studied Kendra's expression and spoke, softly, but seriously. "Honey, if that young man ever asks, I hope your answer is yes." No explanation of Sam's meaning was necessary, and Kendra teared up again.

"That's up to him, Daddy. I know what my answer will be."

SIXTY

K endra and her mother bought boxed dinners in the cafeteria and took
them upstairs. In the elevator, Kendra said, "The nurses may let Jake
get out of bed this evening. If they do, he wants to see Daddy, so maybe
we'll see you in a little bit." Mei smiled and went to have dinner with Sam
as Kendra went to Jake's room.

Jake and Kendra ate and talked of the changes to her home and of
friends. When they were finished, the nurse stepped in and asked if Jake
still wanted to take a road trip. She made him sit upright for sixty seconds,
then stand upright for sixty seconds. When he did so with good balance,
she put his hand on her shoulder and told him to walk with her across the
room and back. He did so without difficulty. She checked his pupils and
asked if his stomach was settled. He said it was. She approved and went
for a wheel chair.

When she returned and Jake was comfortable in the chair, she told
Kendra, "No more than an hour. If he has any difficulty, call the floor
nurse immediately."

Kendra wheeled Jake to Sam's room where he knocked on the door
and called, "Anybody home?"

Sam laughed and called, "Get yourself in here, young man."

Kendra wheeled Jake to the bed, where he stood, shook Sam's hand
and hugged him, taking care with Sam's injured side.

Everyone laughed and smiled and chattered away happily. After a
while, Sam looked seriously at Jake and reached for his hand. "Thank you,

son. You saved our lives … and we're forever grateful to you. Yesterday was more frightening than any day I ever experienced in Special Forces—I was afraid I was going to lose my girls. I don't take it lightly when a man saves my life … and the lives of my family." He didn't release Jake's hand.

Jake was speechless for a moment and looked sheepish. Then, he looked directly at Sam, then Mei, Kendra and back to Sam. "You do me a great honor, sir. I'm glad I was there and that I could help. The three of you are very special to me."

It was very quiet for a long moment. Then, Kendra broke the seriousness when she said, with an exuberant smile, "You two should go into the rescue business." She framed a rectangle in the air with her thumbs and index fingers, and quipped, "Heroes, Incorporated." She kissed Jake, then Sam. "You will always be my heroes."

Later, Kendra returned Jake to his room. When the night nurse saw them, she said, "I have some good news for you. If you don't have any problem tonight, the doctor will check you in the morning and send you home."

She was young and pretty and had a large engagement ring on her left hand. She stepped close to them, grinned and whispered, "Don't sneak sex in your room tonight. A spike in your heartrate <u>will not</u> look good on your chart tomorrow morning."

She laughed and went back to her desk. Neither Jake nor Kendra responded, but they shared a smile and a common thought.

"Would you bring me some clean clothes and underwear tomorrow morning? And some appropriate shoes, please?" Jake asked. Kendra nodded. "And bring me a hat too, will you? I think my half buzz cut and stitches will attract a lot of unwanted attention."

Kendra dropped Mei at her home and drove to Jake's to collect clothes to take for him tomorrow. She let herself in with the key Jake had given her before she left the hospital. The house was warm. She reflexively went to the thermostat and lowered the temperature a couple of degrees. She checked the fridge to see if he needed any items for the weekend at home and checked the pantry for tomato soup, which was Jake's favorite.

She went to his bedroom and selected a pair of nice shorts, a polo shirt and clean boxers. She got the comfortable shoes that he usually wore with shorts from the closet, and opened one of the built-in cabinets to retrieve his small Gladstone satchel. It wasn't there and she remembered that he had taken it to Dallas with him, so it was probably in his car—*which was where?* It hadn't been at her home. She retrieved his boonie hat from the closet peg where it always hung.

She checked to ensure that the sink and shower were clean for his return. She replaced the nub of a bar of soap with a new bar. As she walked back into his bedroom, she smoothed his comforter and fluffed his pillow shams—and felt a familiar tingle inside.

And the reality of the moment suddenly struck her—the only time she could recall ever having been in Jake's bedroom was when he moved into his new home. He had given her, Walt, Kelli and Scott a tour of the home. Yet, she had just walked right to the correct place for his shorts and shirt and underwear. She knew which drawer contained his boxers. And she knew where he kept his satchel. And she didn't know how she knew Jake's favorite soup was tomato.

She sat on his bedroom chair and thought. She knew what brand of shaving cream Jake used, and where he kept it in the shower, and where he kept his backup supply of soap, toothpaste and shaving cream. Of course, she could have recognized the brand and location of his shaving cream when she checked the shower a minute ago, but how did she know where the backup items were? And another thought struck her. Jake always used a blade razor that he kept in the shower, but he had an electric shaver, a gray Remington, that he kept in the back of a drawer for mornings when he didn't feel like blade shaving. She walked into the bathroom, went straight to the correct drawer, opened it, and there it was—a gray Remington electric shaver.

Then, an even more startling memory surfaced. She returned to his bedroom and opened a drawer in his dresser. She found two sets of clean bra and panties, her spare hairbrush, a pair of her shorts, one of her logo T-shirts, a short silk nightgown, and two of her bikinis. She returned to the bathroom. Jake had his and her sinks. She looked in the medicine cabinet above her sink and found a prescription bottle with a label bearing her name that contained several of her pills for her hypothyroid condition, and a birth control patch—*Well, that may answer the sixty-four thousand dollar question*—as well as her deodorant and perfume.

She reached for the patch, thinking to herself, *This might be a good idea. Be prepared, as Callen would say.* She had been told the patch she was wearing when she arrived at the hospital had been left in place. She tried to remember when she replaced her patch. It had ben her habit to replace it the fifteenth of each month, which had been about the time she called Jake and invited herself to his home. She mentally did the math in her head and decided she should be good, but she applied a new patch, smoothing the edges, and confirming the date in her mind. Then, she looked in Jake's medicine cabinet where she found condoms. *OK. Good. Better safe than sorry.*

She looked in a small compartment in her wallet and found a key that she didn't remember putting there. She compared it to the key to Jake's home he had given her earlier that day. It was a perfect match.

Elementary—eh, Watson? I've obviously been here many more times than I know of. And I wasn't sleeping in the guest room. I'm sure we've made love. We must have, but I can't remember doing so. Then, a terrible thought rose in her mind. *Wouldn't it be ironic if his memory of that week is gone and mine never returns?*

SIXTY-ONE

Kendra and Mei arrived at the hospital at nine o'clock. Kendra went straight to Jake's room with his requested items. She was happy to see Jake, but was perplexed by her findings last night.

She kissed his cheek, and he said, "Doc wants one final X-ray before I go. He said he'll read it and not wait for the radiologist; he knows what he wants to see ... or doesn't want to see, as the case may be. So we'll be another hour. An orderly is on his way to get me. I'll call Sam's room when I get back here, if you want to wait there."

Kendra happily went to see her father. An hour later, Jake called Sam's room. Sam answered, talked with Jake for a minute, then handed her the phone.

"I got the all clear. If you will get the car and meet us at the west side lobby doors, the orderly will bring me down there."

She told Mei and Sam the news and promised that she and Jake would be back to visit after dinner. As she hugged and kissed them, Sam said, "You take care of Jake today. If you feel a compelling need to check on me, do so this afternoon. You two take the evening and relax. Go to dinner together or do something tonight. I'm fine, and I'll be out of here tomorrow or the next day."

Kendra met Jake and the orderly, and settled Jake into the passenger seat. The orderly returned to the hospital with the wheelchair. Jake breathed a sigh of relief and took Kendra's hand. "Let's go home. I'll get my car later. It's in front of Kelli and Scott's home." She looked at Jake in profile, sitting in her passenger seat and knew that he had recently been in her car as a passenger. She just knew it, but she couldn't remember when or the circumstances.

They arrived at Jake's home and she unlocked the door. "Thanks for bringing me home," Jake said. "If I could impose on you later, I'd like to get my car, but right now, I'd just like to be home, in my stuff, for a few minutes."

"Would you like some time alone?"

"Not unless you're uncomfortable, or want to go back to be with Sam."

"I'm certainly not uncomfortable with you. I would like to see Daddy later, but he was adamant that, if we come, to come this afternoon. He said we should have dinner tonight and relax together. If you would like company, I'd like very much to have dinner together and to be with you." She laughed. "And we still haven't celebrated the news that you haven't shared with me. If you feel up to it, I think we should do that. I'm very curious."

"Sounds like a plan. Would you like some lunch?"

"I'll fix lunch. You just sit there and look pretty. Then, I'd like for you to rest a little. If you feel like it, we'll visit Daddy later and bring your car home."

She fixed sandwiches and tomato soup and they ate on the patio.

"How is your memory? Is anything coming back to you?" he asked.

"Yes, I think so. But it has all been very … strange, almost weird. I need to think about it, but I'd like to talk about it later—after dinner. I think it's all sitting right there, just waiting to reveal itself."

"Where would you like to be?"

"Here, with you. Some things have happened that make me think I have a better chance of remembering what happened for that week if I'm here. Is that all right?"

"Certainly."

"Would you mind if we retrieved your car before we go to the hospital? That way, I can leave my car for Mother and she can get to my house when she's ready."

"Sure. That makes good sense," Jake replied, then asked, "Can you tell me what happened yesterday afternoon?"

"I can tell you parts of it and fill in parts that I learned from the detective." Kendra recited what she had told the detective and what he had told her. Jake listened attentively, but with an expression of troubled concern. When Kendra finished, he sat quietly, nodding his head for a long moment.

"Thank you. I now have a better idea of why Sam thanked me. I remember Sam giving me the hint by referring to three o'clock to five o'clock. On the way to the deer lease, he told me that three a.m.to five a.m. was the best time to catch bad guys sleeping. I assumed that Mitchell was the bad guy and was at your home then, listening. That's why I said it would take me thirty minutes to get there. I didn't want him to know how close I was.

"I parked in front of Kelli and Scott's house. Coincidentally, Mitchell had parked there also and I recognized his car. I called 911, explained the circumstances, took my pistol from the glove compartment and went to the house next door to your kitchen where I hid behind that huge white oak tree next to your driveway. I looked through the window into the kitchen and saw Mitchell's back and right side. I could see Sam and Mei, but not you. I kept an eye on Mitchell's back in case he turned to look out the window as I moved to your house. I crouched below your kitchen window. I could hear every word you and Mitchell said.

"My intent was to get into the garage, then the laundry room from where I could distract Mitchell and enter, then either disarm him or shoot him. I rose to check his position, saw you, and saw the look on your face when you saw me. I knew he would see it as well.

"I remember Mitchell turning and pointing his gun at me. I really don't remember him firing or me firing, but I vaguely remember the sound of a shot being fired. After that, I'm kind of like you. I don't remember anything until I came to in the hospital. I gather I fired and it was my shot that killed Mitchell?"

Kendra nodded. "The medical examiner put in his report that Mitchell shot first and that you fired in self-defense. The detective told me there would be no repercussion on you."

Jake nodded. "When did he shoot Sam?

She answered and told him about Sam throwing the salt shaker. Jake laughed hard, and said, "That Sam is one brave guy."

Kendra told him of the speculation that Mitchell's turn toward Sam and his shot may have just been involuntary since he was already wounded, but may just as easily been a reaction to being hit by the saltshaker. "Again, that's what the Sheriff and the Medical Examiner believe."

"Thank you. I don't remember pulling the trigger, but at least my shot was straight. I certainly have no regrets ... but I'm glad I didn't have to look at his dead body or his eyes."

Kendra moved to Jake and put her arms around him. *Oh, Jake. You're my hero.* "Thank you," she said softly. She leaned her head against his cheek and sighed as she held him to her. She didn't kiss him or effuse. Her soft sigh, the warmth of being in her arms and feeling her touch said all that was necessary.

She suddenly looked into his eyes and he saw a worried look of apprehension on her face. "Jake, you still have your memory of that week, don't you?"

He smiled. "Oh, yes. Vividly."

"Good." She smiled broadly. "I want to know everything later tonight." She laughed. "Wouldn't we be a pair if neither of us could remember last week?"

Kendra collected their plates, bowls and glasses, and took them inside. As she did, she asked Jake if she could get him anything else. "Did they give me any antibiotics in that batch of medicine they sent home with me?"

Kendra checked. "No. Just pain killers and a mild sedative. Does your question indicate that you'd like a glass of wine?'

"Yes, but only if you will drink a glass with me."

"Excellent timing, Mr. Alder. I could use a glass. Red or white?"

"Red."

She returned with two large, goblets filled with Jake's favorite cabernet sauvignon.

"I really want to celebrate tonight, then talk about my lost week. But, do you mind if I ask some questions for a few minutes?' Jake shook his head to indicate that he did not.

"If this all sounds very disjointed, just bear with me, please." He nodded.

"What color are your sheets?"

Jake chuckled. "I wasn't expecting that. All of my sheets are taupe."

"No seafoam green?"

"No. You have the seafoam green sheets." She nodded.

"Excluding the week I can't remember, can you recall if I have ever been in your bedroom? If so, how many times?"

"You have been there only once and that was shortly after I moved in. You, Walt, Kelli and Scott, and Janice and Alan Purcell came for a house warming dinner, and I gave you the nickel tour. I can't recall any other time before last week."

"Have you ever given me a key to your home?"

"Yes. At the beginning of the week."

"Do you recall ever being a passenger in my car, other than today?"

"Yes. Again, at the beginning of the week you can't remember. Do you want to know more now?"

"Thank you, but not now. That helps me a lot. I'm sure it didn't make much sense to you, but I'll explain tonight." *Now, I know my deductions are correct. I'm sure I've slept in Jake's bed. If I did that, then we must have made love. I just need to remember.*

Jake cocked his head, smiled gently, and asked her, "Did you date much before Walt?"

She smiled a chagrinned smile and shook her head. "I was fifteen when I had my first date. I was asked out a lot. I had a lot of first and second dates, but no third dates. The boys always wanted too much too soon. Dating was a desultory experience. My junior year, I dated a boy that I liked very much and it was nice until he wanted more than I was willing to give.

"My senior year, I dated a nice boy. We went to the same church. I liked him a lot and we made out a lot. I thought it was perfect until just before graduation. He decided we had been together long enough to … escalate our activities. I said no and that was the end of it.

"College was the same—Walt was the only guy in college who came back for a third date. Our relationship was … unusual. He tried hard to be polite, but it was as if his mind was always somewhere else. I think I accepted things as they were simply because I had a boyfriend.

"But, after some things that Mitchell said in my kitchen, I think Walt was getting what he wanted elsewhere, even then.

"I was very surprised when he asked me to marry him. I was naïve … and impressionable. I really don't know why he married me. I think it was because his parents liked me … and I think he thought I would impress the coaches better than some hot chick who followed him around all the time. Mitchell told me that Walt had women on the side when we were married, as well.

"It really wasn't a good marriage, for many reasons. I was too naïve, too inexperienced, and too trusting." She looked at him. "I'm sorry. That was a very long answer to a very simple question."

"No need to be sorry. Thank you for your candor."

Kendra suggested he rest for a few minutes. He did, then they collected Jake's car and went to see Sam. The nurse ran everyone out at four o'clock because Sam had an MRI scheduled. They told Sam and Mei they were going out to dinner and would see them tomorrow. They hugged Mei, and Kendra left her keys after Mei assured her she knew how to get to Kendra's home after dark and that she would be all right alone.

They left the hospital, and Jake took Kendra to her home so that she could get ready for dinner.

SIXTY-TWO

Kendra was excited—very excited, very eager to know all that now eluded her. She ran a warm bath with oil and scent. She didn't know whether he had seen the new items she discovered in her drawer or not, but she chose small, lacy and black. She selected tailored black slacks and a jade green silk blouse that brought out the green in her eyes. She wore simple black flats and simple jewelry. She packed a bag with fresh clothes, a tiny bathing suit, the two robes from her closet, and the four cards she had found in her jewelry box.

Jake arrived at six-thirty. When she opened the door to greet him, she could tell that she pleased him. His eyes widened and a smile spread from ear to ear. "Well, don't you just look beautiful." She took his hand and ushered him inside.

"Thank you," she said softly as she stepped to him and kissed his lips.

"Dinner?" he asked

"Yes. I'm hungry and I want to hear about what we're celebrating."

They arrived and were seated. Jake selected a bottle of good champagne, and she toasted him when their glasses were filled.

"Congratulations! Whatever the reason, I'm sure the congratulations are well deserved."

"Thank you. We just won a seven figure, three-year contract with a new client and renewed another high six-figure four-year contract with an existing client. In two days, we have realized an almost sixty percent increase in our annual revenue."

Kendra knew Jake was an equal partner with two other men, and she had a pretty good idea what this meant for him and his company.

"Oh, Jake. I'm so happy for you. And it is certainly well-deserved. I know how hard you've worked to build your company." She took his hand and squeezed. "Oh, that's just wonderful news. Let the celebration begin.

They talked and he explained the impact of the contracts and the new business. Dinner came and they ate as she asked questions and let him talk. She was happy for him. And it helped to have a normal conversation about something other than herself and the past two weeks.

When their plates were cleared, he asked, "Dessert?"

"This is your celebration. I'll share one with you, or watch you. What's your pleasure?"

Jake took her hand and smiled. "I think I'd rather go home with you now."

She was pleased. She was ready to be alone with him. And to learn.

They arrived at Jake's home. As Jake poured a glass of swine for each of them, Kendra quickly called Mei to check on her. "She's fine. Home with no trouble. I told her not to wait up for me."

He dropped his shoes and sat in a club chair. Kendra slipped her shoes off, sitting on the love seat, her legs curled beneath her. He thought she was breathtaking. He wanted so much to tell her that, to hold her and kiss her.

Kendra took a sip of wine, then said, "I want to know everything tonight, but first, let me tell you about some strange things that have happened. Feel free to comment if you want." He nodded.

"I had a very quick vision of us in bed together, bare and holding each other. I don't know where or when or even if it occurred, but the sheets were seafoam green." Jake smiled and nodded, but said nothing.

"Last night, I came here to get clothes for you. I didn't even have to think about what I was doing. I walked into your bedroom and went right to the drawer where you keep your boxers, and right to the place in your closet where you hang your shorts. I looked for your satchel on the shelf where you keep it, then remembered that it was probably in your car. I did all that without really thinking about it.

"When the incongruity of what I had done struck me, I realized that I know what brand of shaving cream you use and where you keep spare shaving cream, soap and supplies. I looked and they were right where I knew they would be. I had the brand right, as well.

I remembered you have a gray Remington electric shaver that you use when you don't feel like blade shaving. I knew you keep it in the back of a drawer. I went right to that drawer and it was there in the back of the drawer, where I knew it would be. I also remembered the drawer in your dresser where I apparently keep a few things, and where I kept my thyroid pills and perfume in the bathroom cabinet above the sink.

"I went back to the living room and retrieved your key from where I had laid it. I looked in the secret compartment in my wallet and there was an exact duplicate of the key you gave me at the hospital last night."

Jake nodded. "I think everything you need to know in order to remember is right at the edge of your memory, just waiting to come out. How can I help you?"

"Tell me what happened that week, please. Go slowly so that I can massage everything in my mind and maybe find some memories up there."

Jake started with her phone call and slowly described the events since her phone call that Friday As he talked, a memory of telling Jake about the divorce and of the deputy telling her that Walt tried to intimidate him came into her mind.

He saw the look on her face. "Did you remember something?"

"Yes; I have a vague memory of telling you about the divorce."

Jake nodded and continued. He told her about her comment that there were some things she wanted to do over spring break."

"What did I say I wanted to do?"

"You wanted to make flowerbeds in the yard and plant roses. You wanted to go to the Museum of Fine Arts. You wanted to go horseback riding. You wanted to go zip lining. You wanted to lie in the sun and read a book."

"I don't remember telling you that, but I remember wanting to do those things you mentioned. And I did plant the roses. She sat quietly for a few minutes.

"Where did you put my bag?"

"In the guest bedroom."

"Excuse me. I'll be right back." She disappeared down the hall, returning with her bag." She sat, curling her legs under her again. Reaching into her bag, she pulled out the four envelopes. "Is that why I have these?"

"Yes. I wanted to surprise you, to make you happy."

"Did I mention the Cayman Islands?"

"No. With all that was going on in your life at that time, I thought you might need a vacation after the school year and the divorce were over. You said you wanted to lie in the sun and read a book. Cayman seemed like a good place to do that."

"Thank you, Jake. Once again, you're the most thoughtful man."

Again, she was quiet, pensive. She held up the small envelope. "I have a memory of talking about a dress and the cost of dresses. Did that happen?"

"Yes. That was Tuesday. You got the little envelope and were concerned that I would spend too much. We agreed on a price."

She frowned and thought. "You gave me the four envelopes, but told me to open the small one last. Is that right?

"Yes."

"And I said we could get a dress for two hundred fifty dollars and you said we could spend between four and five hundred."

"Yes."

"I told you it had been fifteen years since I had been on a horse."

"Yes."

Oh, bless me. It's beginning to come back. Go slowly. Don't try to rush it.

She looked wistfully at him. "Oh, Jake. You don't have to do all this for me. I hope I thanked you properly, but you don't have to do all this."

"I know I don't have to. I want to. And we're going to do everything you wanted to do. We're going to ride horses, and go zip lining, and you're going to be the most beautiful woman at the Museum of Fine Arts Ball. And we're going to relax for a week in the blue waters of the Cayman Islands."

He smiled broadly. "Obviously, some things are coming back?

She nodded thoughtfully.

A snippet of memory came to Kendra, then more. Tears ran down her cheeks. Jake came to her and she pulled him onto the love seat with her. She put her arms around him and cried. When her tears stopped, she kissed him.

"We were on my deck when you gave me these envelopes. It was nearly dark and you said you hoped there was enough light to read them."

He nodded. "Your memory is coming back," he said hopefully.

"I asked if there was anything else you wanted to do. You said you want to experience warmth and intimacy and intelligent conversation."

Kendra looked pensive. She nodded at Jake and he continued.

"I asked you if there was someone special with whom you wanted that. You said there was. I was surprised, and I said that I didn't know you were seeing someone. You didn't respond."

He looked at her and she nodded thoughtfully for him to continue. "I asked if you had told him your plan. You said—"

She interrupted, holding up one finger. *Oh, my God. I think I remember.* "Wait." She frowned and concentrated. "We were sitting on your love seat. You asked if I had told him my plan ... and I said that I just did. You looked confused ... then, you realized I was talking about you."

"That's right. What else can you remember?"

Kendra looked thoughtful, then blushed.

"I said I didn't want to disappoint you. I was nervous. You gave me a glass of wine and we went to the patio and talked. Then, we went inside. You led me to your bedroom. I was very nervous and you said you were nervous, too. You said that you didn't think we would ever have a chance to be together. That helped me relax, knowing that you were nervous."

As she talked, the single memory became even more vivid to her.

She blushed. "You ... aroused me ... with your mouth and your hands ..." she paused and blushed again, "and you made love to me."

Oh, my God! We made love! It really happened and I remember it now.

"We did make love, didn't we?" she asked tentatively.

Jake just grinned broadly and nodded affirmatively.

SIXTY-THREE

Her memory returned in a burst, a kaleidoscope of images overwhelming her senses, filling her mind like water rushing from a burst levee—image after image of the entire week with Jake.

In her mind, Kendra saw them laughing and loving and working in her home. She saw the perplexed, then happy look on Jake's face when she told him what she wanted and that it was he she wanted. She saw him smiling down at her as he made love to her the first time, remembered the tremor and convulsion that took her to the edge and over, remembered herself nestling in Jakes arms afterward, safe and secure and amazed at what had just happened inside her.

She looked up at him and her eyes sparkled. "Oh, Jake, you made love to me and it was wonderful. I had never …," she shivered slightly, "<u>never</u> … experienced intimacy the way it was with you. We laughed and you held me and it was wonderful. We dressed and fixed dinner together. You grilled salmon for me." Jake nodded affirmatively

Kendra thoughtfully and accurately recounted the events of Monday, Tuesday, Wednesday and Thursday.

She looked thoughtful and Jake was quiet until she laughed out loud. "What," he asked.

"Ruminate!" she exclaimed suddenly. "That was it. That's why I was taken aback when I said ruminate earlier and you said that was an interesting choice of words. It was déjà vu. It sounded so familiar.

"I went shopping Sunday. You saw the *Victoria's Secret* bag, asked what was in it and I said 'maybe I'll show you later.' It was like titillate. You said you enjoyed being titillated and that I was titillating you. And I said that was an interesting choice of words, especially in that context. And ... you also used that word before that day." Jake nodded.

"You said you were distracted and intimated I was the distraction. I said that you could show me why after lunch and you said I was titillating you."

"That's right."

Kendra looked down for a moment and, as if to herself, said very softly, "We made love every night that week."

She finally turned to him and smiled her warm smile. "May we have a little more wine?" He poured and they again sat quietly.

She turned to him. "That Friday, I asked you to help me make new memories in my new bedroom." *And you did, Jake. We made wonderful new memories.* "But, Mitchell has intruded on the happiness and the new memories you gave me."

She paused. "And now I have that terrible memory of being wrapped in a sheet in that dark room, scared out of my mind, and afraid I would never see you again."

She took his hand. "Oh, Jake. You've been so patient with my lack of memory. I'm so sorry for what I've put you through."

"Shh. I'm glad you're back. I'm glad you remember. I've missed you so much the last two weeks."

She kissed him and held him tightly. "I want to put that dark room and Mitchell and the past two weeks behind us. I want you to take me back to what we had before Mitchell."

I remember. I have pictures in my mind, but something is missing. I see us, and watch us move and hear us speak, but something is missing.

He took her hand land and they silently walked together to his bed. Tremulous, but giddy with excitement, she said softly, "I remember what we did, but I need to experience the sensations again. Right now, it's just a memory. I'm eager, but I don't know enough to anticipate the sensations I experienced then."

Jake nodded his understanding.

Kendra sighed and blushed, then purred as Jake slowly undressed her. When his eyes met hers, she stepped to him and just as slowly undressed him. It was not unfamiliar to her.

He tenderly kissed her lips and slowly drew his hand over her warm body. Never taking her eyes from his, she took his hand, turned her hips, and settled on the bed, pulling Jake down with her. She murmured susurrations of eagerness and excitement as he once again brought her along slowly and gently—and it became increasingly familiar to Kendra. They took their time, letting the excitement build until they were moving together in an eager, practiced quest for fulfillment.

For Kendra, each movement, each sensation, each urge was reminiscent of what had gone before and quickly became a foundation on which to grow. Kelli's advice manifested itself into natural reality and Kendra's exuberance was overwhelming. When she reached the crest, she involuntarily gasped, moaned, quivered and cried out Jake's name as they sailed over the edge together in complete physical release and emotional rapture.

And it happened—what was missing suddenly came rushing in. With their lovemaking and her climax, her senses came acutely alive. She didn't just see herself tremble when Jake first made love to her—she felt it and remembered what it felt like. The sensations of Jake's touch, his fingertips and his lips and his mouth on her that week came alive, and she tingled. The male musk of Jake when he was aroused and making love with her, and the smell of him when he came out of the shower teased her nostrils. It all came alive to her.

Kendra was overwhelmed with the magnitude of sensory memories combined with present tense sensations that suddenly filled her world. She felt the heat and fullness of Jake inside her, tasted the beads of perspiration on his shoulder, smelled his musk and hers, and every memory and sensation of the lost week came alive inside her.

Oh, my. That was wonderful. We've done this before—and I want to do it again!

They remained as they were. She held him silently for a long moment, then spoke. "Hold me, please. Just hold me."

He did for several quiet minutes until she wrapped herself around him and asked earnestly as she arched herself into the warmth of their joinder, "Can we do that again?"

Jake chuckled, pressing back against her, and began to move as he kissed her throat and whispered into her ear, "I thought you would never ask." She giggled.

The made love again, passionately, fervently until they were soaked with perspiration and their breath came in quick, halting gasps. As they went over the edge together, Jake groaned from deep within and Kendra cried out his name, "Jake! Oh, Jake!"

A final tremor coursed through Kendra as they eagerly clutched each other, kissing and murmuring until they eventually calmed, rolled onto their sides and quietly held each other. As they lay in the afterglow, she chuckled softly.

"Yes?" he asked quizzically.

"What a lucky girl I am. I had a wonderful, incredible week with you. You opened new doors for me and made new memories with me. But Mitchell made me forget until tonight. And tonight, my memories have returned … we've returned … to … the excitement and the intimacy and to all the wonderful sensations we shared that week.

"I know why I came to you three weeks ago. I remember how you made me feel and how you told me you felt."

She looked at Jake hesitantly. "Has all that has happened changed the way you feel?"

"No, Kendra. I still feel what I told you I felt—even more so. I have no desire for this to end."

She kissed him gently and looked into his eyes. Her expression was serious.

"Find a Scout and make him your friend. Trust him and he'll always be there for you. My brother was right."

She gently touched Jake's wound, and he saw pain for him in her eyes as she whispered, "My poor baby." Tears welled in the corners of her eyes as she again touched his wound, then touched his cheek with her fingertips.

"You said you would never let anything bad happen to me . . . and you didn't. You've always been there for me. You're my hero, Jake."

Her eyes never moved from his as she said softly, "I love you." She kissed him again, and snuggled close to him.

Jake kissed the top of her head, tipped her chin up, looked directly into her eyes and replied, "I love you, Kendra—more than you can know."

She returned his gaze and again softly said, "Jake, where we go from here is up to you. I'll be here for as long as you want me."

They held each other tightly, cuddling, touching and kissing as Kendra cried many happy tears. As her joy became excitement and desire, she pressed against him, giggled and whispered innocently, her breath warm against his ear, "Jake … what's a boy toy?"

On Monday, Kendra's passport arrived.

Printed in the United States
By Bookmasters